CHICKEN IN GREECE

By William Battista

with Prologue from Robert Battista

Copyright © 2016 by Robert Battista and Nancy Morgan. All Rights Reserved.

This is a work of fiction. Names, characters, business, places, events, and incidents are either the products of the author's imagination or used in a fictitious manner. Any resemblance to actual persons, living or dead, or actual events is purely coincidental.

No part of this book may be reproduced or used in any manner without the express written permission of the publisher except for the use of brief quotations in a book review.

This book is a tribute to
Bill and Kay and all the enthusiasm for life that they created in countless many.

Table of Contents

Table of Contents i

Acknowledgements iii

Prologue 1

The Middle 7

The End 10

Chapter One 27

Chapter Two 54

Chapter Three 68

Chapter Four 78

Chapter Five 85

Chapter Six 114

Chapter Seven 131

Chapter Eight 135

Chapter Nine 146

Chapter Ten 157

Chapter Eleven 163

Chapter Twelve 170

Chapter Thirteen	177
Chapter Fourteen	188
Chapter Fifteen	204
Chapter Sixteen	213
Chapter Seventeen	226
Chapter Eighteen	233
Chapter Nineteen	250
About the Author	253
Other books by the Author:	254

Acknowledgements

Robert Battista

This publication is made possible by the great and unending support of my lovely wife, Amada Battista, and our children, Kloey, Rayna, Willow and Moe, without whom I would not have had the courage and stamina to pursue my dreams. And to my sister, Nancy Morgan, for her compassion, nurturing, strength and willpower to help me become a full person and never give up on our dreams.

Prologue

I really do not consider myself what you might call a smart man, but I am a thinking man. I often have many whimsical thoughts, most of which usually surprise and excite me. I suppose that would be right, I am excitable. I was 38 when being startled by some of my own thoughts in a peculiar way. I had just told a story to a friend that would alter my whole life in many ways. It was, however, just a story.

The beginning of a lot of stories looks a lot like the end…and this one is not any different. The problem comes in knowing the difference of when something begins and ends…is born or dies…and in such moments we toggle eternal.

"Ok, so I totally have the movie figured out" I exclaimed excitedly to Cathy trying to counteract a snooze on a late-night drive from San Diego to Los Angeles.

"You know my Dad and Mom moved to Greece from NYC in 1960, right?" I fact checked Cathy's knowledge, for I had told versions of the story to many people. "And, you know my Dad wrote this book, Chicken In Greece," further ground laying on my behalf.

"Well, it is a hysterical book, very colorful. The book is basically a marginally fictionalized version of their life. Anyway…" I looked over at Cathy to see if she was paying attention, and I couldn't tell if her look showed mild interest or if that lifted eyebrow meant she was just being polite. But I plunged on anyway.

"The movie starts with this scene of two grown men at a funeral—my Mom's funeral—one guy, the older one, gives the younger one, me, this gold coin." I remember sounding like a man now believing his own fiction.

"The older guy is a Long Island type," I explained. "A couple of gold chains around his neck but the salt-of-the-earth type of guy. He says, taking one of the gold chains with a coin on it from around his neck 'Your Mom gave this to me as a remembrance of you when I left Greece. It's some kinda Greek coin. I left Greece when you were 1. You were named after me and I am your Godfather. I thought you would want it.'" I was breathing deeply now.

I summarized for Cathy—how confused I was at the cemetery. It had been a long 24 hours, finding out my mother died, making arrangements for myself, my brother and sister, the long flight to NY where she wanted to be buried, the memorial service at the church. The service disoriented me, the Greek incense clouding my senses, the cantor going on in some funereal tone I could recognize but not understand, the wailing of an old woman behind us, us in the first pew, friends and relatives behind, the solemn voice of a priest we barely knew…words of a dear lady, great Mother, inspirer of dreams, national Teacher of the Year, etc. We were all in shock.

So when this guy shows up at the funeral, and introduced himself as Bobby Newman, I felt like I was in some sort of a dream.

I looked over again at Cathy, and I could tell I had her now. The dialog at the funeral was still stuck in my head…

Bob Newman: I am so sorry that I could not come to your Dad's funeral but I was out of the country and heard too late to make it.

Bobby (Me): No problem, I didn't know you and my Dad were such good friends.

Newman: Your Mom and Dad were dear friends of mine. Billy and I grew up together in the Bronx and lost touch after Greece.

Newman: Your Mom and Dad were great people and loved by many. We had so much fun over there, the Greeks, friends from the City that visited—forget-about-it!

Bobby: Yeah, I am surprised we never met till now. I knew my Dad had a partner but you never really came up much. You were the Chicken-man from the Bronx, right?

My sister and brother were huddling together, confused at this intrusion. Or so I thought. I think I remember Nick, my brother, saying, "Damn, he looks familiar." And I'm not sure if it was my imagination, but I believe my sister pulled him away so sharply that he fell head first into the mound of dirt surrounding the casket. But I made nothing of it.

So, then the coin thing happens and fade to black…

"You got it? That's the opening over credits" I wanted to make sure Cathy was on board. "This was actually true and all took place at my Mom's funeral." I then took some time to give Cathy a background on my folks that would go into the movie, fast scene Hollywood style, voice over narration, along the lines of:

My parents were unusual people, unusual in the good sense though, mostly characterized by their magnetic personalities. Everyone wanted to be around them, they were gracious, passionate, funny and fun.

Actually, on paper, they were quite average people that one day woke up and decided that it sucked to be average and they should actually do something about it. I was not born yet, so I suppose in many ways I was a benefactor of their restlessness…my Dad was an "ad-man" on Madison Avenue, for, what at the time was the most trophied of middle America magazines, Family Circle Magazine. He spent many a lunch having drinks at the 21 Club in NYC, laughing with clients, the occasional slap on a waitress' ass. He felt all of the hollowness that must accompany a job selling space, the lack of mission, productivity, purpose…my Mom, Kay, or Katherine Kay, on the other hand was a happy school teacher, giving herself daily to the cause. She was a great teacher, an inspirer of hope, individuality and potential. Later on in her career, as you will see, she becomes National Teacher of the Year.

I continued with my story. I think I was losing Cathy. I had had her when I was talking about the funeral but she wasn't making the connection when I started talking about my parents. What did it have to do with my parents? I went on, because I hadn't figured that out either for a long time, and I wanted to see if she would catch on sooner.

My parents lived in a suburb of New York City, or as my grandpa would say "upstate," in an average home, albeit bustling with chaos generated efficiently by three kids and a collie named Schwartz. My Dad liked the fact that their lawn was messy, ensuring the disparaging eye and muttered "tsst-tsst" of the neighbors. My dad always said that they had reached the height of mediocrity—2.5 car garage, three kids, the dog—the absolute pinnacle of middleclass nothingness. He was in a love/hate relationship with the routine, "the schlep" as he dearly called it…he loved the boundaries and structure it provided, only to despise his routine for the drain on the dignity that it brought to a man. Not that there is anything wrong with 1950's middle-classness, it is just that it caused restlessness in my parents, a yearning for more. Ok, so maybe they were not all that average…

One day, my Dad (after getting fired by Family Circle for hitting on the boss' secretary and sneaking around to class B matinees in midtown artsy theaters during work time), a hopeless romantic and explorer at heart, pitched my Mom on the idea of a new start, an adventure. He told a story of getting away from the mundane, the daily trappings of running here, running there…he thought they should move to Greece and start over, open a restaurant—a NY steakhouse—and live free from schedules and bosses…My Mom, Kay, was 100% 1st generation Greek and wanted to support my Dad and her lover. Bill disdained the materialism of his day, the vapid looks in his peers' eyes, the mechanical trudging of daily life. Greece, he thought, would be different, the people real, impassioned with an air of disdain for the things that wealth summons and not dependent on material things. Kay was all for a change, fearful of the reality that maybe there was no more to life than what she was experiencing daily. So, it was with this spark, this wild scheme to get more out of life, that I was conceived.

Now, you must realize that my Dad was a very persuasive man; a charismatic charmer, schooled with the street smarts of a Bronx born Italian NYC union bricklayer, romanced by the privilege of a Fordham BA in literature and tempered by two years of marine corp. service as a ranking officer…he knew the magic of a stickball bat, the power of a well placed line of Shakespeare and the value of a crate of steaks.

The year was 1960…

…Cut to scene of Bill in Bob Newman's chicken barbeque restaurant in the Bronx. Bill is on his way home from Madison Avenue and trying to convince Bob to close the shop and move to Greece with Kay and him…

Cathy perks up, thinking that I was going to tie it all together for her, but I just continued with the story.

Bill: Common Bob, what's keeping you, it'll be great…

Bob: Bill, I have a great little shop here, people love it.

Bill: Bob, ever since we were kids—you know—we always said there was more, more out there, beyond the boroughs.

Bob: I want to settle down like you, bag a wife, have some kids and run the shop. I didn't go to college like you did Billy.

Bill: Look at me, I went to Fordham, married a great lady and 'settled down'—whatever that means in a man's life. Now what? I'm miserable, bored and taking it out on my family—

Bob: —come on Billy—

Bill: If Kay only knew how trapped I really felt, how regular and scared. It's not fair to her to have me unhappy, I'm distracted. Look what happened at work, I have to get away from it all—

Bob: — Greece is the answer?

Bill: —what's holding us back? You could run the restaurant, I will market it, Kay will schmooze the Greeks. She's got a bunch of relatives there, close relatives. Let's face it, American life is dead, it's empty. Look at us, you stuck in the Bronx, me in the 'burbs. Nobody ever does shit about their lives, we attain status and wallow in it till we suffocate a lazy death of the spirit. You want that? An idiot's death!

Bob: (mumbling) You think we could do this? Could Kay set us up? How connected are her relatives? Don't screw with me Billy—

Bill: —Very! They're Greek aristocracy, look at Ya-Ya. Government people. Generals. Newspaper men, the works. Doctors. Connected.

Bob: Ok, so what if we do pull the restaurant off, you think I can find love over there? Did you sell Kay on it yet? Did—

Bill: —don't worry about Kay, she'll love it.

Roll credits…

The Middle

So, I was born in Greece in 1962. It's all my Dad's fault. I am born in the final chapter of his Chicken book. Strangely, I never read the book till after I moved to Los Angeles, 5 years following my Mother's death. You would think if your Dad wrote a book you might read it, especially if it was about your life. I always knew the folklore of the story and gave the book to good friends to read over the years as a qualifier of their friendship, but never read it for some reason. I knew the story cold because I lived it so I always talked about the fable as if I wrote the thing myself.

As luck might have it, I gave it to a coworker of mine whose dad was this big Hollywood guy, past President of a large studio, Chairman of the Academy Awards, blah, blah. She loved it and pushed me to give it to her dad. Several years passed and I finally gave it to him. Sure enough he loved it too but was too busy to produce it. But he read it! He said "It would make a great movie, but I have no time to work on the screenplay. The problem with the book is that it has no conflict in it, no tension between the main characters. The "B" characters are well developed, very hysterical, but the main ones, the "A" characters, need conflict. It has lots of funny scenes in it: the scene of Ya-Ya and trying to look up her skirt, blessing the rotting chickens in the hopes that the Greeks will come into the store, the scene of the customs agent and the barbeque machine, Nick-the-walk, etc., but it is missing tension and structure, people in Hollywood like to see a beginning, a middle and an end." Then he said, "I'll tell you what, you work on it, find a writer, write the screenplay and I'll help you once you have a draft, we'll take it to Sony and pitch it."

So, I did just that. I worked on adding tension and Hollywood-like intrigue to the tale. It was a weird task, messing with my parents' story, but one I embraced with a spirit of their life, a spirit of drama and fiction. After all, they were in their early 30's when they took flight to Greece. They were reckless, I knew that. They were charming; I benefited from that. Most of all, they were characters—east coast style—and that was my heritage. I forgave myself on the merits to toy with their lives, to spin conflict into it. And in spinning this conflict, I came to grips with who I was, and where I came from.

Now you are in for a real treat. Here is the Chicken story as written by my dear deceased Father, William G. Battista. It is printed here as originally written, unabridged. The Hollywood conflict that I would add to the story is simple, so I will offer it up now…imagine, all the while, that Bob Newman, Bill's best friend is actually having an affair in Greece with Bill's wife, Kay. Imagine that her baby born towards the back of the book—me—is not really Bill's offspring, but rather the product of a torrid love affair between Kay and Bob the friend and partner. Imagine that Bill was in the dark about it the whole time. I know, it sounds so Hollywood. Good conflict though, right? Let's see what you think (timeframe: 1961-1967, Greece):

The Book (298 Pages):

Chicken In Greece

by William G. Battista

It really is hard to follow that story with much, as was always the problem with my flamboyant parents. Tell me it wasn't witty. Tell me it wasn't colorful. Tell me you did not laugh.

Now, in the spirit of making a movie, I casually set out to find a friend that is a screenplay writer. That is not a difficult task when one lives in lala-land. I picked one of my friends who was an aspiring screenwriter and he started on it. We tried to add tension to the story but disagreed over the plot. He did not like my thoughts that it should be a love comedy/tragedy between Bill, the sporadically insolent dreamer husband; Kay, the doting pent up, increasingly resentful wife; and Bob, the opportunistically voyeuristic and not so dedicated friend. Not interesting he proclaimed. I fired him.

My take was that the conflict would start to reveal itself when Kay gets pregnant and you don't really know whose kid it is. Bill is befuddled when he finds out Kay is pregnant; they have not been together in months. He has his doubts but he dutifully rallies and re-embraces his family. The moral is obvious: dreamer wanders in search of happiness only to discover that love was in the backyard all of the time, it had nothing to do with escapes from the accoutrements to far off lands. The audience never really knows what happened but it doesn't matter…great feel good story with a beginning, a middle and an end! I had my movie.

The End

So, back to my movie pitch to Cathy. After telling her an abbreviated version of what you already know, I staged the grand finale!

"The last scene in the movie is Kay [my Mom], Casablanca style, saying goodbye to Bob at the airport in Greece, I, a one-year old in her arms, year 1963, on the runway. She takes the gold coin from around her neck and tells him—'Baby, I want you to keep this Greek coin as a keepsake for Bobby. Your son.' Kay gently folding his hand shut with the coin in it. Fade to black. The End!"

As I told that finish, uttered those words to Cathy, in that very moment I had a thought: "What if it is true!" I thought: I don't look anything like my brothers, I have always been different from them, always the responsible one, albeit like we all have roles in a family. They used to chide me I was adopted but all youngest kids get so chided. I thought. I searched. I am the only one in the family with brown eyes, I had white hair when I was a kid which I always chalked up to being born to Greek beaches (although my Mom, prideful, always said we came from the Peloponisos, where the Turks never infiltration, and the Greeks were fair). I was tall. I was the only one in the family that did not have a substance abuse problem. In my 30s I was going bald! A Greek and Italian man going bald (although my Mom always said that you need to look beyond your immediate father to the Grandfather, which in this case was bald in his old age). My

Mother always said I was born unto that classic Greek song, Never On Sunday. I never really understood what that meant other than it sounded forbidden. Now I thought: forbidden how?

Ok, so my parents were dead. I met Bob Newman once at my Mom's funeral. I did not even know him. He appeared out of nowhere, gave me a Greek coin, and disappeared again. That was 10 years ago. I hadn't given him another thought. But now, all I could do was think of him. The next day I called my sister. She was the family record keeper and matriarch since my mother had died. I told her I finally figured out how to tell the Chicken story, how to make it a great movie with conflict. She heard my pitch, the phone space between us oddly quiet. Nancy said, "Do you think it's true?" I said, "I don't know." I needed to find and call Bob Newman. Nancy found his number in Mom's old stuff, now 10 years gone by, and stoically gave it to me.

I sat on the precipice. All of my human frailty rested in my still hands. What was I to do? My parents were dead. What was the truth? Would anyone tell me? Did any of it matter? Was Bob Newman still alive? How was he positioned? Was he a friend or foe? Was he to be honest? Did he have a conscious? Did any of it really matter? What if he was senile and anyone that called him became his son? All these thoughts cycled around in my head like electricity being called to a light switch when someone flicks it. I had always lived a life of constant motion. Activity—any type of activity—was a whimsical escape into a self controlled reality. Now I was still.

I made the phone call to his Florida home after dinner the next evening. I had a predicament in figuring out what to say? If it is true there is a good chance he will not tell me as they obviously never intended that I know, their beguile making witness to my life. We small talked for a minute or two. I told him I was happy, married, kids, stable, financially secure and, oh yeah, I had a bizarre question for him. I said before asking it:

"If it is true, don't say a word. Don't say anything. Ok?"

"Ok" he capitulated.

"If it is not true, just tell me," I continued.

"Ok," he mused.

"Ok. Is there any chance that you're my father?!" I boldly stated.

1.5 seconds lapsed.

"It's true."

An eternity passed.

"It's ok" I said strongly. "I figured it out."

"I'm so glad it's out in the open" he confessed. "I'm so glad its out." You could walk on the words.

"So how's the health on that side of the family?" I quipped.

We went on from there to fill in the details. How did it happen? What happened? Who knew? What did they agree on? Etc. Turns out my Hollywood story superimposed on my Dad's book was dead on, almost verbatim. He said that he and my Mom fell deeply in love, that my Dad worked in the daytime at the store, and he worked at night (I chuckled a thought in my head: 'yeah, in more ways than one'). He explained it like it was yesterday, as if finishing a recent conversation, that my Dad and Mom were estranged at the time, were not sleeping together and when she was pregnant they all knew what had happened. Listening to the story was like peering in on a bustling fish tank. There was lots of activity but it was deadly silent and I could not do anything to get involved. A dull numbness filled my brain. I meandered a bit like a dingy being towed in tether to a boat drifting and accelerating, remembering its course only when being lunged by the taught rope. The details were like a hard hail storm pelting the windshield while you sit safe and cozy in a plush car. The storm was happening, it would pass, and these small ice balls that braved the elements, proud and strong, imploring their concerted message on the entrapped, would magically be vanquished by their new world, perhaps not without leaving small dents about which their origins would only be known to those that braved the storm, the aftermath of which to be duly afforded as a mystery to others. Hail is a natural phenomenon that we witness in awe, such now was my news. I also realized that I could really only hear his story at this point, my parents were poor players on his stage. His message survived, it was given an opening through which he was releasing his hail storm, weighing me to my station immobile in the nested life that my parents provided acting as a protectorate like a windshield. In this storm I was oddly feeling safe. Here I was, 38 years old, getting told from a man I just met for all intensive purposes, no, my dad technically, getting told about how he and my mom, no, his lover, were going to take me and run away with the other kids to a life of happiness. But then my Dad rallied. He punched Newman in the nose, broke it, sent him to the hospital claimed me as his son, as part of his family. He became my father. I was listening, chasing the story all the while seeing three confused people, in their young 30s trying to make sense of their unfettered detritus.

Here, at 38 I was evidently a new-man. A Robert Joseph new-man, as was his name. I already had the Robert Joseph part, just not the Newman part. Over the coming weeks I pondered on a lot of material. I grew up Greek and Italian. Now I was Greek, German and Irish. I always did get along unusually well with the Irish I thought. I talked to my brother and sister. Nancy grew up suspecting it all along, being 8 years older than I she remembered the fights between Mom, Dad and Dad at the time. She remembered the time my Father (who will remain Bill Battista) broke Newman's nose and took him to the peasantry public Greek hospital instead of the better private one. (It's funny how kids remember things that don't make sense.) On his death bed, my Dad officially confessed to Nancy under an oath to secrecy. After finding out the truth myself, I remember calling an old family friend, the kind of friend that even as an adult you still call "Mr." I was explaining how it was all a little different now. How I am not really who I thought I was.

"It's weird," I said. "I am not really Italian. I loved the idea that I was some hot blooded Greek and Italian. I cook great Italian food."

"Bobby, you are Italian," Mr. Iannocone asserted. "Your Dad was Italian, he loved you so very much and you are Italian. You know I am 100% Italian, ok. I go to Italy every year to visit relatives, the old country."

"Yeah? Uh huh—"

"I say to my relatives, 'I'm Italian!' They laugh. They say: 'You're not Italian. You're American Italian!'"

It was a great fable for me. It grounded me. It neither offended my biological father nor did it diminish my paternal father. Besides the story helped me preserve my morphing identity, it made me gain perspective. I thought, 'huh, I should find like reckonings to as many of the open issues that avail me.' I should celebrate the fact that I had two dads, one that raised me in unabashed, albeit dysfunctional love to the best of his abilities and one that was happy to be found. I did, however, have a lot of thinking to do. What was the essence of family? Was it blood? Was it nurturing? On the one hand I had one dad that lived a pontificating ponderous existence, diverted by the occasional grandiose scheme and on the other hand, I had a dad that lived a blissfully happy sensate life over the countertops of his serial food establishments. One lived romanticizing life through literature and one became alive through the realities of literature. Nevertheless, accompanying my ambient sense of confusion was a luminous sense of relief. Feelings of clarity coursed through me like a magical dye clearing a body of water of its opacity.

I had always yearned for one event, one magical bullet to kill a demon. The demon was of a peculiar sort though. It was the demon betrothed to lack of acknowledgment and as such very illusive. That was the entry of the bullet, the mere fact that I found the target. The exit was that one event itself—one meaningful event—would assuredly rip all the injustice out of my life. As one impact it was perhaps a decisive wound that would heal the two, acknowledgment with atrocity. It is generally hard to find one ethereal event to accomplish all of that. The New-man discovery was it. It was large enough. A total loss and found of identity. A blank check to write all bad debts to. I was gifted that in my news. "I'm adopted! I don't belong here and I don't belong there!" I just belong. I felt cleansed, admittedly in kind of a dirty way. To this day I am not sure why; and, in that it is one of the only things I don't question in life. It is one of the few things I leave in the sanctity of a sovereign state for my base emotions. Maybe it is because I found an answer to a pestering emotion. I always felt this open ended aspect to my life, a missing link. Don't misunderstand: my interpretation of not belonging is not a license to stray; it is an emblem for groundedness, an absolution, of self and others.

My dads gave me many gifts, of this I am sure. In their un-proclaimed struggle to find meaning, find love, they made me. Made by consequence, reward, sacrifice, neglect and commitment. I guess what I realized is that, unbeknownst to me, I was ½ made till I discovered the truth. I always felt like I had a missing piece and figured that everyone felt that way, it was the human condition. Upon discovery of Newman I thought that truth meant honesty. I felt quenched by the honesty only to be soon parched by the arid reality that honesty only facilitated enlightenment. Truth has more to do with meaning and how we reconcile facts, honesty/dishonesty, into understanding. I have come to realize that truth is understanding which sits just atop of honesty. An obtuse set of semantics admittedly but ones I cast fairly and ones that I am compelled to figure out in light of my news. The big question being: Does it matter? Does the truth matter? Why? Well, it all rests on the meaning of the "truth." The truth is not the fact pattern. The truth is not a compilation of true statements. There was so much deceit surrounding my life that I always felt I never knew truth. I was missing ingredients to gain understanding. Very frustrating. There is no greater loneliness than the feeling of isolation in the company of others. It was, however, this very trait, or tolerance I should say that made me so successful in life. Successful in relationships, in challenging situations, in my career. I was both very tolerant of injustices and also always vigilant on finding clues to a more fulfilled life.

 You must ask: "But don't you feel betrayed?" "Don't you feel lied to?" "Duped?" "Bitter?" No. Why would I? How would I cycle to such ground? It would be an idiot's wind that I would draft to get there. And now, when I was looking to affront such a draft, I would not be relegated to that space. I did feel a tinge bit irrationalized in the world of faithful woman though. None of our moms really had sex.

We were all immaculately conceived. Right? I had to think: 'Who was unfaithful?' My Mom? My paternal Dad? My biological Dad? I suppose they all were. In this sense I still struggle. I feel through people all too often. Always have. 'What would so-and-so feel? How would so-and-so feel?' Things were generally discombobulated. My discovery did help to correctively focus me on me. I found my missing piece. It forced me to think about how I felt about events, particularly since my parents were dead and interpretation lay on my shoulders. I suppose I always felt through people as a means to try to spy the truth for myself like a ferret earning its name. If I could always trust people to be dishonest, or more aptly be honest to the best of their ability as bound by their circumstances, then I always trusted people and ultimately relied on myself to find the truth.

As the ensuing months passed I came to grow into my new-man story. I used it as a crooked crutch in times of fain togetherness. Perhaps the most disconcerting time was when I actually went to meet my biological father a few months after I discovered the news. It was a microcosm for what it all meant I guess. I looked just like him. I cooked like he cooked, we liked the same food, had the same strange metabolism that was the envy of my friends. I remember feeling like I was a monkey raised by lions that actually thought I was a lion until I met another monkey. I felt this strange sense of righteous betrayal of my heritage when I actually saw him. In a good sense though. The feelings had balance for me. I felt self delivered, through my own vigilance, to this place. I actually was a monkey but I belonged with the lions. I knew their ways, their pride traditions, was conditioned by their haunting habits and would die by their veldt, ah, alas, but with monkey genes.

I also met a half sister, aptly named Nancy. Fancy having two sisters named Nancy. It was a little strange. She was as kind as a sister would be. That is one thing that I learned: family is family no matter what. Maybe because we are all searching for more, or maybe because it is a matter of blood, but family has an aura to it, an energy and a claim to more. It is a puzzle though, as we have all heard, "you cannot pick your family!" I never knew anyone had a choice but in a strange sense I, for one did. A choice of perspective, for my reality was my reality. Of acceptance. And, in that acceptance a choice of understanding. I understand that the world is a broken place. I understand that people make mistakes. I understand that we make the best of situations. I am such a situation.

Recently, Bob Newman died. He died for what in my family was an old age of 75. He died young in the standards of his family. Most of his people lived into their 80s and 90s. When I got "the call" of his passing I was very sad. In a funny way it completed the meaning of the whole discovery for me. I was alone and I knew it. Years before my discovery, in my early 30s, I went to a Rabbi that I respected and vividly recall telling him: "I just want the sky to part and a pair of hands to come down, assuredly, to give me a badge acknowledging that I had a tough life." I said that I just wanted some definitive authority to acknowledge that sometimes it sucked, sometimes it was ugly and I did okay, I made it. The Rabbi said to me: "No doubt you had a tough life, suffered great loss and were robbed of a childhood. But, I would suggest that unless you find meaning in all of it, unless you accept how all those experiences shaped you, you will be lost." I was magnetically puzzled to this idea of finding meaning to my life through acceptance. Only I was unsure of what to accept. I lived a life pummeled by receptive acceptance, passively accepting my lot. To accept pro-actively though, what would I want to accept? I had a choice? On the day that I found my new-man news the sky parted. On the day Robert Joseph Newman died I got my badge. I was irrefutably alone. I accepted that. It calmed me. I was cut loose. There is no worse suffering than a pain unfixed to a source. Such pain is without meaning and therefore without cure. My pain began to gain a source and as such it flowed directly out of me like a ribbon might wisp free off a fence by catching a determined wind. It was made real. I have always lived in a resilient world self created by rationalizations. My news was blessed news. It was a gift. I felt blessed to have figured it out. I loved my Dad and I loved Bob Newman for the short time that I knew him. My Dad made me resilient and Bob Newman made me rational. His absence in my life gave me a yearning to learn the truth and in doing so gave me a behavioral skill that was now mine.

 Oh the oddities come and go. How many people can say they buried two Dads? I hated funerals, having been to too many prematurely. I knew I had to go to his. It was oddly enough the only one I wasn't afraid of and kind of excited to attend. I knew it was critical to me for closure. I also knew for once, it was my decision to go. It was my mourning. No family pressure because there was really no bond with family on that side. I was free to mourn as I pleased. Nevertheless, age and adulthood status does not change the childhood impressions we have of certain social obligations. Funerals are untouchable, they are like going to bed, you have to do it. Going was another trip altogether though. I packed my bag for Florida. There I met my ½ brother, Robert Joseph and other ½ sister, Janet, both of which I never met till the day of his funeral. Reflecting, it is ironic how many immediate blood relatives I met at funerals. It rings of the old cliché: with every death there is rebirth. It is also ironic that both Bobby Newman and Janet did not speak to their father for some 15 years because he ended up leaving their mother to an affair with the cashier at his store. They being incensed at the deceit and indecency that surrounded his departure. He initially married in the year after coming home from Greece, in 1964, had the three kids and divorced 10 years later. He then remarried to the cashier in his store following his divorce and lived a happy life to his death 20 years later.

 When I showed up to his funeral it was like Mick Jagger appearing at a teen party, except the teens were all seniors. Everyone knew me. I knew three people, Phyllis, his widow; Nancy, my sweet ½ sister and her husband, Sandro. It was like playing a role in a movie, people came up to me, not even knowing who I was, but the combination of standing next to his widow and looking exactly like him, would say:

"Your father was a great man, we loved to work with him. We are so sorry for your loss." He worked at a supermarket up until he died. At my previous parental funerals I was always angered by the overtures of consolation and the "sorry" brigade. This time, I felt rested, actually calm enough to accept the consolation, even strong enough to console them with a haughty mourner's phase. I really felt like his spirit was in me and I was providing a service to the community. To say that mourning is a personal experience is pejorative. To be called to mourn without personal emotions is bizarre. It feel like when you got a hall-pass to roam the empty corridors in grade school and all of your friends are getting tortured in their classes, but you, you were free. You know what it feels like to be in the class, in the control of the teacher, but you were somehow stealing time and missing—forever—the material being covered. For those brief "hall-pass" moments, you were invisible. Such was the feeling of being at his funeral. I was there, in my station, first pew position, the honored seat, but it was not really real. I envisioned the funeral parlor as a school, with me walking in this neutral zone, though kids I did not know, maybe 7th graders, walking these safe corridors, hall-pass in hand right through everyone. I tried so hard to feel what my ½ sister Nancy was feeling, she was crying, weeping in peaks and valleys unintentionally synchronized to the chorus of his widow's dignified, albeit valium induced, corps speak. Where else than a funeral can speaking to nobody be so accepted. It is a blissful license afforded to the primary survivors. The widow is Queen at a funeral. Anything goes. In this case, with a touch of "it's ok" humor, her valium high was confessed in a pew murmur. Nancy said: "She took a valium to help out, she has been a mess," and then Phyllis would chime in, "I've never taken these pills, they're great, oh well, who knew…" The valium seemed to help her in very social-like manner come in and out of the turret's of mourning. It was actually endearing in the way that it took the awkwardness of her transitions from "Bobby, how was your trip" banter to "oh, Bob (her husband) when are you coming home" and then in a lower voice… "You know he loved to work, he loved the customers and the people at the store."

One of the most amazing benefits of the funeral was this old couple from the Bronx, married 55, yes 55 years. Between the two of them, equally summed, they might have been eight feet tall. They knew my parents and Bob Newman as kids. I melted into their tales and was coddled by their discreet intones of childhood confessions. "Your Mom and Dad were great friends, we all grew up together…yeah we knew your Dad well." No name was mentioned. A Niagara of history coursed down the lineages that they represented. They knew my grandparents (Grandpa Billy and Grandma Nancy and even the ones I didn't know on the Newman side) which made me feel like I had family there at the funeral. We all like to feel represented. After all, that's the essence of funerals—representation. I felt my Mom and Dad there through their stories. This little couple, preserved in Florida, was a connection to everyone. They were also beautifully colored by the obvious grief over my dad du jour. It was a peculiar feeling feeling so engaged in talking to them amidst the home court backdrop of the local fans. We were both connected from the old school ties of the Bronx. Images of family covered me as I stood listening, towering over these sweet, adorable sentries of both worlds. Until we met we were both marginalized by the nouveau Florida community of mourners. The trip had purpose. Meeting them was really special and, but not for a moment, the din of the parlor was muffled by the blanket of warmth that covered me with the soothing magic that a dense still-life snowfall makes on a bustling city park.

We buried Bob Newman in one of those "condo" tombs that they used to stock cartons of cigarettes in behind the counter. 'Uh, I'll have a carton on Marlboros, and oh yeah, um, can you put my dad in the 4th row, eight up.' It felt good to put the services behind me. Of course there was an "after party," Bronx/Florida style. These were "Deli" people. People of the counter with a license to slice meat. I was assigned to Nancy and Sandro as my priority escorts in that sobering postmortem parking lot negotiation that reminds people they have to move on and function. Ah, the jarring and comforting aspects of logistics and small concerns. It was agreed, I would follow Nancy and Sandro to the hosting house, the house of the widow's sister. The elongated and nondescript carpet of sun blanched Florida communities that we drove through were perfect to cleanse the mind after the funeral. Life went on. Cold-cuts would be served. We choose life. We would eat to live; perhaps even tip the Chablis a little early if the widow leads the charge.

I prepared for phase II: the return to social conversation that cannot happen in the mourning parlor. People would want to get to know me. My family instincts prepared me for the situation as I docked my rental car along with the early arrivers on the lawn of the house I was entering. I figured there had to be a drunken uncle in there somewhere and if I was lucky, I would get out before he reared so I could spare myself of that side of this family. The house was perfectly Florida. Ranch bungalow with trinkets resting on shelves that only retirement can populate with such precision. It was sweet, the people were so nice. I was still under the grandiosity of the first family. I had a flight back home in four hours, which gave me about an hour and a half at the party, just enough time to lush through the first nectar of the tier one epitaphs and not enough time to have them tarnished by any breaks in the veneer of a wayward mourner. Everyone was delightful. People changed into Florida casual wear, which in and of itself is like a sedative. Funeral's over, respect Bobby Newman—production time, deli style. The General was dead, Sergeants became First Lieutenants and the food was laid out in great pride. "Bobby loved parties, this is great roast beef, you want some? Try the liverwurst, he loved this…" In the milling around of the kitchen, I was first told about the spread, where they got all the meats from and who pulled in favors from whom to procure Newman's favorites. The communal feeling of aloof nobility surrounding the meats and the cold-cuts was regal. Bobby would have loved the party.

Moments like when I was reaching for a sandwich and one of his nieces (a teenager) started to tear up because my hands looked just like his, were, well, a bit strange. They were endearing though. "Look at his hands, they look just like his. I'm sorry, it is just amazing though." Then Nancy and Sandro blurted out, "yeah, he drives like he did too, its weird, we were laughing so hard, he is all over the road, crossing the line, it is remarkable. Just like pop did." I felt proud and I felt like I belonged.

So, this is my story. Oh, I could go on…how it affected my life, my marriage, my subconscious choices in life. You will have to wait on all those ditties as they remain unscripted until I am relegated to my cigarette carton in the sky. My parents. They moved to Greece in 1960 in an attempt to "start over." I was born in Greece. I have three sisters and three brothers, two alive, one dead. It really is a simple little story after all. So life begins on this day.

– The End –

Chapter One

At thirty thousand feet the Peloponnesus looked like a shriveled four-titted udder limply hanging down from an old over-milked cow. At twenty thousand feet the udder became indistinguishable and was swiftly replaced with the triangle of the Attican peninsula as the big jet raced to finish its journey to Athens from New York.

 Bill Treekerson looked down past the wing at the changing picture below. For him, until recently, the Peloponnesus wasn't a place, it was a vague war between unknown combatants—possibly Greek. And Attica was the name of an itchy movie house on Eighth Avenue near Forty Second Street which traditionally showed Class B films. The wonder of knowledge, he thought, squinting at the thin line of the Corinth canal. Only three months ago the Peloponnesus was a mysterious myth, now in addition to being a war it was a solid tangible patch of brown and green, a piece of earth with people and trees and towns and cities. Treekerson was not what might be called a thinking man, but he delighted in acquiring knowledge. It was exciting for him to think that just an instant ago ancient Sparta was directly beneath the plane. To be sure, not the Sparta that was—that fierce fatherland of superbly disciplined warriors—now it was only a small lonely village. But then...then...thousands of years past. He bit his lip and concentrated on the sky for a moment. He was reasonably certain Sparta was in the Peloponnesus. Or was that Macedonia? No, he was certain! He took a deep breath and sat back in his seat confident Sparta was below, before.

Treekerson was about to light up his 93rd cigarette in fourteen hours when the sign in the front of the cabin flashed on. He buckled his seat belt and affected a nonchalant landing air as the stewardess passed checking to see if all the passengers were strapped in. He was glad he didn't use the cigarette, he had had too many, his stomach and mouth felt crummy and sour from smoking so much.

The jet banked softly, dropped altitude and glided in on a path between Mount Hymettus and the Attican coast line where the blue Aegean lapped quietly at the sandy beaches of Greek ship owners.

Treekerson's fatigue and belly ache, a result of too little sleep, too many cigarettes, breakfast at midnight, sunrise at two in the morning, left him now, giving way to a strong feeling of anxiety. The pain and uncomfortable knot in his stomach moved up to his trachea, there blocking some saliva he was attempting to swallow. He had had this trachea problem before, when he finally made the decision to remove himself, his wife and his large family of little children to Greece. The decision had not come easily, it took months to make, but helping immeasurably was the fact that after he lost he rather well paying and soft job, he had been unable to make contact for another one. The style of living to which they had become used, had become outmoded and some kind of action was demanded. The problem was a serious one— they were in debt—but no more serious than that which afflicts thousands or even millions of people each year. What made it more serious was that Treekerson was glad. An opportunity for escape had been offered without the utilization of his unproven courage. For Treekerson had not lost his job bravely standing fast to his principles and spitting on the boss's desk, but ignominiously in the lobby of The World on 52nd Street after a Brigitte Bardot pre-acting flick, for grow incompetence and neglect of duty and for sneaking around movies while he should have been calling on clients. The fact that the boss had been there too made no difference to either Treekerson or the boss, they accepted that Treekerson as the junior man would have to go.

After that he concluded that he was not a young man in a hurry, able to compete, drive to the top; and concentrated his energies and talents on thoughts of escape.

"But why Greece?" People cried. "Who ever heard of Greece? You can't make a living here – you're going to make one there? You don't speak the language, its poor there…poor…undeveloped. You're too old for the Peace Corps."

The arguments against going to Greece were sound and his sanity was questioned. Kay, his own wife objected. She screamed loudly when he told her. "You're an absolute clod! Are you mad? Are you? Tell me, I'll arrange for commitment…are you just stupid or mad? Why can't you just get a job like everyone else?" She kept fighting him for weeks. "Five kids…five kids overseas. In Greece yet. I don't know anybody in Greece. How do we know about the water…and the fertilizer? Do you know anything about the fertilizer? No, you don't know about anything…you're insane."

But because she was equally dissatisfied, the spirit of an adventure, of a life away from suburbia, the women's club, Saturday marketing, had a strong built-in appeal and ultimately she capitulated. Once she did she threw herself into the project wholeheartedly and pushed Bill whenever his resolution waned.

Thus he had left, with five thousand dollars in travelers checks in his pocket, representing a loan on the house and the small drippings of an unemployment scathed bank account; an American-Greek dictionary and glossary of terms most used and useful, and a letter of introduction written by a Greek-American friend to an uncle in Athens. The friend said his uncle would help him, although he wasn't certain – he had never met his uncle. "My pop says they're the kind of people that like to help," Mike had said when Bill went to his house to say goodbye. "I don't know though, you know the old-timers, they forget. Take this letter, Pop wrote one too, this gives a little more information, Pop's no letter writer. We'll wire them when you leave, they'll probably meet the plane. If you really insist on going, you'll need all the help you can get…you don't know the Greeks." He showed Bill a picture of his uncle, "He's a doctor and speaks English, that's all I know about the guy. Well," Mike had put out his hand, shaking his head as if to say Bill was crazy, "that's about it. I wish you luck…Pop says you're foolish for going, he wouldn't go back if the deported him.

He also had armed himself with a number of research bulletins printed by the United States Department of Commerce which contained such pertinent information as: National per capita income…230 dollars per annum; trade balance…deficit; unemployment…large and chronic; production…the last year, poor, 20 percent of the crop destroyed willfully by dissatisfied peasants protesting a government ban on delivery of the crop to market by donkey; transportation…by sea – small leaky boats; previously on land, by donkey; economic forecast…excellent – the bottom had been reached.

That was the research-wise, creatively-wise he had in his head a comprehensive plan on what to do in Greece.

He tucked the book of traveler's checks deeper into his pocket as the wheels of the plane screeched contact with the runway.

The stewardess led the passengers into a bright April Greek sun to the airline terminal and customs where they were asked to form a line in front of a long wooden table and pick out their luggage from a pile behind a seated customs official.

The customs man wore a dark brown uniform. His hair was a black oily mass of waves and curls and his eyes were black and evil. Hiding most of his face under his nose was a thick shoe brush mustache.

There were a number of people at the far end of the customs, outside the gate, greeting visitors. Bill craned his neck to look for anyone fitting the picture Mike had shown him, but no one looked like the uncle.

The tourists were processed quickly, the customs man simply stamping the passports and filing the statements they filled out on the plane. When Bill handed over his passport and declaration the customs man looked up at him, his eyes riddled with suspicion and said, "You are not a tourist? You have here, purpose of trip—business. Is that not so?"

"Yes, I'm here for business," Bill said.

"what business? You have not listed what business. What business do you intend in Greece?" The customs man tilted his head and waited for an answer.

Bill wondered why the questions, the others had gone through without a word. "Business," he said innocently, "just business." He smiled. The customs man looked at him stonily.

"Which are your luggage?" he asked, nodding his head in the direction of the pile behind him. Bill pointed out his two worn brown bags and the customs man said something in Greek to a tall assistant standing nearby. The assistant asked Bill for the keys and opening the suitcases started rummaging around inside.

"I didn't smuggle anything."

"What business?"

"Business…I told you…look, just plain business."

"You have nothing from our consulate in New York. How can you be admitted without papers…you cannot be admitted?"

Bill was getting nervous; this was an inauspicious start. "Look…sir," he said, "what can I tell you. I mean...it's just that I'm coming to Greece...you know…for business. I honestly didn't know about the consulate. You can let me through, I'm legitimate. There's nothing wrong, is there? I mean...businesses..."

The customs man's face, evil, colored slightly and he said quietly through clenched teeth, "There is no business in Greece. What business?" By this time the assistant was deep inside the suitcases. He picked up a pair of torn underwear shorts from one of them and threw them back into the other. Bill again looked around for Mike's uncle. Hopefully he said, "Err, why don't you put me down...I'm a tourist."

The customs man's bushy black eyebrows arched upward, "You want to be a tourist?" he said.

Breakthrough at last. "Yes," Bill smiled, "put me down as a tourist."

"You can't be a tourist," the evil one hissed, "you wrote down business."

Some complaining noises came from the rest of the line. People wanted to get started on their vacations. The customs man jumped up suddenly and started to help the assistant, but changed his mind, returned to his chair and said, "You will have to wait. We will finish with the others first. You may sit there." He pointed to a wooden bench near the luggage.

Dismayed, Bill said, "I'm not smuggling anything." He desperately watched another plane planeload of people form up in line. "I'm a tourist. I swear I'm a tourist...look, I have travelers checks."

"You wrote business." The customs man was final. "Sit."

Bill saw it was futile trying to reason with the man and cursing himself for putting business on the declaration, started for the bench. Just as he was about to sit down, he heard a loud shot from behind him. "SAS PARA KOLO? ENA LEPTO ETHO! ! ! TI KANIS? EH? TI KANIS VLAKA?" Simultaneously he felt two strong hands grab his shoulders and whirl him around. He was engulfed in a storm of wet sloppy kisses and tried to pull away, not knowing what was going on, but the hands had too powerful a grip. Through blinking eyes and heavy spray of saliva he made out the source of the shout and what was holding him fast. It was an elliptically shaped man in a rumpled brown tweed suit. His face, where the features, tiny blue eyes, small piggy nose, and rosy, wet lips occupied a triangular space of perhaps three inches in the center of a round mass of cheeks, jowls and chins, quivered and folded with emotion. Bill, ducking from spit of the kisses identified him as the man in the picture his friend had shown him in New York, the man scheduled to meet him at the airport in Athens.

The little blue eyes looked at him levelly, as if linking a written description with the reality. The little mouth smiled. "I am Doctor Klones," the fat man said. "Is it you? Are you Beel? My brother wrote to me...you are you?"

Bill nodded slowly, "uhh...Dr. Klones?"

"I knew it was you," the fat man shouted happily. "I recognized you immediately." He grabbed Bill again, swept him into his stomach and kissed him loudly on both cheeks like a French Marshal awarding the Croix de Guerre. In happiness, he pushed and pulled Bill back and forth like a child playing with a rag doll. Then, releasing Bill's smarting shoulders, he turned and faced the customs man, who had risen to his feet respectfully with the initial shout. He directed a furious stream of turgid Greek at the customs man, shouting and gesturing wildly. He drew tourists, passers-by, the customs assistant and baggage handlers into the one-sided argument. His voice was filled with authority and all motion around the customs table ceased. The Greeks, who understood what he was saying, held their heads down, red-faced. The roaring diatribe lasted a full two minutes without a pause for breath.

    The customs man's face lost its evil dark look as it became an innocent beige, and his mustache, once a crisp shoe-brush became a wilted shine rag. He sputtered, "Kirio Klones...Kirio Klones...signome...signome...amesos...amesos."

    Bill watched in wonder as the elliptical man, still shouting and cursing, the chastised customs man and his assistant neatly repacked all his shirts, underwear, socks and research bulletins, ironing each layer out softly with their hands. They delicately closed the valises and carried them carefully out a door beyond the customs gate. The evil one rushed back to stamp and obsequiously hand Bill his passport. "Thank you, sir," he squeaked, bowing awkwardly.

    "Thank you," Bill said, stunned by the sudden change in events, and, feeling the grip on his shoulders once more, allowed himself to be escorted out of customs by his benefactor.

The suitcases were outside on the sidewalk next to the a very odd looking compact European car. Dr. Klones opened the front hood and with a wave of his thick arm directed Bill to put the bags in. He once more made for Bill. "I am so happy; I cannot tell you. I was afraid I would miss you. I was late, I am sorry." Strongly he wrapped his arms around Bill. "You have much to tell me. My brother wrote to me, he told me were a nice American. You are real American?" His eyes narrowed slightly, "my brother, tell me, his is rich? He tells me that always business is bad, his restaurant is only hetsi-ketsi." Doctor Klones spoke English well, accented but perfectly clear to Bill. When he was at loss for a word he interjected Greek. "We have much to talk about, "he continued, "I must know exactly what you will do, and I must help you," He rubbed his hanging chin with a hand that looked like a blown up rubber glove. "Is my brother's business so bad? He cannot even come for a vacation...I would like to see him, it has been so many years." He shrugged his massive shoulders and sighed. "Come, we will go to Athens."

Bill got into the car and watched the fat man throw himself violently into the driver's seat. The small car rocked back and forth with the load and settled into a ten degree list to port. He put the car in drive and lurched onto the highway to Athens. The back of his seat, suffering the immense burden of the driver for thousands of miles, was broken and tilted back on a forty-five degree recline. Doctor Klones held the wheel tightly with arms stiff, partly to steer and partly to hold himself from falling into the back seat. It looked as if at any moment he would wrench the wheel from the steering post.

Bill cleared his throat and said, "I don't know how to say thanks...for meeting me... for helping. I think I would have been stuck there for hours. I don't understand why...."

"Because they are stupid," Doctor Klones interrupted "what can I say...only malakas. Fools." His face puckered up in contempt and he waved a thin wisp of blond hair away from his eyes. "They are stupid because they only see what is written down on paper. They have no heads to themselves. You say hours, I say many hours you would have been sitting there. Bah, those people...so idiots."

"What did I do?" Bill asked, taking out his passport and looking into it for a clue as to why the customs man gave him such a hard time. "Oh..." he said, taking his letter of introduction from the passport, "by the way, I have a letter from Mike." He gave it to the fat man.

"Ahh...Mike, my niece. He is a wonderful boy. I have never seen him, but his father writes he is a good son. He is a lawyer? No? You must tell me, does he make a lot of money? Does he have a good business? I am sure he makes money, he is smart." Doctor Klones nodded his head knowingly.

Bill didn't want to get into Mike's economic situation. Firstly, he didn't know too much about it and secondly he knew Mike to be closed-lip anyway. He felt it wasn't ethical to say too much. "He does all right, I guess...I mean he's young yet, new in the field. It takes times." He looked out the window at the Aegean Sea moving in the opposite direction. Calm, soft...millions of tiny suns tinkled off the smooth waves. It was a good day for a swim, he thought. I can't figure out why they wouldn't let me in," he said, returning to the evil one. "All I did was write down business on the paper they gave me on the plane."

"You were honest," Doctor Klones chuckled, "you were a mystery to him. You are not with a company, the customs know the business companies in Greece and their three representatives. You are alone, he was confused." He pointed silently ahead drawing Bill's attention to the Acropolis in the distance. For a brief instant it was visible and then the road curved and it fell from sight. "I am glad I was there," the doctor repeated, "I am very happy you have selected my country to come to. You, an American. from a rich country. I am grateful. When I received my brother's letter, at first I thought it was a bad idea, but now seeing you... You are young, healthy, smart—you will do well here. I can help you much, I have many friends. The police, government. Everywhere I have friends. The malakas at customs," he grunted, "they know. They know who I know." He paused and turned inquiringly, "what business will you do? My brother doesn't tell me."

"I don't know specifically yet; I have a couple of ideas. It'll take me a week or so to formalize my plans."

"Hmm. Yes...good...very good."

They wove down the highway. Doctor Klones was an atrocious driver. Bill was frightened at his recklessness. As they approached

Athens, traffic became thicker and he zipped the little car in and out of line.

"They are stupid at customs," the doctor laughed. Last year there were men from America, a big company I think...PCA...RCA. They came to put television in my country. They wouldn't let them in. It was in the papers. The Americans waited three days at the airport and then they went away. There were pictures of them sleeping by customs."

Bill shuddered. He was appalled. It might be a joke to Doctor Klones, but if a big operation like RCA couldn't function in Greece, how could he? They were an established, internationally known entity—he was nothing. Why had he not read the department of Commerce bulletins more closely? "But why?" he asked nervously, "don't they want business?"

"It is very strange, I know. To outsiders it is hard to comprehend. But you see, we are very poor... the occupation...the civil war. Greece is a very poor country." The highway curved again and the Acropolis came back into view. The Parthenon stood magnificently on the square hill of rock. The sun was reflected so brightly on its marble columns that it was difficult to look at.

"But we are proud and jealous," Doctor Klones nodded, pursing his lips. "It is mostly that we want to keep our poorness clean. And also, it is true – there is no business is Greece."

Bill was grieved. The words fell like a rain of lead cannon balls on his ears. His mouth went dry. If there was no business in Greece, what was he doing here attempting a new life?

When they got to one of the main squares in central Athens, Bill attempted to get out of the car. He thanked the doctor for all his kind help and asked him which one of the many hotel ringing the square he would recommend. He was extremely tired, new fears pervaded him and he wanted to get to sleep as quickly as possible. But the fat man would hear nothing of the sort, he started a tug of war with Bill's arm and shouted that it was apogorevita, forbidden that Bill would stay at a hotel when he had friends. He demanded Bill go with him to his house and stay.

"But sir….," Bill protested, "I can't put you out like that. You've been very good to me, I don't want to wear out my welcome."

"There is no such thing in Greece. You are forbidden to go to a hotel. You are my philos, my friend."

"But...sir...Doctor Klones…."

"My name is Theo, everyone calls me Theo... uncle."

"My arm...Doctor Klones...please, my arm."

"Theo," the fat man insisted, "Theo."

"O.K. , Theo! My arm, Theo…it doesn't bend that way...whew…thanks." Bill rubbed his shoulder, it didn't seem cracked. "Theo…I just can't see putting you out. Give me your address, I'll come over when I'm a little squared away. I would appreciate your help when I'm formalized, no kidding…but I can't bother—"

"Bah…" Theo waved his hand, dismissing the idea, "We are happy. You are my new niece, I am your Theo. You will stay with me…it is settled. This is the way it is done here. We have much to discuss. You would waste money at a hotel, when I am here? Bah!" He stepped on the gas to prevent any attempt at escape and aggressively tore into the traffic.

Theo's apartment was located in the best section in town, where most of the ambassadors of the wealthier nations had quarters. The streets of the neighborhood were packed with big luxury cars and ultra-modern terraced apartment houses stood cheek by jowl and marble façade to chiseled cornice. The whole area, its modernity, richness and cleanliness gave the lie to Greek poverty.

Theo bumped the car into a tiny space between a Mercedes 310 and a right hand drive Jaguar.

"We are here, come Beel." He rocked back in his seat to grab a little momentum and then hurled himself out of the car like a boulder shot from a catapult.

They entered a building lobby which looked as if it were hewn out of solid marble. Theo walked very close to Bill and taking his arm, the twisted one, ushered him into a small open elevator. Before it had stopped at the top floor he started shouting, "Maro, Maro, ela…Maro."

A young woman opened the door to the penthouse apartment and rushed madly into his outstretched arms. "Theo," she cried. Her face was covered with worry. "Ise arga. Imme stenahorimenis." She knew what kind of driver he was and wrung her hands when he was five minutes late.

"I am late Maro," he said, stepping aside to reveal Bill, "because I have brought a friend to stay. From America! Beel this is my wonderful wife, my Maro. She speaks English. "Maro, speak English," he commanded.

If Bill had known Theo all his life, he would have found it hard to select a congruous mate for him, but Maro seemed perfect at first glance. Bill guessed her age at thirty, about twenty years younger than her husband. But in Europe, he knew that to be par for the course. She was tall, chick and striking. Her reddish hair was set in a Christine Keeler style. Two solid, round breasts, the right one a full three inches lower than the left, stood firm and pressing against a low-cut cashmere sweater. Her skirt was just above the knees, stylishly revealing a nice pair of legs. Her charming appearance was strangely made more so by the fact that her eyes, like her breasts, bulged. She was afflicted with a Bette Davis-type thyroid condition. And due to a severe nearsightedness, she wore very thick-lensed, green tinted glasses which magnified her popping eyes. Because of this interesting combination her eyes looked like two tennis balls erroneously driven into a net. In order to properly distinguish anything—despite her thick glasses—Maro was forced to lean very close to it. She leaned over to Bill, and he noted with a barely perceptible raised eyebrow, how remarkably clear white her skin was above the unaligned tits. "Beel?" She put out her hand. "I am pleased with you."

"You see," Theo beamed, "how well she speaks." He squeezed her proudly. "Maro, Beel will stay with us. He is the one Pracitellos wrote about from America. He is our friend. He is going to live in Greece."

Maro, who had forgotten all about the letter from America in the press of her daily activities of visiting hairdressers, playing cards and being fitted for clothes, said, "He will live in Greece?"

"To do business. He is a business man. He loves Greece. Puinne Antony, Maro? Puinne?" He turned to Bill, "You must see my son...my gold...Antony."

As they entered the apartment, Bill saw how far it was from anything he ad anticipated finding in Greece. The living room, large, airy, tastefully furnished, had a floor of exquisite, shiny, black marble with blue and white streaks. Two wide French doors led to a terrace which overlooked the Acropolis. The kitchen, on the right as they entered, was modern and utilitarian.

Theo pushed Bill into the living room. A little boy, about six, stood on an armchair placed against the wall. He had his back to them and was diligently doing something to a picture – an oil of Militiades, the commander of the Greek forces at Marathon, sending the runner Phidipedes, on his famous race. Alarmed, Bill saw that Antony was knifing the painting.

"Antony", Theo cried, "Ella tho. Aftos inne Kirio Beel. Ella."

Antony turned slowly, showing a round angelic face. A huge bread knife was in his hand and he looked at Bill with eyes capable of emitting a laser beam.

"He speaks German," Theo said proudly. "Antony, speak German." Antony silently turned back to the wall and resumed carving. Theo shrugged and waved Bill to a chair.

"You will like coffee?" he asked.

"Yes, I would like a cup, thank you." Bill was happy, he needed something to revive, he was getting more tired by the minute.

Theo shouted toward the kitchen, "Voula, thres cafedes."

After a few moments, during which Bill watched, fascinated, Antony convert the picture canvas into thin strips, the maid shuffled into the living room carrying a silver tray with three small cups of Turkish coffee. If Bill, after seeing the neighborhood and the apartment had expected Theo to have a pretty uniformed maid, he was mistaken. Voula was not the petite French-type maid that he knew so well from watching foreign films at the Plaza, the type that are always doing it with the master of the house or his son or sometimes even with the wife. Voula's uniform consisted of a very old, faded, short housecoat and a pair of bloomers.

She looked like an incestuous child of Daddy Warbucks and Little Orphan Annie, with the wild, wide eyes that remained unblinking in a head surrounded by bristly red hair. Her work-hardened, sinewy arms were just a little longer than normal and ended in red dishpan hands which hung disturbingly at her knees. Unlike most people, she walked on her arches, as her sheer density had long relegated them to be the closest things to first hit the floor.

Bill sipped the coffee she served.

"You like Turkish coffee?" Maro asked, straining her eyeballs to see him.

"Yes," he lied, his body screaming from the syrupy sweetness of the coffee and the powdery taste of the grounds lying in the bottom of the cup like sediment on a river delta. The grounds wended their way in between his teeth and covered them like stockings of chalk.

They drank their coffee without conversation, Theo slurping loudly, Maro smiling in the direction of where she thought Bill was seated and Antony, who had finished with the picture proper, working on the frame.

Bill was surprisingly comfortable in the midst of this Greek family, their slight imperfections and deviations from the norm notwithstanding. He felt tired, but at ease. The normal inhibiting factors, the strained feeling of people newly met, were not present. He was possessed with enough insecurity to not want to be surrounded by perfect people. And this family had enough crooked seams to make him feel at home.

Nevertheless, he felt obliged to ask to be released from their kind hospitality. "Doctor Klones," he said, putting down his cup, "I can't bother you this way. I think I really ought to go to a hotel. I appreciate what you've done for me...I mean it; you've been very kind." It was probably a good thing, he thought, to meet a Greek family right away, but he wanted to adjust more slowly, deliberately. Everything had happened so suddenly that now, to get to a hotel seemed an end in itself. He rose to shake hands and make his way out. "Really, thank you. I know where you live and I'll be by in a few days..."

Theo's eyes rolled upward until the pupils disappeared into his head, his eyebrows rose an inch and he made a clicking sound with his tongue—Greek for no! "You may not go to a hotel, we have room. We want you to stay."

Maro nodded her head violently in the direction of Theo's voice.

"But you don't even know me, I can't barge into your house and plop all over...You have your family, it's just not right."

"But there is no bother as you say," Theo said softly. "You will do business in Greece, how will you learn of Greece in a hotel? You will be a tourist, seeing only the shell? You will spend a lot of money and learn nothing." He got up and walked to the French doors. After a pause he said, "You are married?"

"Yes, of course."

"Children?"

"Five...we have five children."

Theo went into an ecstasy, "Five children," he shouted, "Five children...po...po...po. Na sazisoun., congratulations...five children. Ah, in America you have wonderful large families. You are rich there, you can do it. Here we are poor, it is hard to have children here." His small eyes had doubled in size and as he spoke his jowls flowed back and forth like a water filled plastic bag hung on a swing. "But," he shouted, "You must stay here. You must have help to do the right thing...now it is more impossible that you may leave! Five children...po...po...po. I will help you find the exact thing to do."

"Theo knows all the people to help you," Maro said, still nodding her head, "to the President."

Theo couldn't get over the five children. In Athens, in recent times, it was virtually unheard of. "Five children...now no more of leaving. It is done...egena. It is forbidden to leave. What would my brother say—that I threw you into the street?"

Bill was too tired to argue, tomorrow there would be time to make other arrangements, for now he would accept the doctor's kindness.

"You need to sleep," Theo said, "rest. It has been a long trip for you. We usually sleep...a nap...in the afternoon. Would you like to sleep?"

Bill almost fell over in gratitude, "I really would, I'm pooped. If I could take a quick shower and lie down even for a few minutes...I'd feel a lot better."

"Egena, it is done." Theo shouted once more to the kitchen, "Voula, ela." Voula tip-toed in on her arches and stood respectfully in front of Theo looking blank. He directed her to fill the tub and lay down Bill's bed. "Go Beel, bathe, relax. You must feel in your own house."

The hot bath in the extra-large marble tub felt good and he let himself relax and luxuriate in the warmth of the water. When he got out saw that Voula had unpacked his bags and turned down the bed. It looked so good to his tired and confused eyes, that he crawled in and in a few moments was fast asleep.

"Beel, Beel. Come...get up. Beel." It was Theo bellowing into his face. Bill's eyes slit for a second and then snapped shut.

"Come, you must get up. We let you sleep, but it is almost ten o'clock. We must have to eat."

His eyes cracked open again and he glanced around suspiciously, for a moment forgetting where he was. Theo's hulk was hovering over him. "We must eat, come."

He got up sleepily. He didn't want to eat, he wanted to sleep. All the cells in his body were twisting his nerves, trying to force him back to unconsciousness.

"Hurry, Beel, we are going to a wonderful taverna—the food is megalio...you must have food." Theo started to pull Bill from bed, twisting his arm a fraction.

"But Theo..."

"Ah, you do not wear pajamas in America? How democratic."

Maro popped in and she and Theo waited impatiently while Bill got dressed. There was no embarrassment with Bill in his underwear shorts as Maro couldn't see him clearly from where she was standing—five feet away. When he finished, they hustled him out of the apartment and into the elevator. Downstairs, impossibly jammed into the back of the car were Maro's mother and father and sister and brother-in-law. Bill was introduced and he, Theo and Maro got into the car, a confusion of arms, elbows and random body parts. Bill sat indelicately atop the gear stick, his legs intertwined with Theo's and his face pressed against Maro's chest. He noticed that her lower breast sagged even lower tonight and attributed it to the late hour and hunger.

In the back seat it was worse. There they sat, varied and crushed like the insides of an Italian hero sandwich. Someone in the back whispered in Greek, "don't move."

Theo shot the car forth on the most hair-raising ride Bill had ever experienced since during his high school days when he took a dare on the roller coaster in Coney Island. The discomfort of the gearshift especially when Theo changed gears, was all but covered by fear. They raced over paved roads, bumped and jumped on dirt washboards until they reached their destination—the Megalo Taverna. Every time the car turned a corner or dodged to miss an oncoming truck or motorcycle, the wedge in the rear seat let out a collective grunt.

Outside the taverna, Bill was hastily introduced, it seemed to him perfunctorily, the relatives were not in the least as friendly as Theo. They were hungry, and the social amenities, even for Greeks, lost precedence to the desire for food. The excursion fast became the wildest dinner party Bill had ever attended.

They were met at the door by the obsequious owner who possessed a handle bar mustache the width of his shoulders and wore a full length cutaway and a butcher's apron. Since he was also the maitre d', he ushered the party inside. The dining room was crowded with well dressed, dignified looking people who were eating in the midst of a low hanging black cloud of smoke. Something, Bill couldn't figure out what, was different about the smoke—it fell instead of rising. It was heavier than air.

Rather than seating themselves at a table, the group rushed into the kitchen. When the kitchen door was opened the heavy fog in the dining room was replenished with a gust of foul, oily smoke from the grill.

The proprietor-maitre d's wife, a sloppy counterpart to the mamma in American tomato paste ads, was in the kitchen, sweating into her cleavage over an antique coal stove, grilling fish, frying potatoes and skewering shish-kebab. An old arthritic and bent man in a striped uniform helped.

Bill learned that it was Theo's habit to select his food raw and have it weighed before his eyes to ascertain the cost before being seated. Each person in the party was delegated a particular responsibility in the selection of dinner. They went seriously about fingering meat and smelling it to judge its age, opening iceboxes, handling fish and appraising vegetables.

Theo and Maro got into a fierce argument over the raw fish—Maro wanted it for herself, but Theo fought her very hard. The fish slippingly changed hands a few times before Theo gave in and Maro took it to a corner and held it close to her eyes to study exactly what she had won. After a few moments of mauling the fresh food Mamma was advised precisely on how it must be prepared.

Theo abstractly wiped his hands on the proprietor-maitre d's apron and said to Bill, "At the better places, one always selects his food fresh." He eyed the scale and suspiciously and on the back of a cigarette package, jotted down the exact weights of the meal they had chosen. "In Greece we have price and weight control," he said, "so we are not stolen."

They now ran to their table in the dining room. The proprietor-maitre d'-waiter, assisted by a small boy who wore a jet black cotton jacket to conceal dirt and wipe silverware, set the table. The boy draped a long sheet of waxed paper over the table. Evidently, thought Bill, to protect the patrons' arms from the oil and the stains of the greasy finger wiping's on the table cloth. The waiter brought out pitchers of cold clear water, fresh, chewy, dark village bread, clay jugs of retsina wine, white lumps of salty feta cheese, plates of shiny red calamata olives, tomato salads and stuffed vine leaves smeared with a heavy lemon and egg sauce. The table came alive with color and smell. Ubiquitous thick olive oil, covering everything but the bread with a thick film, picked up and diffused the light from naked bulbs hanging above and gave the food a rich sheen.

Almost immediately, as they were being seated—the water was gone. It was gulped...inhaled...absorbed.

"Nero," Theo cried. Water.

"Ela micre," Maro's father, a thin vinegary faced man with an inordinately long head, shouted. Come, small one, water.

The party attached the food; bread, cheese, tomatoes, and olives disappeared almost as swiftly as the water in a lightning fast assault of hands, knives, forks and mouths. "Psomi, psomi...grigora," Maro ordered. Bread...bread...immediately. Her tennis ball eyes darted around the table in search of an unclaimed crust of bread.

Theo, wiping the drippings of an oily tomato from his mouth on a corner of the table cloth, demanded, "Ta fagate...pou ine?" The food...where is it? As he was about to get up and see about the food, the proprietor-maitre d'-waiter and the bus boy barged out of the kitchen, staggering under a load of platters holding steaming fish, fried baby squid and bowls of shrimp in a cheese and tomato sauce.

Maro's brother-in-law, Nick, cleared a place in the center of the table for the main course. Bill thought his face an interesting one. It contained many chins under his mouth, but quite unlike normal double chins on ordinary fat people—for he was not that fat. His chins differed from most in that they ran in a perfectly straight line from his bottom lip to his upper chest. He looked like a pelican which was storing a ruler in its pouch. The rest of his body was generally normal except his stomach, which, because of the connection of chins to chest, gave the appearance of rising to claw down the food when he opened his mouth. Nick, the Chins ate with both hands and only spoke when asking for more food. Brutally, he grabbed the bus boy and ordered more bread, tomatoes, oil and wine. As he spoke, his stomach agitated up and down, clutching at his esophagus.

On Bill's left was Nick the Chins' wife Nota. Maro's sister. She had given birth to the family heir two years ago and was still exhausted from the experience. She was twenty-five, beautiful in a hairy sort of way, and pampered by Chins and her mother, a quiet grey haired lady with deep set, sad eyes. The heat bothered her and she sighed constantly. She carried a big fluffy powder puff and weakly thumped her chest to relieve her condition. "oh," she sighed, patting her chest and eating with her free hand, "Theo, nero para kalo." Theo, water, please.

More fish and squid were brought out as the platters were emptied. There was a steady hum of chewing mouths and Bill began to enjoy himself. The fish was good and the rich ripe tomatoes swimming in the golden olive oil were delicious. And the bread...he had never eaten such wonderful bread. He found himself, like the others, dipping it into the sauces and savoring every bite.

Except for a few questions, asked through Theo, about how rich the brother in America was, he was left alone to enjoy the meal. The talk, he saw, was light; anything that could delay eating or cause a fork to be laid down for thought, was not brought up.

Later, in bed, he felt well satisfied. The jet travel syndrome was still present and his body didn't quite know what time it was in Greece yet, but he was confident that his metabolism would adjust itself. And the retsina wine—different from any wine he had ever tasted—helped. The suddenness of the events of the day, the argument at customs, Theo and his family, dinner in Greece were like pieces in a Pollack jigsaw puzzle, and like someone putting together the puzzle he wondered why he was doing it in the first place.

As his conscious level dipped, he reflected on the question of his presence in Greece. An odd thing that he was there. What to anticipate? Better not to anticipate anything...it never comes out the same.

Hi last thought was back at the dinner table: there was Nota, weakly sighing and brandishing her powder puff all evening. Nonetheless, but adroitly offering her open mouth to her chinny husband who dutifully filled it with food every time, she had out-eaten everyone else.

Chapter Two

The next day, Theo gathered his in-laws together in the living room for a comprehensive interrogation of Bill on his business intentions. Theo sincerely wanted to help the young American as much as he could—he liked Bill. The letter from his brother urged him to help. Since his father-in-law, Vinegar-face, was an influential newspaper publisher with many ins and Nick the Chins was in business in Athens and had been to America, he thought it a good idea to have them give some advice.

Voula, vacantly staring, served Turkish coffee. "You are rich?" Things were very basic to Vinegar-face - one was either rich or poor, good or bad. He was so far right in his political convictions that he once declared editorially that the Royal Family of England were Communists for having recognized the post war Labor Government. He was under the impression that to be American was to be rich.

When Bill answered no to his question, he lost interest and suspiciously turned his attention to his coffee, holding his stomach gently. He had many ulcers.

Nick the Chins spoke excellent English, having studied at M.I.T. on a scholarship his father-in-law had gotten for him from the American Ambassador. With the knowledge gained at the institution and Vinegar-face's pull with the current right-wing government, he was getting pleasantly fat and rich manufacturing defective light bulbs for all the public offices in Athens. Nick who was forty and his wife, Nota who was twenty-five, were of the "smart" set. They were adept at the twist, bossa-nova and hully gully. Nick the Chins ad a great deal of admiration for himself for his business acumen, worldliness, ability in bed and as the father of a boy. With the air of an interviewer he scratched the skin of his chin and said, "Theo tells us you're going to stay in Greece and do some business. What kind of business?"

Bill enthusiastically explained what he had in mind. With all the tourists Greece was not getting, an American-style supper club would have great potential. There was no such place in Athens. It was needed. Tourists get homesick. They don't like the food of the countries they visit. What Americans want are good drinks and steaks...cocktails...martinis..."T" bones. Now, he reasoned, with proper promotion in the tourist guide books, at hotels and agencies, is the time for it—before Athens got too mobbed and a lot of big time competition moved in. Every city in Europe had its American lounge. "A kind of Carousel room...you remember...in Boston...Scully Square," he concluded to Nick, "You know...good food...hot steaks...soft lights...music."

Chin shook his head slowly when Bill finished. With a pained expression on his face he said, "I understand, after all, I lived in the States and I've been to a thousand places like that. But this is Greece. I may enjoy a place like that...but I know Greeks won't. They don't like dark places."

Bill thought of the taverna the night before— naked light bulbs, unfrosted to squeeze out as much candlepower as possible.

Nick the Chins lifted his coffee cup to his mouth— his stomach rose in anticipation and after a sip said, "Steaks, no... no. The Greek likes a variety of foods, not just steaks...not steaks at all."

Bill tried to tell him that such a place would be catering no to Greeks but to tourists, who crave steaks and things American. It wouldn't make any difference if the Greeks didn't patronize the club, the tourist market was booming—that's where the business was.

Nick couldn't understand. "Why would you come to Greece if not to deal with the Greeks?"

Theo, who didn't know what an American supper club was, also felt it was a poor idea. "Why don't you get a job teaching English?" he suggested. "You must be segura...sure. You have many children to care for." He turned to others and said proudly, "Beel has five wonderful children."

With Theo's announcement there was a visible reaction in the living room among the Greeks who like the French consider one child enough—if it is a boy. Maro's mother, who had been sitting quietly in a corner brooding into her coffee grounds, turned her melancholy eyes to Bill and whispered congratulations. Vinegar-face's lips tightened with more suspicion and Nota whipping out her powder puff, fluffed her chest rapidly.

It was no use, thought Bill, to get them to understand what he had in mind. It was too vague for them. The pessimism written all over their faces made him feel a little sick inside.

After switching the conversation to a probe of Theo's brother's worth, they filed out solemnly. Vinegar-face was still holding his ulcer and Nick the Chins tended to Nota, helping her on with her coat and running out into the hall to make sure there were no drafts that she couldn't endure. The spectacle of the young American with five children depressed them. If he were rich or even had been of Armenian blood, there would be a chance. But he seemed to have nothing. On the way down, Nick told his father-in-law, "We've got to get Theo to convince the American that his idea stinks."

His third day in Athens, Bill tried once more to separate himself from Theo and Maro. He argued that it wasn't right for him to sponge off them this way, they had their own business to attend to without him using their apartment as a headquarters and messing up the place for the flat-footed Voula. He whined that he was a bother. They beat down his arguments by ignoring them. He was no bother, no mess. In Greece he must stay with friends, not hotels. He was stuck with them. If he wanted to go out on his own and see Athens, that was all right, he need only make sure he was in the house near ten o'clock every night to join them and their relatives for supper. Other than that he was free.

Theo took him on a two-day driving tour of Athens and its environs—Marathon, Chalcis, Piraeus, Sounion. They wildly tore up to Delphi where Theo joked that Bill should have consulted the oracle before traveling to Greece in the first place. Theo's driving gave Bill another attack of trachea trouble and he estimated he said three hundred prayers to get him through the tour. After that he was left alone except for the nightly dinners.

Methodically he covered Athens proper for a solid week, walking through every inch of the city. He liked Athens, it was clean, modern. Everything old—save the fascinating Plaka, the medieval city under the Acropolis—was being torn down to make way for new buildings. As his focus cleared, as he acquired a perspective, he began to feel more than just six thousand miles from America.

Bill was not an ex-patriot in the normal sense. He had no inclination to cut his cultural ties and then sit around dark European coffee bars sipping exotic drinks and scribbling bleak commentaries on the emptiness of life in the Crystal Place. He was neither equipped with talent or temperament for that. The effort required for such an expatriation clashed with his desire to relax. His motive was simple—change! The reason people take vacations.

It in no way explicitly implied a resentment of the suburban rut from which he ran or the sterile way he had earned his bread. He accepted, with a philosophical shrug, that de-humanization was necessary in a highly complex modern industrial society. It was just not for him. He was lucky on two counts; he recognized he was suffocating early—he was twenty-eight—but more importantly; his wife was game. Her ability to adjust was vital.

Bill had chosen Greece because from what he read and knew, except for a few scattered South Pacific atolls, it was the furthest place from prosperity and mechanization. In addition, he still had to support his family and there was a tidy little tourist boom predicted for Greece. Not a gigantic wave that would destroy simplicity and bring the supermarkets along with it, but enough of a slosh to make a small investment rewarding. From his studies at the Department of Commerce he knew that a huge sum of money was not required for investment.

But before he could relax and enjoy the fruits of his idea he had to find some specific way to keep his family alive.

The idea of a small supper club, despite Nick the Chins, had merit. Living like a Greek but earning money from tourists would be, he thought, an ideal combination. He and Kay had discussed the notion of an American supper club in detail before he had left. They agreed that by drawing on his experience of five years on an expense account in New York combined with a comprehensive effort, they could do it.

After a week he wrote to Kay, confirming their general plan. It was an optimistic letter, he raved about Athens, its beauty, the weather and squeezed in subtlety line about maids and their abundant availability. He told her how hard he had been working, sweating on the preliminary research, going to restaurants, Greek night clubs, tavernas, to see what existed and what was needed. Because Theo had taken him to a very famous taverna where the food was rotten but a balding, three-fingered piano player was packing them in, he asked her to check with the New York Musicians Union and see if some unemployed jazz man might be kooky enough to join them. He thought that a rather good idea.

Then another week went by. And, typically, he accomplished nothing. He continued to tour and learn Athens. He also toured and learned the beaches. The magnificent weather, the clear Aegean water and the well endowed Greek girls in skimpy bikinis thwarted his will to work. He had not, as he was supposed to, lined up a location for a business, priced or bought any furniture or fixtures or any equipment which would be needed. He had no idea of where the club should be located, how much rent would be required or where to find mechanics to do the work. He had done nothing but walk around the city and swim. He was overcome with sloth and a guilty conscience simultaneously. He resolved strongly one day at the beach that after only one more swim the next day, he would begin to create the supper club and settle down to the work at hand.

He awoke on the day of resolve, the early morning sun brightly filling the room with a creamy yellow. It was a wonderful day and he felt charged with enthusiasm. He even drank the coffee Voula served him. His whole body crackled with power and lust to get things done. The days of lethargy and research were gone, now to work...to work. He would price equipment, chairs, tables, silverware, refrigerators, china...price and buy...price and buy. Find a location in the center of town...haggle...be tough...business-like. Rent, price and buy. Work.

The language barrier would be difficult but not insurmountable. With American know-how he'd fix up a place in short order, send for Kay and relax once again.

He dressed speedily, building up a savage momentum and threw himself out the door and into the open elevator. Songs of work and determination surged in his breast. He was an orchestration of labor as he pushed the down button.

The elevator started, lurched, coughed, dropped a few feet and abruptly halted. It was stuck. And so was he. For twelve hours the elevator remained stubbornly in place a half story from Theo's apartment. The symphony of work and determination degenerated, as the day wore on, into a mournful roll of muffled dreams.

After his screams were heard the fire department and the police were called. The electricity was turned off, put on, turned off again. At mid-morning heavy pulleys were called for and attached. With fearful grinding noises and sudden tugs the elevator jerked up a few inches before the pulley chord snapped and it resume its locked position. The pulley man and his hunchbacked assistant were forced to leave in disgrace, followed through the building and out the lobby by a stream of critical catcalls and whoops from a crowd of police, firemen and anxious tenants.

Throughout Bill's imprisonment the Athens emergency squad milled around excitedly on all floor landings cursing and shouting, getting very little done. A great number of police officers, supervising the rescue mission, clumped up and down the stairs and on top of the elevator, sounding to the entombed Bill like a mob of Mediterranean revolutionaries.

Two alert firemen finally hack-sawed a small hole in the top of the elevator. They were only prevented, in their excitement, from severing the main holding cable by Theo, who kept in general charge of the entire operation with his head sticking into the elevator shaft above.

Someone thoughtfully lowered a big bottle of ouzo through the hole and periodically through the day cheese, bread and olives were tossed down to Bill.

They worked noisily, aimlessly, all morning to extricate him from his cage. At two o'clock the din from above and below diminished, crowbars clanked to the floor, ropes were tied, the light in the elevator-cell went out. Bill heard the sound of retreating footsteps. All became silent. It was repose. Everyone went home to nap.

When he was finally released to Theo and all the necessary forms filled out and signed he groggily noted that the halls and stairwells were packed with wide-eyed Greeks staring curiously. Word had traveled up and down the neighborhood that a stupid Amerikanos was trapped and everyone wanted to see.

The combined effects of the long hours of solitary confinement and the deadly ouzo—only a drop remained—caused Bill to collapse. Voula cradled him in her long, strong arms and carried him gently to bed, moving him from breast to pillow mercifully.

The next week, besides visiting a number of new "Megalio Tavernas", suffering severe leg cramps from the positioning in the car, being afflicted with acute indigestion from eating salads of oily eggplant and mashed garlic, Bill tried to get something done.

At the American Express office, where he cashed a check, he struck up an acquaintance with an official guide because the man spoke a number of languages and wore an armband with the words "Official Guide" marked on it with black crayon. The waiters at the sidewalk café next door to the office where he spent most of his time sipping water, called him Haralumbus.

A Greek by blood, he had lived in Egypt until recently. He had come to Athens from Cairo, where for sixteen years he had owned and operated a plush private club. The club had been a haven for select French and English officials, imperialists and rich Egyptians. In a crowded amphi-theater in the rear of the place, he had staged with subtlety and taste, authentic belly dances and exhibitions. To be a member of Club Haralumbus, or a rarely invited guest, was to enjoy the finest in liquor, cuisine and erotic shows. The patrons were so refined and Haralumbus so smooth that in the history of the club there was never once recorded and untoward event.

Through diligence, hard work and high prices, Haralumbus had built up a fortune in English gold sovereigns. Unfortunately, the Nasser Government had decided to nationalize the club, accused him of spying for Israel, tortured him and gave him a choice of repatriation to Greece or death. The money he had in the bank, his block of apartment houses, ranch and tourist hotel were also expropriated and he arrived in his homeland with only the clothes on his back and four small, uncut diamonds secreted within his body.

He was fifty years old, had a sharp, intelligent face and was immersed in cynicism. Although he had but still the one suit, it was always clean and freshly pressed, albeit shiny. He carried himself with the dignity of one who has seen the very best make fools of themselves. He had taken to loitering around the American Express office, because, as he explained to Bill, he had an earnest desire to help misguided tourists and the proceeds from the diamonds, being small because of their uncut nature, were gone.

Bill paid him for translations and guided tours with drinks at the Grande Bretagne bar where they were privileged to observe the cream of Athenian society. Haralumbus would frequent no other place and refused to even look at the new Athens Hilton.

They had long discussions regarding business potential in Athens and Bill was encouraged that Haralumbus thought well of his idea.

"I like your idea of the club," Haralumbus told him. He spoke English with a combination French-Welsh accent. "I've seen enough of stupid tourists to know it would succeed."

"My adopted relatives say it won't go," Bill said, thinking of Theo's daily lecture on why he should give up his business aspirations and get a job teaching English.

"What do they know, the stupid Greeks."

"They treat me like a son...but a retarded son."

"Here the rich sons are retarded. They're not supposed to do any work. Like in Egypt when Farouk was in. Bob around all day, go to Oxford till they're ninety..." Haralumbus waved his hand in disgust, dismissing the rich.

"Every time I say I have to get started, ask them for a little help, advice where to go...what section of town they think best...where to rent a place..., they tell me avrio, tomorrow...there's always avrio...or I have to be segura, segura...They worry about my children, and I'm getting nothing done."

"You ignore them and do your work," Haralumbus advised. "Now you can pay me for today's translations. It comes to four scotches and two cocktails but I'll trade the cocktails in for a sandwich."

Bill found that Haralumbus was not absolutely infallible when one noontime they made the horrible blunder of calling on a prospective landlord during repose. They barely escaped being thrown bodily down a steep flight of stairs.

"I thought we could catch him before two," Haralumbus said, embarrassed by the treatment. "But we missed, and a Greek will not discuss anything during repose...not even business."

"Maybe that's why it's a poor country...maybe they have the right idea."

Haralumbus nodded, "If you want peace, not money, you come to Greece. That's all right for you but my bloody diamonds got me nothing on this stupid market." He sighed and stared off into space, thinking of days gone, of valets, gin and pinks, gyrating dancers.

Coming out of his reverie he said with a shrug, "Well, I have a date...some rich English woman wants to see the Acropolis. A skinny dowdy thing...big thick shoes, but I can't pass it up. Who knows maybe I'll wind up married one of these days. I'll see you tomorrow at the office." He walked away to his date, trying to remove his "Official Guide" armband which had slipped down to his elbow with dignity.

After a period of much fruitless effort in search of desirable site for a supper club, Haralumbus had an idea. One morning as they made their way across Syntagma Square to the Grande Bretagne, he said, "We're not making any progress." It seemed to Bill the understatement of the year, something too, that his old boss might say.

They entered the hotel, turned right in the lobby to the bar, appraised the tables to see who was drinking early and seated themselves in front of the bartender. Haralumbus ordered his usual, double scotch and Bill had a Fix beer.

"It's not that we're not working, "Haralumbus continued, draining his glass and nodding for another. "God knows how we've covered this town...my feet are all worn out. By the way I need a new pair of shoes, so starting tomorrow I'll credit the drinks to shoes." He turned to watch some members of Athens Jet Set enter and noisily take a table by the big window overlooking the square. He swiveled back to Bill, "It is possible though that our approach is wrong."

Bill blinked and waited for the new approach.

"To be logical, first...we know there's money to be made with the proper effort. Second...we also know that a place like ours is needed. It is, if I might say...extremely needed. Next...if we are to set up this club we need excellent location. We will not hide our light under a bushel." He paused, drank and ordered another.

They had seen many possible locations for the club, all centrally located, on the beaten tourist track and of the right size. The problem was not so much finding a suitable spot but finding one with a suitable rent. The rents they had been quoted were fantastically high, creating a situation with a strong potential of bankruptcy. The Department of Commerce had not led Bill to believe that real estate would be such a big headache.

"I think, what we have to do," Haralumbus said, getting to his idea, "is to send for your wife now. Now wait...let me talk. She could be of great help. A Greek will think nothing of stealing all the pounds in your pants, you're a man, but when it comes to women they're still old-fashioned. We need to get the rents down... perhaps she could do it. I say this even though it means our cocktail hours will be finished. I'm convinced you have to call your wife. Besides, from what you say she's smarted than you anyway."

Chapter Three

On Pine Oak Lane, in a small suburban development outside New York City, Kay Treekerson was hard at work, packing and preparing to pack some furniture and small pieces which she had no use for any more now that her husband was away. Small items, especially his, like the round three-tiered walnut ashtray table which stood next to his Niagra vibrating chair. She had gotten it for him a couple of Christmas' back. From the hall closet she took out a boxed telescope and carried it into the living room where she placed it carefully in a big wooden crate sitting in the middle of the room. She smiled to herself as she packed it. Her husband had ostensibly bought it for the children, saying they had to be made aware of the cosmos around them, and then hogged it for himself and wound up using it to keep tabs on the neighbors. He always knew what was for dinner in ten houses up and down the road. Unfortunately, he was bitter that the neighborhood was so dull that there were no juicy scandals to spy on.

Kay had just received a call from the telephone operator warning her to stand by for long distance from Greece. She wanted to speak to her husband very badly. She wanted to tell him what a heel and stinker he was and how she would get even on him for leaving her with all the work of packing up the house and children while he flitted around Athens. She was completely dissatisfied and fumed at the number of letters he had mailed—all too few, vague, stupidly optimistic. She was not normally a vindictive person, but this time she would make him pay.

Little beings milled about her feet. Arms, legs and chocolaty fingers and mouths. Two of the children were at school, but the three remaining took up any slack. "Don't touch me," she screamed, quickly backing away from their dirty clutching hands. "Come on, inside...inside...Popeye...Sandy Becker's on." She herded the three little boys—twins of two and a surly four-year old—into the den and turned on the T.V. and their faces assumed vacant expectant looks.

She went into the kitchen and started wrapping dishes with thick sheets of newspaper and dumping them into a card-board barrel the movers had supplied. She left out only enough china for day-to-day use.

Kay was a ping-ping girl, five three, a curvy 112-pounds and wore her sandy hair in a flapper bob. Her nose turned up and her chin came to a sharp point. Her eyes were a bright blue-green and dreamy and even when she was angry and scowling, they would give her away as an easy touch. She didn't like the way she looked, she thought her chin was too sharp and ugly, but Bill did. He couldn't resist the combination of her high behind and low waist and he spent a lot of money on dressing her, insisting on being present whenever she bought clothing. He called her tannenbaum—Christmas tree.

In her twenty-seventh year and after seven years of marriage with many children she still liked to neck with her husband and even though she often considered him brainless and she had to suffer with his difficulty in supporting his family, she loved him a great deal. It had been relatively easy for Bill to talk her into moving to Greece because she was bored with her life. She was not the type for the PTA and the women's club and she wanted to do something, see new things before she became irrevocably stuck.

She knew that her husband needed her, that he was grossly inefficient and that once the original flush was off one of his frequent hair-brained ideas he fell into lethargy. The request in his most recent letter for a musician was a typical example. It was a good idea, but she was certain that he had forgotten about it by now. She hadn't, it seemed logical to her that if they were to open an American club they should have an American Entertainer. So she contacted the musicians' union, auditioned and promised to send for a young colored jazz pianist who happened to hate his job of teaching music in a New York City junior high school. And, she had pulled off what she considered a major coup. A college friend of Bill's who had dropped out of sight for awhile had heard of their plans and asked Kay if he could join them. When Bob Newman had called at the house one evening not long after Bill had left and made the suggestion she was a little shocked that there was someone as foolish as her husband but he convinced her that he was sincere and, just as important, a good man to have along. "Kay," he had said, "let's face facts. We both know Bill...he's not going to be able to do it himself. I mean, I know he's got talent and all that...but you know he's the collapsible type. I'm sure he's thinking with the supper club he'd be some kind of Toots Shor, hopping around from table-to-table, wrapping arms around shoulders, talking light...resolving some of the problems of the world. That was the way he was in school...unfortunately business was not like that. I know at least what running a business is. He thinks he's going to retire. I think the idea's great. The little I know about Greece and from what Bill had said last time I saw him tells me the thing has a good chance. But not by himself." Bob seemed anxious, but Kay didn't want to be responsible for him going broke on a wild goose chase.

"What about your store?" she asked him.

"Sold it...don't have to go into it now, but I got rid of it. Five years in the chicken Bar-B-Que business is enough." Kay was keen enough to sense that Bob didn't want to go into why he gave up what she knew was a successful little business in the Bronx which all of his friends in industry envied him for, so she restrained her curiosity and didn't press him.

"So I'll be leaving New York anyway," he continued, "Don't think you're dragging me away. I have nothing here." Then he said earnestly, "Write to Bill, see what he says. Tell him if you're going to sell food you need me...I think he needs me even if he's planning to sell garbage, so see what he says. Besides—I'll have a few thou to kick around as soon as the new jerk with the store comes through."

When the telephone call from Athens came through, the twins were in the midst of slaughtering each other and the two older children arrived from school and wanted to speak to daddy, so Kay had to content herself with hearing only a garbled, "Pack up and come right away...need your help...I love and miss you...remember, as soon as you can...tomorrow...the next day."

The big day arrived. Bill lay, propped up on one elbow, in bed drinking the coffee the omnipresent Voula had served. "Do you know what happens today, Voula?" he asked her Little Orphan Annie face. "Do you know that tonight my wife and family join me in the sun-swept land of the Olympians? Where Socrates taught and did other things, where Athena ruled and Byron died." Voula tittered and rocked merrily back and forth on her arches.

"After today, Voula, You'll have no Kirio Beel to bring coffee to. Kind of breaks you up...eh?"

Voula laughed heartily, picked up her small handles-less broom and commenced sweeping. As she bent to her chore her short tattered housecoat rose up in back and revealed a holy pair of bloomers. Bill was always fascinated at the sight of Voula and her broom—and the way she bent from the waist, not bending her knees at all, causing the housecoat to ride up to her low slung hips.

Theo and Maro were almost as anxious as Bell to meet Kay and were nervous all day. When evening came they rushed him out of the apartment and to the airport to wait for the TWA flight to land. Bill could only think of what a wonderful thing, an almost sacred thin, is reunion. His arms ached to hold his wife, to squeeze her.

The plane had not rolled to a stop when they pushed past the evil one, still on duty, through the customs gate and onto the field. And then suddenly Kay was in his arms. The ache got worse as he held her and pressed and her back ribs dug into his forearms. They kissed long and wetly. Bill felt children tugging at his trousers, trying to shinny up. He sighed and kissed Kay again...reunion...Then the sigh turned to a cry of pain as she maliciously dug her chin into his ribs.

"Ugh...what...?"

"Don't you touch me. You are worse than a bum." Kay cried. "And get your greasy hands off those kids." She backed up and spread her arms protectively to shelter the children.

He couldn't believe what was being said. This is a reunion? "But...I...what are you talking..."

"you...you...what can I call you? You left me alone. You left me to sell a house...pack all that junk...all your junk...get the kids ready with shots and vaccinations...passports...ship a dog. My insides are falling out." She was very angry. "I...I...have to hire a piano player...I have to do all the work...while you...why look at you, your nose is peeling."

Theo looked on curiously. Maro had remained at the gate. With her eyes training up against her glasses, she had erroneously greeted some tourists and was hugging and kissing then in mistaken welcome.

"I just don't have any words for you..." Kay fumed, "if it weren't for Bob I don't know what I'd have done. You bum."

Bill looked sheepishly at Bob who was carrying a child and four open airline travel bags. He knew Kay was right, that he had been a rat fink about leaving all the work to her, but how was he to know that he would need her right away. But that was illogical—no matter when she joined him, she would still have to pack and do the same work. To get away from Kay, he went over to shake bob's hand but he couldn't find it so he took the child, one of the twins.

Bob looked tired and his face was pale. His eyes were deep in their sockets and he needed a shave. He had never been so proximate to so many children for such a long period and his lap was wet. Glancing at the canvas bags hanging from him, Bill noticed that they held jugs of water. "Don't tell me you brought your own water. They've got the best water in the world here." He laughed. "Bob, it's great to see you. When I heard you were coming I couldn't believe it. I still can't. There're so many questions to ask."

"What questions," Kay said, "Never mind the questions, I want to get these kids to sleep. They were terrors on the plane...they need sleep."

To quiet Kay Bill quickly introduced them to Theo who was entranced by the children. They were equally delighted with him and like hunting dogs hearing the far off sound of thunder, tilted their heads and eyed him wonderingly. To them he was a real Thanksgiving day balloon. "Come, come children," he said, "come to Theo. I have children like you...Antony. You will like him...come."

When they got to the car, Maro was there, holding tightly onto one of the tourists she had captured. The woman tugged and pulled, trying to escape. "I have your Kay, Beel," she cried triumphantly. She let up on her grip and the woman tore away and ran hysterically back into the airline terminal.

Theo directed the baggage handler to place the bags atop the car and Bill suggested, "We'll have to lie criss-cross in the car, the children in last."

They squeezed in, Theo started the car and was about to drive off when Kay's muffled voice came deep within the pile, "The dog...the dog...get the dog." Schwartz, the dog, a big white and brown collie, was rolled past customs in the cage they had imprisoned him in for the journey. He was barking hoarsely and the Evil One respectfully stood back and waved the cage through.

Theo told Bill to jam him into the front trunk and they rode off to Athens. With the dog's head sticking out the front like some giant emblem, Theo had difficulty seeing the road ahead and asked Maro to lean out her window and direct him. With her help he delivered them to the small furnished house just outside of town that Bill had rented the week before. The only thing, Haralumbus had scoffed, they had done efficiently since they had met.

Theo had prudently hired a maid fro them, Bill had insisted that she be ready when Kay arrived and she was waiting at the door. An ox-like hulk, she lacked only a ring in the nose, but with a combination of speed, force and salty Greek she got the excited children fed and into bed.

Theo and Maro quickly took their leave after bombarding Kay and Bob with kisses and hugs. Theo saw how tired they were and explained that he had work to do at the Kliniki and that only his mother, YaYa was there to take charge and that she was old and feeble and no match for any emergency that might arise.

Before the front door had closed behind them, Kay and Bob, exhausted from their ordeal of fourteen hours of traveling with five children, collapsed in the living room. Bob sprawled out in an armchair, his long legs half-way across the room on top of a coffee table. Kay lay on a couch rubbing her temples to relieve the bite of a headache. Bill went into the kitchen to make them a cup of coffee.

There were so many things to say, so many questions awaiting answers. Puzzling Bill was what motivated Bob to come to Greece. He was glad he had come, about that there was no doubt. Bob's knowledge of the food business would be indispensable, and it would resume a long friendship dating back to their first year in college. Well, Bill thought, whatever prompted him, he was here. He felt so much stronger with a partner and, of course, with Kay at his side. He wondered, would Kay like Athens...would she see the things that he was beginning to enjoy? And the children...oh...he thought, they would adjust, there was no concern there. Well, the die is cast...if any time could be selected, this was the turning point in their lives.

Kay was almost too tired to think, but she did muse on the glowing optimism in the letters she had received from her husband. She was frankly skeptical; she knew his enthusiasm more often than not clashed with reality. And this Haralumbus, he sounded confident that a supper club was a good idea as long as he was being bought drinks. She had doubts and she wondered why she had permitted this to happen but she, like her husband was inexorably drawn to something new and fresh.

Curiosity about the amount of money needed to invest, filled Bob as he sat quietly. He liked Bill and he liked Kay—they were fun people, it would be good teaming up with them, but he hoped they had enough.

The only thing that bothered him since he had seen Kay that night and asked to go along was the money. Moving out of New York to Greece or Timbuktu was for him no more difficult than moving to Hoboken, he had no ties and was tired of making the scene in New York. But the money...things would have to really be cheap in Greece, he felt, for them to get anything started. Like, he thought now, shifting his weight from one bony haunch to the other, I'm not going to build up any anxiety about it, dad...I'm done with anxiety.

They all wanted to ask questions, discuss the logistical problems; Greece, Supper Clubs, money, food, water, Theo, Maro, but Kay and Bob were so fatigued that Bill suggested they drink their coffee and put the session off till they got some sleep.

Chapter Four

Although he was six feet four inches in length, Bob Newman tended to sleep wrapped in a ball, curled up with his knees tightly drawn under his chin and both arms around his neck holding his head down. His feet, the ankles of which were double-jointed, folded backwards against the natural curve of the bones and he had won many bets in his lifetime by touching the calves of his legs with their soles.

He awoke, scratched the back of his leg with the nail of his big toe and painfully unrolled himself. He felt as if he had been hit in the head repeatedly with a barrel of wine. Which was in fact, almost true.

Clear, sharp sunlight was bursting into the room through a large window on the left of the bed, hurting his bloodshot and light sensitive eyes. On a night table next to the bed rested a cup of cold instant coffee and a glass of fresh orange juice. With long clutching fingers he brought the cup trembling to his mouth. Last night had been bad.

The door opened with a bang and Bill in his underwear entered the room. He looked hung over. "You awake?" he said.

"Awake?" Bob said huskily, "I'm not even alive. My mouth feels like the Greek army marched through it last night. All dirty boots and everything."

"Drink the juice."

"I feel very poorly."

"You are not used to retsina," Bill said.

"It was the food, not the wine...don't you know it's never the wine." Bob shuddered, closing his eyes. "Pull the shade, will you." He turned and balled himself up once again.

When Theo and Maro left them the night before, they sipped their coffee and went wearily to bed. There was not even a question of a bath, sleep is what Kay and Bob most wanted. Kay had observed through half closed eyes the maid's deft handling of the children and had told Bill with a trace of hysteria in her voice, "I don't want to see the kids for forty-eight hours...you hear...no less than forty-eight. You and the maid take care of them...you haven't seen them...eh...eh, you forgot. My arms are all black and blue from carrying them and my insides are falling out."

They were just settling in bed when suddenly Theo, Maro, Chins, Vinegar-face, Nota, the mother burst into the house filled the downstairs with commotion and boisterous Greek. Theo trotted upstairs where they lay terrified. "Come, come, you have rested," he bellowed, "Now you must get up ...get out. We are going to give you a proper Greek welcome. We must eat. There is a new taverna...the food is megalio. Hurry...grigora...hurry.

Bill, Bob and Kay were forced to dress, driven out of the house and squashed into the car. Theo properly introduced Kay and Bob to the others who had already seated themselves in the car and although it was difficult with nine people sitting all over one another, everyone shook hands, except Vinegar-face who was wedged into a corner covered by his wife and Nota.

The taverna which had been selected was a smoke-filled, roofless, plywood shell in Marusia, the ancient pottery producing area of Athens. In the center of the dining room was the kitchen, an open, greasy iron stand and grill. The grill served to cook food, warm the patrons in winter and through the catalytic effect of meat and fat on the charcoal fire, destroy insects—flies, roaches, lice—in the summertime.

The specialty of the house was a famous Greek dish called kokoretsi; hog intestines stuffed with lungs, liver, pancreas, spleen, kidneys, brains, eyes, ears and throats.

Bob, normally very fussy about what he ate, was unable to see clearly what was in front of him because of the smoke and he ate a huge amount of the kokoretsi as every time his dish was empty, Nick the Chins happily filled it. Chins also dispensed a great amount of retsina.

Strangely, the lack of oxygen in the place had very little effect on Kay and she revived. It was as if she had been given a shot of adrenaline, which, Bill was sure, the kokoretsi contained. She relished the food, the whole atmosphere of the smoky taverna and most of all Theo. She made a friend of him for life. He chatted gaily away with her, a stubby arm over her shoulder and fed her like a baby.

Nota once again out-ate everyone else, sighing loudly and fanning heavy black smoke into her chest with her powder puff.

When all the kokoretsi had been consumed and every globule of oil wiped clean from the salad dishes, Nick the Chins ordered another kilo of retsina, ceremoniously filled all glasses, wiped his mouth and chins on the table cloth and rose to address the assemblage. He held his glass high in a toast and spoke in formal Greek. He was interrupted by applause and glass banging twice which brought on a barrage of two waiters and four busboys with more wine, bread, feta cheese and water. When he reached h peroration, Chins turned to the Americans and said, "Herita, ke kalo erthite...Eptitikia...Our warmest greetings, we welcome you heartily. We wish you success."

Kay, feeling the warmth and sincerity of the words, Theo's arm about her shoulder and his tender squeeze of affection, had tears in her eyes. Bill, who had been all through welcoming, choked up nevertheless. Bob looked sick, he had discovered what he had eaten.

No, the morning after, he felt even worse.

"You going to get up?" Bill asked his balled figured. "We have lots of work to do."

"Don't talk," came the grunted reply. Bob pulled the sheet tightly over his head.

"Did you really mean it," Bill asked, "last night, why you came to Greece? Was it you or the wine talking?"

"Why?"

"Don't get me wrong, I'm glad, really glad you are here."

"What'd I say...last night, why I came?"

"You said your psychiatrist made you," Bill said, sitting heavily on the edge of the bed. Bob hunched further away, trying to escape the down pull of the mattress, his curved body looking like a giant worm.

Then giving up any hope for more sleep, he slowly and painfully sat up.

"Yeah, he did," he said defensively, "he advised me to get away."

"Talk to me, Bob...nobody in the Bronx goes to a psychiatrist."

"He said I was alienated from my work," Bob said, huffily, "Besides, his office is in Riverdale."

"How could you be alienated from your work? You had a one-man chicken shop...I mean it's not like you were at a factory or IBM or something like that."

"Yes," Bob said, almost sadly, "I told him that too, but he insisted I was alienated. Told me my best bet was to sell and get out. Look, for four hundred clams, I'll take his word for it."

"I don't care why, but I'm happy you came. No kidding, I don't think I could do it without help." Kay came bubbling in, trailed by Alike, the ox holding a tray with three cups of coffee. Her face was scrubbed and shiny. She wore a blue T-shirt and short shorts. She was full of pep in sharp contrast with the two men.

"Morning...morning," she said gaily.

"Gimme that coffee!" Bob demanded.

"Where have you been?" Bill asked. He had missed her form next to him when he woke up. "Where are the kids? I didn't hear any screaming this morning."

"Quiet. They're all outside playing. There's a beautiful garden outside. We have to get a gardener. I've been supervising the maid all morning while you two have lain in bed. How can you lope around on a day like this?" She wrung her hands in glee, "I'll never do housework again...a maid...a maid...never again."

She bent and gave her husband's cheek a peck. "I'm going to love it here." She got business-like, "Well, that's neither here nor there, what do you say you both get dressed, we have to see Athens."

"Oh, come on Kay," Bob protested, "We're not even here yet, let's rest today."

"My dear husband's partner, we don't have that much money to rest. I figured it out...all together it's less than ten thousand."

"We can wait till tomorrow," Bob pleaded, "My head hurts. Besides, if I remember last night and what that guy with the funny face...the neck...what's his name—Nick—told me we don't stand too much of a chance anyway."

"What'dya mean?" Bill asked.

"He said your idea stinks." Bob looked intently at Bill.

"What does he know..."

"I don't know what he knows, but I do think he lives here. By the way, where did he get that neck. Did you ever see chins like that?"

"What did he say?" Bill interrupted.

"He said Greeks don't like steaks...the beef is lousy here. It's not like in the States. He said they like a place like the one we were at last night. Ugh..."

"The guy's a jerk," Bill snapped. "The tourists, he doesn't know about the tourists. That's where the money is."

"He had some words about that too. According to him the tourists in Greece are all beatniks or school teachers from England and Germany—they run around with packs on their backs and sleep in rotten old bags. They're too cheap to go to hotels. He should know. Where did you get your information?"

"You wrote me that Theo and everybody liked your idea," Kay said. "You said they all thought it was great, it couldn't miss." There was a slight edge to her voice. "By the way, where is this Haralumbus character?" She turned to Bob, "I think you had better get dressed, we can't wait to start tomorrow."

Chapter Five

It did not require a super intelligence to realize, as Kay and Bob did after two weeks of studying Athens, that there were other business ventures with more potential for them. They agreed with Bill and Haralumbus, who was faithfully at their side every day, that there would be an American-type club in the city, that there were enough American tourists and members of a large American Nato community living and working in Greece to fill such a place. But to get this market, things would have to be done just right. And they had neither the wherewithal nor a goodly sum of money to make it perfect. There was no Sherman Billingsly in the group.

There was no thought of giving up or packing and going home to America. People do not commit themselves so strongly for a short vacation. Although Bill was depressed with the realities of the situation, he never mentioned retreat, and Bob, who soon became convinced that Athens was good for his mental health, would have let them leave by themselves. Kay saw the whole move as a remarkable adventure, with more to come and took almost as much delight in discovering that a supper club was not for them as she would have had it become a booming success.

What they did was not important to the three of them. That they did, was.

The two distinct paces of Athens became evident to them as the days went by. The one, slow, Mediterranean, with its siesta or repose hour, where things must be done avrio—tomorrow—and the other helter-skelter, confusing, jostling and violent. Greek blood surges through Greek veins like foamy Niagara rapids in the morning, and then because of custom and climate, slows to a muddy Mississippi crawl about two in the afternoon. People in downtown Athens are so exhausted about mid-day from fighting one another and the insane automobile traffic that a nap is necessary. Traffic, mechanized and pedestrian is new in Athens and there is no tradition to guide the city that each day swells with émigrés from the villages or horios where cars and trolleys do not exist. At each street corner, hordes of people line up to wait fro the lights to change, or not waiting, destroy the order shiny-helmeted traffic cops try sweatingly to maintain. The automobiles and busses which use the two main boulevards, Panipistimeou and Stadiu, are a constant hazard. They screech and squeal and swerve at breathtaking speeds. If these menaces to life are caught at a red light and do not stop exactly behind the designated pedestrian cross walk, they are savagely trampled upon. If, in turn the pedestrians are trapped by a quick changing light they are brutally run down. The amount of traffic is out of kilter with the economy of the country.

The three Americans were taxiing near Omonia Square one day, marveling at the warfare between the hordes of walkers and cars. Bill pointed out that Omonia was the geographic center and rapidly becoming the business center of Athens.

They stopped for a light at the busiest street corner in the city on the way home after a particularly depressing morning in which they learned that a place Haralumbus had chosen as a great location for a supper club, had a monthly rent of two thousand dollars. Even Haralumbus who had offered his services as Maitre'd cheaply to the, had to admit they'd never make it with that kind of rent.

The cab lurched forward after the light turned green and rolled past a newly erected office building.

"Stop...stop...stop the car," Kay and Bob shouted simultaneously.

"Get out..." Kay cried excitedly as the frightened drive hit the curb. Bill paid him and jumped out after Kay and Bob who were already running back up the street to the office building. They obviously both had the same idea.

"Here," Bob said in front of an empty store.

"here," Kay repeated, breathlessly "is were we set up our business."

"What are you talking about?" Bill stammered.

"Here," Kay said again, "is our new idea— a chicken Bar-B-Q." She waved her hand to the corner, "Do you see those mobs? Do you see how many people pass here?"

"Do you know what a Chicken Bar-B-Q could do here?" Bob shot out.

"Wait a minute," Bill said, "Let me get with you. I'm not psychologically set up for this idea, I'm still thinking supper clubs. What about the tourists?"

"The tourists..." Bob said, "What do we care about the tourists. You see those Greeks. Weren't we saying we should think of something else?"

"Nobody knows the chicken business better than Bob." Kay said, and looked into the window. Bob and Bill peered in and a crowd of curious Greeks, having followed their animated conversation at the curb—a thing they thought strange for foreigners—elbowed their way closer to also get a look at the store. They found this a tendency of Greeks; if they had nothing to do, they would matter-of-factly make other people's business their own, staring, nodding approval or shaking disapproval and contributing words of advice or criticism.

"I've been thinking of this the first day we got here." Kay said.

"I have too," Bob said, "We haven't seen anything like an American Bar-B-Q here. We could have a monopoly."

"You think the store is large enough?" Kay asked.

Bob cupped his hands around his eyes and took a good look into the store. "Looks OK. About forty feet. That's enough, my store in the Bronx was just a little bit bigger. It all depends on how many chickens you sell and where you clean them" Bob expertly scanned the store and mentally positioned sinks, refrigerators, Bar-B-Q machine. For a moment he had forgotten the advice of his analyst and his alienation.

"Make sure," Kay said, again glancing at the crowds of people tramping up and down the sidewalk. "You're going to do a lot more business here than in the Bronx."

A big, red-lettered sign was pasted on the window, with some numbers —obviously a telephone and a long word none of them could make out. "It has to say for rent," Bill ventured.

"Brilliant," Kay said, "You can see you've been here for a while. Get the number and let's make the call." Kay was organizing. Bill walked to a sidewalk kiosk a few steps from the store to make the call, sticking a finger in his ear to muffle the traffic noises.

"He spoke perfect English, his name is Grapus and he's very anxious to talk," he reported on his return. "He's upstairs on the eighth floor."

"Let's go up right away," Kay said.

"Can't. He said after five, he's going home to repose now."

There were two Grapuses, brothers of forty and forty-three. One was cross-eyed and the other beetle-browed and shifty looking. They were two of the most wealthy men in Greece, having inherited a great sum of money from their father who had been a member of government. They had just finished the eight story office building and were in the process of renting offices and a string of stores on the ground floor.

Cross-eyed asked Kay and Bill why they wanted the store while Sneaky worked on Bob, showing the dimensions and quality of construction of the building.

"What's the rent?" Bob asked directly.

"24,000 drachmas, eight hundred dollars." Sneaky replied, looking more sneaky.

"Eight hundred dollars...what's that a year?" Bob said.

"Eight hundred dollars a month," Sneaky said softly, shrewdly rubbing his hands and looking out through the tops of his eyes.

"Let's get out of here," Bob cried, "Eight hundred for that midget store is ridiculous."

"That's absolutely too much," Kay said to Cross-eyed, taking Bob's lead. They rose to leave.

"Wait...wait...I'm sure we can work something out." Cross-eyed said, quickly locking the door.

"You've got to do much better than eight hundred dollars," Bob told him. "Look, in the States rents aren't that high. They don't pay that kind of money on Times Square."

The two brothers went into a huddle, whispering softly in Greek. Cross-eyed kept one eye on them all the time.

Kay leaned over to Bob and asked, "How many chickens would we have to sell to make eight hundred a month?"

"I don't know what the wholesale price is here but we'd have to keep the same spread as in the States. Let's see...working on 34-40 percent, figuring shrinkage; we'd have to sell somewhere around a thousand chickens a month. It all depends on the size. Naturally, the bigger they are the more you charge, but offhand I'd say about a thousand average ones."

"With all those people, the mobs...don't you think we'll do it?"

"You don't have only rent, Kay. There's labor costs, gas and electric, taxes."

"The tax structure here is much as it is in the States," Bill said, proudly quoting the Department of Commerce.

The Grapus brothers finished with their esoteric conference and turned to their visitors. "The best offer we can possibly make profitably," Sneaky said, "is four hundred fifty a month." He added quickly, "You know when you rent the store, it includes the use of a big store-room in the back of the building. You could use it to put away beer and soft drinks and anything else. We won't charge you for it." He pointed with a pencil to the blue-prints on top of his desk.

"What if we wanted to expand," Kay asked. "Would that go with the store, Mr. Grapus?"

Sensing he was about to make a deal, Sneaky smiled and said, "You'd be able to have that for only a nominal charge, if you want to expand later on. It's big enough to do anything with." He tapped the blueprints, "I'll give you an option."

They all huddled around the plans and looked at the layout. The large empty storeroom was separated from the store by only a partition. "That's good," Kay said. "We'll need to expand." She was certain that business would be good.

"All right, Mr. Grapus." Bob said non-committally, "Let us think about it for awhile, we've got some other places to look at."

"Four hundred is the best possible offer we can make with a profit," Sneaky Grapus said.

"We'll call you when we decide," Bill said, "When are you here?"

"Everyday," Cross-eyed said. "Seven to two in the morning and five to seven at night. Three-fifty is the best offer we can make...we won't make any profit."

Later, when they had gotten home, Bill said, "Well, what do you think?"

"I think the rent's way out of line," Bob replied. He took a pencil and a box of cigarettes out of his pocket and jotted down some numbers.

"It's in the center of town, Bob. It's like Forty Second Street," Kay said. Alike, the maid brought in three coffees. Every time they sat down she dropped everything and served coffee.

"How's she doing with the kids?" Bill asked Kay, nodding his head in the direction of the ox.

"Fine, just fine. I don't think we have anything to worry about as far as the kids are concerned. They're still in the backyard and she's telling them stories in Greek. Nancy and Billy are fascinated. She's very good."

"Thank God for Theo, could you just see us lugging the kids around renting a store?"

"It's a great spot," Bob said, continuing to write on the cigarette box. "There's no doubt about that, but it's a lot of chickens to sell just for rent. What's the cost of gas, do you know Bill?"

"Nick the Chins says electricity is cheaper. They have no natural gas, only unnatural." Bill roared at his bon mot. The others only looked at him.

"Well, I don't know," Bob yawned. "Let's think about it awhile. I'm gong to take a nap." He tucked the cigarette box into his pocket and with a long slow strides went to his room.

"That's a good idea," Bill said leering at Kay.

"What are you crazy? We've got work to do," she said, ignoring his hint. "You'd better get used to it honey, we traveled 6,000 miles for you. Now you'd better put something good together." Then she relented, smiling sweetly and dug her chin affectionately into his chest. "You know I really missed you when you were gone," she purred.

Kay was to become in the next two months a tiger, a fierce practitioner of the curse: "By the Sweat of Thy Brow Thou Shalt Earn They Keep." Dedicated totally to success. She was able to work like no one Bill or Bob had ever seen before, driving them both relentlessly, sparing neither their feelings nor their hides. When many times they contentedly were willing to sightsee or sip a Tom Collins at Zonar's, a popular sidewalk café, frequented by luscious Greek girls in tight short skirts, she would have none of it, constantly reminding them of their purpose. There would be ample time to sit. From a bored suburban housewife, who needed an occasional tranquilizer or martini to cope with the children, the house, her husband, the neighbors, she turned into a sort of chain gang boss, pulling Bill out of his natural laziness and pushing the nervous Bob hard. It was the first time in her life she had an opportunity to do more than change diapers, chauffeur kids to school and put dishes in the dishwasher. And she wisely took advantage of the chance.

While Uncle Theo was still saying "Segura, you must be sure...go slow...tomorrow..." in their nightly forays into the tavernas of Athens, the three Americans worked like madmen during the day. They began to see Greece as no tourist can possibly, and after awhile began advising an American Embassy attaché who lived across the street from them.

Bob and Bill, having both squeezed by college Spanish with D's were no match for Greek. Except for their knowledge of various fraternities, the alphabet was incomprehensible to them. Kay on the other hand caught on very quickly. She learned a lot from the children who in turn were taught by Alike. Coupled with her skill was the use of Haralumbus and the language barrier became less formidable an obstacle.

They signed the lease with the Grapus boys, using a fish-eyed lawyer Theo recommended. With a dramatic rustling of the blue prints and a thin smile from Sneaky they took a three-month option on the back room. Kay insisted.

They planned to buy as much as possible with the use of gramatia—Greek time payments—and Bill thought of suburbia and shuddered. A thousand dollars was quickly dispatched to America for the purchase of an ultra-modern electric Bar-B-Q machine. Nick the

Chins closely advised them on the type of current, voltage requirements, ohms, amps and watts fro the machine.

While Kay shopped for a refrigerated showcase in which to stock raw chickens, beers, sodas, Bill traipsed around the Plaka looking for a carpenter to build the necessary shelves, counters, stools and cabinets. Bob, as the chicken expert, was assigned the task of establishing contact with a chicken wholesaler and to price and grade the best fowl Greece produced.

After ten days of exploration, selection and haggling, they made some concrete deals and one afternoon gathered in the garden over retsina on the rocks to discuss their efforts.

"I did well this morning," Bill said. "I must admit I'm getting along very well in Greek. Everybody I spoke to understood exactly what I wanted. Besides Haralumbus was along in case of emergency."

"What about the bar?" Bob asked. It was their intention to use one wall for quick lunch trade.

"I went to six underground places in the Plaka before I got a carpenter who can do what we want. I told him we needed a cashier's table and two bars with built-in shelves." Bill would have been happy to spend every day in the Plaka. The old buildings, winding streets and alleys and the underground shops manufacturing and selling everything from shoes and spinning wheels to goat skin rugs and tourist pottery was to him a combination of the best in antique auction sales and Greenwich village.

"You or Haralumbus told him?" Kay asked skeptically.

"Haralumbus translated very little. He understood exactly what we want. I made a drawing. Anyway at first he said that the whole job, including the display counter with glass doors would cost 30,000. Naturally we walked out and he followed us, screaming down the street. So after an hour of haggling he'll do the job, using English formica, for 18,000 drax."

"That's six hundred bucks," Bob moaned.

"I think it's a good price," Bill said. "I know it's best the guy could possibly do and make a profit, because the eight time we walked out he didn't come running after us. I'm a real pro when it comes to haggling. I immediately divide by two what they quote and work down from there." Bill felt proud of himself, for his crafty encounter with the carpenter and wanted Bob to realize his worth. "Besides, for free he's throwing in the stools."

"I didn't have any price difficulty," Kay said. "Refrigerators are standard and I bought a Kelvinator. It's just the size you wanted, Bob. It'll be delivered tomorrow. All charge...a hundred dollars down and two years to pay the rest. Now how about you?"

Bob looked very glum, he sat with his chin on his chest and dejectedly pushed an ice cube around in his wine. He took a deep breath before answering. "The chickens in this country are atrocious. I visited every wholesaler in the Agora and from what they showed me, I'm convinced that we're out of business before we start."

"What do you mean, what's the matter with them?" Bill asked anxiously.

"What's the matter with them?" Bob said, his face taking on a vomity look. "They're ill. They're just not like chickens. They don't look like chickens. They're scrawny, no meat, undernourished. To top it off, you have to buy them live. You should see it down there...all kinds of old ladies shopping...carrying live, screaming chickens wrapped in old newspapers, like bouquets of flowers. It's the Bronx terminal market sixty years ago."

"Theo says that until recently the only people who ate chickens were pregnant women and sick people." Bill said.

"I can see why they're sick," Bob said with a sneer. "And the cost...my God...for such garbage we got to pay forty drax a kilo. I'm going to have a nervous breakdown."

"What's that American?" Kay asked. For all her managerial ability and her skill in language, she still had difficulty translating drachmas into dollars and cents.

"Comes down to about 65 cents a pound. To think the A&P sells retail for twenty-nine. No kidding, I really felt alienated down there."

The chicken problem was severe, all the formica bars, shiny showcases and barbeque machines were useless without good broilers. And buying them alive...the thought terrified them...to have perhaps a hundred or two live chickens pecking around the store everyday. It seemed a little crude and unmodern...and what would Cross-eyed say. Who would kill them? Who would clean them?

Theo plugged the breach admirable when they told him of the problem that night at dinner. "Of course, we have good chickens here," he said. "Eviscerated, American style. Your Government set it all up for us. Where do you think I buy the chickens for the hospital? At the Agora?" He shuddered at the thought. "There is one dealer in Athens from whom you may get all the chickens you need, and big ones also...he gives them hormones. But you must never tell anyone that...he and you will go out of business. The Greek male is very proud of his virility and is afraid hormones in chickens will take some of it away." Theo was very serous, his jowls and chins jiggled emphatically as he spoke.

Chins said "I agree. I never eat chicken which has had injections."

Bob wanted to know how Chins asked a chicken if it had hormone injections, but only said, "You'd have to eat three or four chickens a day to be affected by the hormones, Nick. They proved that in the States."

"I don't care," Nick said pompously, sticking out his chest, causing his head to jerk downward from the tension created on the chins, "any depreciation of manhood would be sinful."

Nota stared at his chins, sighed and frantically fluffed and powdered her chest.

The Grappus brothers dropped down to the store each day to check on its progress and to make sure the Americans were not defacing the walls or cracking the terrazzo floor or in any way depreciating their property and thus cutting into their profit. Cross eyed showed Bob where they could get aluminum foil for wrapping the cooked chickens. He thought the foil idea a stroke of genius and when Bob told him that such wrapping would keep a chicken hot for hours, he shook his head in respect and mumbled, "American know-how."

The store itself was crowded every day with work, men putting it in shape for business. Only thirty-six feet long by eighteen wide, it became a scene of complete confusion. The painters rigged up scaffolding between ladders and gaily swished away, dripping paint on all who passed beneath them. Four plumbers were needed to attach a small sink and tap for cold water in the rear. It was a simple job essentially. Bob said there was terrific feather bedding going on, but the large crew was useful when it became necessary to smash down half the back wall to find the main and connect the one pipe. Grapus sent down a marble polisher who noisily scrapped and ground the floor, spewing marble dust over everyone the three days he worked. Curious passers-by who wandered in from time to time to look and approve or disapprove of what was going on wadded to the chaos. Located immediately next door was a coffee shop where men idled away their day drinking Ouzo and Turkish coffee discussing politics. To break up the routine and stretch their legs, they dropped in periodically through the day. They were frankly horrified when they learned the Americans worked during repose and swore darkly that Bob, Bill and Kay were Fascists or Communists, having no respect for the established order and traditions of Greece. When not arguing politics with the working men they gave orders, encouragement or criticized. They thought the painter was a butcher and wanted the electrician shot in the back of the head for his inept wiring.

After a few days of relative calm, in which they scrupulously avoided one another, the carpenter and the painter foreman had a violent fight over paint drippings on the formica. It was resolved suddenly when the carpenter took away one leg of the scaffold and left the painter hanging from a florescent light fixture fifteen feet in the air. That Same day the plumbers walked out completely dissatisfied with the plasterer who had mixed gypsum min the sink and plugged up the drain and pipe in the wall.

There were curses, shouts and vendettas, six fist fights, three broken noses and a dislocated shoulder when the painter finally came down to earth. The casualty toll also included one passer-by who was carried out in shock after showing the electrician how to properly put in a fuse.

The neon sign Kay had bought for the outside, showing Bob and Bill's in red, white and blue, was demolished and splintered into thousands of pieces by the feet of hundreds of inquisitive people when the worker who delivered it left it on the sidewalk for a moment while he got a cup of coffee.

Kay, Bob and Bill daily rushed from worker-to-worker pleading and threatening. They tried to get some organization and system going. Kay's hardest fight was to get the painter to believe they wanted flat and not a high gloss paint used and he didn't like her choice of colors at all, preferring his own bright reds and purples. Bob complained that every time he showed someone a mistake, they would say, "then birazi,"—it doesn't matter, or "avrioa", we'll fix it tomorrow.

They made the acquaintance of a number of retired Greek American waiters living in Athens in relative luxury on Social Security. They were interested in the endeavor and offered advice and encouragement: "What are you paying rent? That much. Whew. Too much, you'll never make it. I know, I've been in the business. Naw, these people will never go for Bar-B-Q chicken. What the hell did you leave the States for? You nuts? All the Greeks go there to open restaurants. What did you come here for? Wait 'til the help cheats you. What's the carpenter charging? You got took. Chicken Bar-B-Q...no...no...they can't afford it. Frozen chickens? They'll never buy frozen stuff. These people are old-fashioned. Whatd'ya mean they're fresh—they ain't got nuthin' fresh here except the women. Tell that painter he's dripping. Jesus...what a smear job. Who's paying the painter, you or the landlord? What did you say the rent was? Oh Christ, you'll never make it, the place is too small..."

They finally took to locking the door and soaping the window, but there was no escape - whenever the door was opened for some worker to go in or out, fifty or sixty shouting people would plunge in, advising, touching paint and plaster, or simply staring at the three Americans, an unfathomable puzzle, opening a business in Greece.

The store ultimately did take form. The two formica counters were in place on either wall. The long refrigerated showcase was hooked up to its motor and working. Behind it were the bench and sink for cleaning and spitting chickens. The cashier's table and register were at the end of the bar on the right hand side and in front, facing the window stood the display case of shining chrome and a shelf for despitting cooked chickens. The only thing lacking was the Bar-B-Q machine and it was confidently expected to appear in Pireaus momentarily. As soon as it did they were ready for business.

Bill noticed some marked changes in Kay and Bob since they had joined him in Athens. While Kay had always been an excellent household bookkeeper in America, he was astounded at her now, her skill and managerial ability. Her latent talent, which her husband had never recognized, burst forth like a geyser under the pressure of establishing a business in a foreign country. But it was more than that - she threw herself into the life and tone of Greece; it was as if she were reborn. If they were to live in Greece she wanted to squeeze every drop out of its traditions and customs. Nor would she give up her American heritage; she simply saw the richness and fulfillment to be gained by consuming more and more of the world. She lost any shred of the parochialism forced on her by the circumstances of her past life.

Bob too now had broader horizons. Any abnormality suggested into his head by his doctor, was gone. To be abnormal in New York, he discovered, was to be a block of conformity Greece.

Bill, on his part, lauded himself for his scheme. Taking a side-seat now and watching his wife at her best became a great part of his happiness. No matter how much he had ever loved her he had always thought in terms of self; will I be happy in this or that new job; will it be interesting to me; will I grow unhappy in a small town; will I enjoy perhaps living in the city; will I, will I, will I. That was gone now with a new maturity of recognition of others' needs for growth.

While they waited for the machine to sail into Piraeus harbor, they relaxed from the daily trial with painters, plumbers and plasterers. They took the children to the beaches on the coast, to Sounion, and in town to the Acropolis. Bill was crushed that the two oldest children agreed that the Parthenon was only a pile of rocks, but took some solace in the fact that they were fast learning Greek.

They toured some of the Aegean islands in seaworthy, if not ancient touring boats. Once they hired a caique and were excited at their ability to maneuver it when the fisherman let them have the helm. On the sandy islands they noticed something that did not happen in a democratic country like America: the rich—the fantastically rich—and the poor lived the same on vacation, ate at the same smoky tavernas, swam at the same magnificent beaches, dressed alike in blue jean comfort, so much so that it was impossible to distinguish the status of one from the other. They fraternized in such a sincere, matter-of-fact manner that it showed the Americans that in Greece there is more in common between people than wealth, job and station.

They enjoyed the large verandah of their rented house. The weather was guaranteed good that Bob slept outside.

"You're turning into a real Hellenophile," Bill told Kay one evening, while they sat on the verandah, absorbing the beauty of the soft summer night and the bright starts. Bob had already set up his folding bed and sat in his pajamas, smoking and sipping retsina.

Kay sighed and said softly, "I like it here. I like the people. I like the spirit. Believe it or not I enjoy the work too...of putting the store together. It's a good experience for all of us. I keep seeing Marcia and Rita back in good old suburbia USA, grinding it out. Every day the same thing, every week, every month. Here, I don't see that for us. I think we're going to be a great success. We'll be the first anyway. Even if we're not, we've gained something. You know, it's funny, we're strangers here but I feel close to the people. Something I couldn't feel on Pine Oak Lane. I like learning the language too. It's a tremendous challenge by the way, I finished those two Greek crossword puzzles you and Bob gave up yesterday.

"Smarty."

"I see something different in store for us here," Kay continued, "and I want to thank you for thinking of it and dragging us here." She reached out and touched Bill's hand.

"You're a sentimental existentialist," Bob said from the darkness. "But I feel the same way. I'm really grateful to my doctor. Tomorrow I'm going to send him a note and a case of retsina."

"You guys are getting maudlin on me," Bill said. The pleasure of Kay's words and the sight of her beautiful face silhouetted by the moon filled his heart with gladness.

After some careful thought, Bob declared that they would need a master electrician to hook up the Bar-B-Q machine when it arrived, the one they had hired to install the florescent lamps in the store was to inept to do a major job.

They ran up to see the Grapus boys and Bob asked Cross-eyed, "Mr. Grapus, will you be able to help us get a good electrician? We'll be needing him soon, our machine is going to be a little tricky."

"We can hire ours out to you for a fee," Cross-eyed said, locking both Bob and Bill in his stare.

"We're willing to pay as long as he's good," Bob said seriously, "The machine has got to function perfectly."

"We'll give you the lowest possible price with a profit."

The man Grapus delivered was named Tikidoras and wore a blue serge suit, white-on-white shirt with French cuffs and a conservative Italian silk tie. In his hand he carried a rich leather briefcase. Bill was startled to notice a long Fu Man Chu type fingernail on his right pinky. The man reeked with mystery and Bill was exceedingly curious. "Is this your electrician?" he asked. "He looks more like a lawyer."

"Well as a matter-of-fact he was a lawyer, but he lost so many cases that people at court used to call him "Tikidoras the loser" and laugh at him. He grew so despondent that he gave it up for electricity. He says he prefers to deal with electrical current than people, it's less dangerous.

"Why does he have that long fingernail on his pinky?" Bill asked, his eyes riveted to the talon. Grapus laughed, his eyes twinkling merrily in front of one another, "You know the Turks were here for four-hundred years. They brought many customs, and a long fingernail symbolized that station of the owner. A status symbol you call it. People with long fingernails would never be taken for common laborers. It was a sign that one's work was clean; that of business, law, politics. It's a carryover from the past. Nowadays the long fingernail is used for scratching, pointing, cleaning the ears and a lot of other things."

Bill was fascinated as he watched Tikidoras picking his nose with fantastic dexterity.

The notice informing them of the arrival of the Bar-B-Q machine finally came. While Kay and Bill rushed to Pireaus to redeem it from customs, Bob waited with Tikidoras at the store. They trembled with fear at what the day would bring, for they were informed by the American Economic Attaché that Greek customs were impossible; they would be lucky if they got the machine out off the dock in a month, and that it would be best to anticipate a duty charge of somewhere in the neighborhood of 1,200 dollars. They had not figured on this new difficulty or the possibility of being wiped out in a single blow at customs and arrived at dockside with an empty feeling in their stomachs. Bill was so nervous eh chewed up the pinky nail he was developing.

The port of Pireaus is noisy, active and teeming with life. Every major shipping line in the world uses its facilities. Because of these giants of industry and the vast sums of money involved in the business, Pireaus it is out of harmony with the rest of Greece. It is a busy and commercial place where the citizen knows he is different, more worldly, better paid, more sophisticated than Athenian. The people of Athens' port city even speak differently, a strange dialect centuries old. By the Athenian they are called Mangas—sharp. When politics are discussed in the cafenia rimming the port, it is not to idle away time aimlessly, but to change systems of government. There is power and force in the open-collared dockworkers and they know it. They know their vote is important, because they are so numerous and they know their work is important because Greece, as it has been through the ages, is a maritime nation and the bulk of its income is derived in the activities of the sea.

It is a puzzle to people that the customs houses are so rotten. They use a system, accredited by some, to have been old in Periclean times. Their activities are not duplicated by any civilized nation on earth, and their authority is broad and overpowering. The longshoremen have an inordinate amount of influence with official customs, partly because of the government's recognition of where power lies and partly because most of them are related to customs officials. If the politics of the flag of a carrier are in too much variance with those of the longshoremen, it is possible that a ship will be forbidden to be unloaded. It is a carryover from the Golden Age of Greece, when the importation of cargoes from far-off could make or break the economy of a foreign nation or tribe.

The Persians themselves and their Great King, recognized the usefulness of Pireaus and even in war paid yearly tribute to its people. The customs officials do not seem to be aware that all that is past. Here and there on the dockside are precious cargoes rotting away because of insurmountable difficulties in redeeming them. Visitors wait in long lines for bags and baggage to be checked and released after enormous payments of duty. Greeks coming back to their homeland after many years, watch as their possessions are ripped apart, pawed over, registered in innumerable books and lists, and carted away to dark corners, not to be seen again for periods ranging up to two years. Chaos and inefficiency reign. The simple act of importing an automobile can bring headaches for weeks and months. The petty custom's officials and bureaucrats are so powerful they are despotic.

Small groups of retired dock workers and custom clerks dot the custom houses; men who, through long habit cannot escape the lure and fascination of the place, meet their old cronies and sometimes earn a drachma or two from particularly harried tourists by helping to translate the demands of the tyrants into welcome to Greece. Kay and Bill had experienced frustrating difficulties. They had run from one customs house official to another waving the notice of the machine's arrival, only to be turned away repeatedly with: "it is not here, it has not arrived, you must wait, come back in a month, do not bother me..."

The higher up the bureaucratic ladder they went the more agonizing the effort. They were shunted aside, pushed and ignored. Out of such a group came a savior. Exhausted, they were half planning to leave the country with curses upon the Hellenes when they were selected from hundreds of dissatisfied and weary people milling around the customs house amid tons of baggage and trunks, broken crates, bundles, cardboard suitcases, electric dynamos, splintered wood, excelsior by a figure who did not walk like any other human in existence. He shot out of his group of hangers-on with a gamboling, left-handed gait—a cross between Cary Grant and Henry Armetta—and moved like a heavy tank attacking, slits closed, intent on the kill, unconcerned with obstacles in front, puffing and rumbling. First left thread, then right, then left. He ground to a halt in front of the astonished Kay, threw out a hand, shook hers, threw out another to grab Bill's and they were friends.

Nick the Walk was a retired minor customs clerk. He had grown up on the docks of Pireaus. He was the complete Mangas, a man of indelible sharpness. He was George Raft and Demosthenes combined. He knew of frustration, having witnessed it for years at customs, although he never experienced it himself because he could change the world and knew it. During the occupation, with a small band of guerrillas, he tried to kick the Germans out of Greece. And succeeded in part, so many Krauts were decapitated in the quiet evenings around his village that the Nazi authorities felt it more prudent to leave that area to the Italians.

He had fought on both the communist and loyal side during the civil war, it depended upon where he was at the time, and was personally responsible for removing from the scene the more fanatical of each group. In his defense he said he hated extremism. For these efforts he spent five years imprisoned on a small island in the Adriatic.

There he nurtured hatreds and brined feta cheese. He was an anarchist politically and now hated both right and left with equal vehemence. Richly confident, eloquent, he possessed a golden tongue with which he could talk anyone into anything, although he lisped atrociously because all his front teeth were missing, due to communist torture. He used his power sparingly, not for material gain, but for sheer joy. He wanted to help Kay and Bill, because, as he explained later, he liked Kay's face and out of all the people at customs they looked the most exasperated. They grew to love Nick the Walk, his stubbly chin, horn-rimmed glasses and his completely disarming toothless smile.

Because he was so active, he tranquilized himself by fiddling komboloy—Greek worry beads. He had the reputation, no mean thing in Pireaus, of being the greatest worry bead flipper, either one bead or multiple, on the docs. His fingers were so sensitive that he was capable of flipping the famous and difficult Pireaus Gambit: a cross over top of first three beads, then string, then in rapid succession, two, one, and four beads, over and under. On his name day one afternoon in 1956 he made history by performing this intricate maneuver behind his back and the President of the Board of Trade, who was breathlessly watching along with most of the population of the city, declared a city-wide holiday.

He gently took the papers Kay held and said, "Dose mou ekato drachmae, ke ela." Give me a hundred drachmas and come. They followed his interference, watched him block three stewards and two ship passengers to clear a path, push a guard into a pile of Singer

Sewing machines, move a fork lift and commandeer a decrepit motorcycle and sidecar for a ride to the main custom's office.

There they moved with him through a maze of offices and waiting rooms. There were people shouting and screaming, waiting in noisy lines to be agonized by the clerks. Nick the Walk did not wait. Unhesitatingly he pushed and shoved people aside and cut a swath to the main desk around which grown men were pleading, weeping and pounding their breasts in despair.

His voice was full of command as he buttonholed a clerk, slipped him twenty drachmas and immediately ascertained the location of the machine. By some idiotic consequence it was loaded on a sea-going barge which the Port Authority used to store highly volatile and explosive material. It was floating around somewhere in the bay of Salamis. "Then birazi," mumbled Nick the Walk, and Bill loosely translated in his head, it doesn't matter? Oh no, not him too! But everything mattered to Nick and soon they were surging out to the barge in a stolen customs launch. Using the barge's own crane, Nick lowered the crated machine to the waiting launch and amid applause and bravo's for his skillful handling of the derrick they shoved off for port. He then helped Bill and Kay fill out twelve forms and declarations pursuant to the regulations, and they were ready for the uncrating in front of the untrusting eyes of the superintendent of custom's inspectors.

It was at this point that Kay did something for which even the cynical Nick was proud and would later congratulate her. Noticing that the custom's man was ogling, she vampishly lifted her skirt, baring her dimply knee. While the superintendent was thus concupiscently eye-balling her tanned legs, Nick covertly removed the machine's electric motor—customs duty US $475 dollars; electrical heating elements, customs duty US $512 dollars; glass doors, custom duty US $47 dollars; long steel rods. He piled them into an old garbage can innocently standing nearby. Since what was left was just a pile of molded chrome and steel, the customs man looked, said, "Tin afto?" What is this? He smiled at Kay and released to their trembling hands the machine for a total cost of twenty-three dollars, quickly replaced by Nick the Walk with a direct offer of ten in cash to the waiting palm. For another ten dollars they rented a stolen custom's truck and two longshoremen.

With horn blowing furiously, they zipped back to Athens and the waiting Bob with the Bar-B-Q machine standing majestically in the back of the pickup. What might have taken months or even years to redeem at horrible cost was delivered in a matter of hours with very little outlay. To Nick the Walk they owed much, but when Bill tried to give him fifty dollars, he looked hurt, and said it was too much. He liked them and it was his pleasure. He finally accepted ten dollars just for luck and to keep his professional standing.

Now it was to Tikidoras the electrician they turned. He was already pouring over the diagrammed instructions for the assembly of the electrical components and suddenly screamed, "Inne thra fasiko, afto eki ena fasiko. Ine ekato deka voltas, afto eki diakosa ke."

Nick the Chins, the eminent MIT electrician had given the wrong information about voltage requirements and electrical phases. The machine was useless.

Bob was confused, "You mean Nick the Chins did this to us? Why? I ask 'why?'" His eyes glazed, alienation descended upon him like a vatful of molten tar.

"The idiot," Bill swore. "I'll kill him."

Kay, who in the past became hysterical if the TV didn't work, calmly asked Tikidoras, "Can it be done? Can it be fixed, Kirio Tikidoras?"

In answer, Tikidoras put down his briefcase, rolled up his jacket sleeve and whipped out his fingernail. With its point he started to unscrew the bolts on the side of the machine. They stared as the lawyer-turned-electrician labored. After some deft slashing of wires with the cutting edge of his nail and some adjustment of terminal screws, he cried, "Etimo, bravo. Etimo." It is done. He plugged the machine to the socket, turned the burners on and stood back. There was a loud explosion, the lights went out and a thin line of smoke wafted out of the fuse box. "Vlakas," stormed Tikidoras. "Vlakas, vlaka, zorn." He sat down with his head in his hands and wept unashamedly. Kay put her arms about his shoulders and said soothing words. He mumbled something into her sympathetic face at the tears flowed out of his eyes. His fingernail was nicked and scraped and twisted near its apex.

"He says there's not enough electric power in the store," Kay said, "the machine consumes too much power. Please don't cry, Mr. Tikidoras."

"What are we going to do?" Bob moaned.

"We must have more electricity," Tikidoras said, looking at them with a tear stained face. "More electricity." Then an idea struck and he jumped to his feet. Suddenly he was Clarence Darrow and Thomas A. Edison again. He said something to Nick the Walk and they both rushed out of the store.

A few minutes later an electrical cable came dangling down in front of the store and Tikidoras and Nick marched triumphantly back. "We needed more electricity, and now we have more electricity, "Tikidoras gloated. "I have taken the liberty of borrowing the electricity we lack from Mr. Grapus. This man," He pointed to Nick the Walk, whose gums were out in a thick smile, "talked him into it."

Bill looked out the store and his eyes followed the twisting cable up to where it disappeared eight floors above in to the Grapus office.

Thus it was with jobbery of customers, with jobbery of electricity and the benevolent repose of the Grapus brothers that they were able to open a Chicken Bar B Q store and serve chicken in Greece.

Chapter Six

To merely throw a store's doors open to the public and commence selling a product is forbidden in Greece. First, must be suffered the Engenia.

When Bill, Bob and Kay excitedly told Theo they were opening for business the next day and if he wanted to make sure to get a chicken in the expected crush of customers he had better get there early, he threw himself upon them, shaking his head vigorously and shouted, "Apagoreveta, apagoreveta...it is forbidden. It is forbidden that you may open without Engenia. You must have Engenia!"

They shivered, they needed to open immediately, they were down to their last few drachmas, and this seemed like a new delay. "What is Engenia, Theo," Kay asked patiently, "and where do we get one?"

"Engenia is not a thing to get...it is a rite - a religious rite in which you receive blessings for the success of your enterprise," he told them solemnly. "I will make all arrangements for the pappas', the priest and guests. Yaya knows all the pappas' in Athens." Yaya, Theo's ancient mother, spry and crafty in her eightieth year, had endless contacts in Athens. She was a matriarch in a patriarchal society. As her parents had come from Constantinople - she never called it Istanbul - she was through blood a master of the art of Byzantine intrigue. She was both respected and feared by the Athenian oligarchy. Her chief interests in life were assisting Theo in his Kliniki, where she toiled as head midwife, and acting as a marriage broker for homely rich spinsters with large pricka or dowries.

"For what hour will you be prepared?" Theo asked. He thought of the preparations Yaya must make for a good Engenia.

"The first chickens will roll off the machine at twelve o'clock," Bob told him happily. Despite what the psychiatrist had told him, Bob was chaffing at-the-bit to cook up a big batch of chickens.

"It is good that you will have chickens cooked," Theo said, "The pappas will be hungry and you must give him to eat. Also money," he added quickly.

The morning of the big opening dawned and Bob, Bill and Kay rushed down to the store to prepare for the Engenia and the early rush of customers.

The employees were lined up in front of the store when they got there, all bright and clean in their white uniforms and blue and red caps. Theo had relieved them of an immense burden by hiring all the help for them. He would have none of their interference in this phase of the work. "You will be stolen. I will hire the people you need," he had said, stating a simple fact of business in Greece. "You can trust no one. No one."

He had chosen young people, two boys, Chris and Yianni, which were classmates in Athens University, studying medicine, and were known to him through colleagues. Chris spoke English. He was a clean-cut, curly-headed youth, supporting his widowed mother and five sisters. His only apparent fault was a tendency to occasionally stare into space and abstract himself from reality. Preoccupying him was the rigid custom in Greece which demanded that in a fatherless family the older brother was responsible for the dowries of the girl children.

Yianni was a slow-moving boy of seven feet, an oddity among the short Mediterranean race. Bob was certain he would bring in customers out of curiosity if for no other reason.

It fell to the boys to learn the cleaning and cooking of the chickens. Bob carefully showed them exactly how to place five plump chickens evenly on each steel spit so that they would both look good and be properly exposed to the heat of the electrical elements in the back of the machine. He rehearsed them for days beforehand. The boys were also expected to wait on counter trade, mop the floor, keep the machine clean and boil and peel potatoes for salad. They were good boys, anxious to please.

Katina the cashier was a mustachioed girl of thirty, who, Theo swore, was absolutely trustworthy. Yaya had taken her on as a client some years back but her dowry was so low that even Yaya and her list of eligible bachelors could not get her married.

Kay had gotten around a dishwasher by coming up with the idea of paper dishes and plastic knives and forks. Again Cross-eyed was impressed with American -know how, saying he couldn't bear so many firsts from just one source.

Bill unlocked the door and let the labor force in. They quickly assumed their positions. Bob, putting on an apron, worked with the boys, hooking up spits and picking out an odd pin-feather or two. He was completely in his element and hummed happily as he hooked.

Katina moved to the register and Bill took his self-assigned place next to her, on the right side near the compartment for higher denomination bills. Kay nervously roamed around supervising, flicking dust from the scale and shelves and squaring away the stools facing the counters at least a dozen times. Since it was she who had done the most to create the store, she was most apprehensive. It was as if, she said later, she had given birth. She was proud of her baby.

If there were mobs of people looking in when they were preparing the store, there were armies now that they were ready and cooking chickens. Scores of eyeballs watched the chickens going round-and-round on the machine. They had never seen anything like it before. The seven spits of chickens gently turned, slowly turned to a delicious and mouth-watering golden brown. The upper and less cooked spits dripped hot fat on the ones beneath, constantly basting, and precluding drying out.

The giant chrome-and-steel machine was spotlessly clean and the special heat resistant glass doors of the oven magnified and highlighted the succulence inside. Mouth outside the window fell open and dripped saliva when Bob took off the first spit of five red-hot chickens.

But they could not open the doors, for the Engenia had not yet happened.

Suddenly, a line of cars screeched to a halt at the curb, doors flew open and Theo, Maro, Chins, Nota, Vinegar-face, his sad-eyed wife, Antony, Voula and some forty or fifty of Theo's relatives, aunts, uncles, and friends, whom he had rounded up, pushed their way through the watching crowd and into the store. Many held beautiful and colorful flowers, roses, hydrangeas, gladiola, potted plants and climbing ivy. The women immediately started arranging them all over the store on the counters, refrigerator, cash-register, machine, in Bill's lapel, Kay's hair and Bob's apron. People and flowers flooded into and around the store like a blazing rainbow wave 'til there was no room to move.

Then, as if warned, there was a measurable decrease in chatter and movement as all eyes in the store turned to the curb outside. There, from a big black limousine, came a regal, white-haired old lady. She was dressed completely in black silk shantung. Her hair was held high with a magnificent diamond-studded tiara. A black silk shantung veil flowed and floated delicately behind her. The crowd became absolutely still and people moved back respectfully to make a small path for her.

In her right hand she held a silver-knobbed, ebony walking stick and by adroitly smashing shins and elbows she made the path wider. Yaya had arrived.

Directly behind, following her footsteps with great care came a tall, bearded, Greek Orthodox priest. He too was in black, with flowing robes and vests. His hair was tied and braided in a thick knot under his high kamilaffe. A little altar boy in white lace trailed on the priest's heels, holding a golden mortar and pestle.

The Engenia was on.

The priest flowed on past Yaya who stopped next to Kay, and dipped the pestle in the mortar which contained water. He sprinkled the people lining the walls and blessed them. He sprinkled the walls. Getting on the altar boy's shoulders he sprinkled the ceiling, intoning blessings in Archaic Greek and Byzantine rhythm. He proceeded further into the store, wetting everyone in range. When he got as far back as he could, he stopped wetting and gently placed the pestle back in the mortar the little boy offered.

Theo leaned over and confided to Bill, "Yaya has gotten a special dispensation from the Archbishop for an outside Engenia inside your store. It is the first time in my memory that an outside rite will be used inside. It will assure your success." Theo, to ward off any evil spirits that might have attempted to interfere with the Engenia, wore a necklace of fresh garlic cloves around his neck. Bill didn't know what he could possibly be talking about but he watched the priest with marked attention and moved as far away from Theo as he could in the press of the crowd.

The priest reached deep into his gowns and girdles and after a little struggle his hand came out holding a ball-pean hammer. He gave it to the boy. He reached in once more and there was a great rustling and fuss inside around where his liver was located. Quickly he whipped his hand out holding a live rooster by its scrawny neck.

Bill's eyes widened. He wondered.

With a malice rarely seen in a man of the cloth, the priest took the ball-pean hammer and bonked the rooster on the head, causing a horrible chicken scream from the chicken-hearted chicken.

The chicken bled profusely, awkwardly hanging his broken head in a figure eight. Mercifully the priest tied a not in the neck to stop the flow of blood. But the chicken did not give up the ghost easily and he frantically pumped his feet in a rapid scratching motion. Maro, who just happened to be standing close, had the bodice of her dress completely scratched off. Her dislocated mammillae, held by a specially built brassiere, were revealed for all to see.

The priest gave another blow, this time using the pean edge of the hammer and the chicken's heart beat once, a big beat, and stopped forever

Bob fainted.

"It's an outside ritual," Theo again whispered, moving closer to Bill, who had a sudden and violent attack of vertigo from the stench of the garlic, "the chicken would be buried in a hole specially prepared." But there was none so the priest simply tucked the chicken back into his robes and once more took up the pestle.

He went back to sprinkling and intoning. Bob remained on the floor sobbing.

The priest moved behind the counter, blessing glasses, plastic silverware and paper plates. Four dozen paper plates turned into a soggy mass after the assault. He got to the cash register, opened the drawer with knowledge, looked in, saw little of interest and didn't bother to bless it although he did give Katina a squirt and took some of the wax off her mustache.

The priest now had come full circle and he made his way to the machine which was roaring at 500 degrees Fahrenheit. He opened the doors, took the mortar from the little boy and with solemn incantations threw the entire contents into the raging fire.

He was instantly driven out the door by a solid wall of flying fat and flame.

"Never put water on a greasy fire," bob said from the floor, holding his head in his arms lest he be killed in the stampede of terrified guests making their way out to freedom.

That first day they took in 2,000 drachmas gifts of good luck from Theo, chins and the horde of relatives. The priest originally wanted five hundred fro his effort, but Nick the Walk got him down to two, thus the net was equivalent to sixty dollars.

"True," Bill thought, they didn't sell any chickens but that could readily be attributed to the interruption of the Engenia and the ensuing three alarm fire. "Tomorrow will be different," He said optimistically. "We'll normalize tomorrow. Did you see those mobs of on-lookers? I've never seen such a mass of people - even in front of Macy's."

They were sipping gin the living room, relaxing from the day's events with retsina.

"We'll run full tomorrow," Bob said professionally, "I'll have the boys hook up a hundred and fifty chickens and we'll have them cooking all day. There's absolutely no merchandising like a loaded Bar-B-Q machine full of dripping spits."

"It was nice of Theo and the rest to give us gifts. Gee...they're really good people," Kay said, reflecting on the generosity of the guest. "I even saw Tikidoras give Katina twenty drax for luck."

The second day of business as Bob planned, they cooked 150 chickens. The help was starched and anxious to serve, ready to pounce on the expected customers. Yianni, looking like an escapee from a freak show, squeamishly letting Chris clean chickens, draped a napkin over his arm and waited at the counter. Katina was clean-shaven, smiling at the cash register. She kept cracking her knuckles to loosen up her fingers to better handle cash.

Again there were mobs of people outside, they counted eighty-three noses pressed to the window. Ugly Greek-Americans, ex-waiters from some of the greasiest joints in continental America, jealous of the real Americans and their enterprise, stood at the curb laying bets on when the first chicken would be sold. Bill was bluntly informed that the noon time odds were 745-1 - they'd be out of business within two weeks.

So the chickens cooked, browned and basted, spit after spit: 150 of them in total. At the end of the day's business they counted, there were 147 left over. One they gave to an emaciated beggar, one they sold to a cousin of Theo's who hadn't made the Engenia and wanted to wish them luck and one they ate themselves.

After a solid week of no business, they closed the shop early one night and called an emergency meeting at home on the verandah. Despite a clear sky and bright moon, the atmosphere was pervaded with gloom. Despair was creeping into their souls.

Kay, whose attachment to the store was most manifest, felt as if she had given birth and been informed by the doctor that her offspring had six toes. With effort she kept herself under control.

"Why aren't they coming in?' She said with a tremor in her voice, informally calling the meeting to order.

"I can't understand it," Bill said, shaking his head. "I just can't. The potential is there, the chickens look beautiful, the price is good, the store's clean..."

"Maybe it's too clean," Bob said, then he added incredulously, "I don't believe it. We stand in the store fifteen hours a day and nobody comes in. I've had bad days in the Bronx but never a total zero..." He put his hands symmetrically on his temples as if to ward off shooting pains in his frontal lobe. "I may have a nervous breakdown." The lack of business was deeply affecting Bob's newly found joie de vivre and he was seriously thinking of going back on equinol. Paradoxically, he was eating and sleeping better than he had ever done in the States. He rationalized his appetite with the logic that it is infinitely less taxing to go broke in Greece than it is to put up with the terrific daily pressures of a successful one-man operation in New York.

"I've been listening to some of the comments outside," Kay said, "They think the chickens are frozen and they won't buy frozen food.

They say that everything in America is frozen. And a lot of people are afraid of the machine, they've never seen anything like it...I don't think they trust it."

"The way they line up at the window with their mouths hanging open," Bill said, "I'm sure they think we're from another planet."

"Another thing," Kay continued, "somebody in the crowd asked why we left such a rich country like America to come to poor Greece... he said the police are after us, we stole something and now we're stealing form them."

"Communist," Bill said.

"Well, I don't care about the reason," Bob said, jingling the change in his pocket, "but I know that if we continue with the present trend, we won't have what to give old Cross-eyed, the first of the month."

"I have a good idea," Bill said, "we could hire one of those sidewalk hawkers...every other store has one."

"Oh, Bill...you'd only cheapen everything," Kay cried.

"We've got to do something, Kay," Bob said, "we've got 617 cooked chickens piled around the store. They're starting to smell like they died."

They lapsed into silence. Bill thought of what Bob had said and how difficult it is to stop a trend. Perhaps, he wondered, the supper club was the better idea after all, perhaps Haralumbus was right in warning them not the cater to Greeks. That is was, as he had put it, "clumsy and undignified to attempt to sell anything to the stupid Greeks." Perhaps not even coming to Greece was the best idea.

If they had opened a supper club, Bill mused, with proper promotion they could have packed it. Suddenly a thought struck him and he shouted, "Promotion, that's it. I have it. We'll kill two birds with one stone. We'll get some publicity and dump the old chickens at the same time." He explained to Kay and Bob; they'd gratuitously give the chickens away to some old lady's home or orphanage. Theo would find some suitable and deserving organization. Then they'd contact all the Greek newspapers and the English language <u>Athens News</u> and inform them of their philanthropy. Of course, if the newspapers wanted to write it up and take some pictures, they would modestly permit it, if only to give some notoriety to the charitable organization and perhaps stimulate a wave of gifts from the newspapers readership. "It'll be our way of showing the strong bonds between America and Greece, you know, NATO partners and all that," Bill concluded. "Good?"

"Perfect," Kay said, getting up and giving him a kiss.

Bob chuckled softly the idea of setting off a wave of charity in Greece was amusing.

The next day, Haralumbus reluctantly called all the newspapers. He was unhappy with the idea, thought it gauche, but since he was promised a visit to the Grande Bretagne for his work, went along in his best con man's voice.

The newspapers responded almost 100 percent, only the extreme left wing <u>Truth</u> stayed away. <u>Truth</u> explained that it was covering an anti-American peace march that day and advised in a long harangue that if the three American capitalists who were in Greece to bilk the population had any souls at all they would turn the chickens over to the marchers as they would be tired and hungry.

The day of the give away the store was crowded for the first time since the Engenia with the reporters and photographers standing around or sitting at the bars eating chicken and potato salad. They waited noisily for the directress of the orphanage Theo had selected to receive the gift.

The smelly chickens were wrapped well and set apart in a prominent spot atop the refrigerator for the benefit of the photographers. Katine and Kay had affixed blue ribbons bows to each package in the great ceremony of gift giving.

At the appointed hour a battered jeep pulled up outside and a tall athletic woman with short hair and sweat socks and sneakers trotted in. "Oooh heloooo," she said in English, wringing Bill's hand as he met her at the door. "I'm sooo thrilled that yoooou would do this wonderful thing for the poor children at the orphanage."

"You sound American," Bill said, looking down at the floor and her ragged sneakers.

"Ooooh but I am, I certainly am. If you're wondering why I'm in Greece it's because there's so much good to dooo in the poorer countries, don't you think?"

"Of course," Bill agreed, "to do good."

The reporters moved in, getting their story about the orphanage and the good done there. By weaving in and out the circle around the directress, Bill was able to softly interject some pertinent facts about Bob and Bill's chicken Bar-B-Q prices, store hours, telephone number for home deliver. He whispered some openly contrived verbal testimonials from steady customers raving about how delicious they thought this new food was.

The photographers waited patiently and then asked Bob and Bill to present the chickens. Bill, a modest grin on his face gestured with a wave of his hand to the chickens. Yianni, on cue, stumbled up behind holding a crudely drawn sign BOB AND BILL'S BAR-B-Q OMONIA SQUARE TEL 236 222 NO MUSS NO FUSS LEAVE THE COOKING TO US!

"Oh, they're cooked," the directress said sadly.

"Of course, they're cooked," Bill said. "Do you think we'd trouble you with the cooking when we've got that big machine there." He motioned the photographers to the machine to take some more pictures.

"Oh my...oh my, that certainly is a lot of work for you but I don't want you to think we're so much trouble, sooo if it's all right I'll be happy to accept an equal number of raw chickens. Besides the children do sooo like soup. We can make so much good soup with the raw chickens. Soup is sooo healthy you know, it does so much goooood." Aggressively she counted out 168 of the largest raw chickens and fast-balled them to the waiting arms of the jeep driver outside.

The newspaper publicity emanating from the act of charity and Nick the Walk's had once again saved the day, prevented bankruptcy and the untimely folding of the store. The papers broke containing the story of American generosity, and the Greeks, intrigued by such an idea, cautiously entered the store and finally bought. Coupled with this was the fact that the gawk Yainni quit his job. He had been having fainting spells because cleaning chickens didn't agree with him. He approached Bob, his long head as white as his uniform and using Chris to interpret asked to be released. The bloody raw chickens turned his stomach, Chris explained as Yianni slumped to the floor and the work was interfering with his medical studies. He was also depressed because the pictures in the papers showed his headless body holding the sign. Nick the Walk was immediately informed of the new need and one hour later entered the store leading a short dapper man of serious countenance.

Nick introduced them to their new employee, Jimmy, one of the most experienced counter-men in Greece. An ex-merchant seaman, Jimmy had spent fifteen years in the United States after jumping ship in Houston, Texas. He escaped from the law in Texas, made his way up the Mississippi by barge and wound up in Detroit where he worked as a short order man in a coffee shop which catered exclusively to immigration officials and FBI men. For fifteen years he served hot coffee and westerns to the very men who were charged by the state to remove him from American soil, and would still have been there if he had not decided to officially immigrate and become a citizen. He was totally unaware that the Greek quota, although having been increased to 400 that year, was filled. His petition was refused by a court which couldn't understand how he had foiled the authorities for so many years, even though he proved he had voted for Governor three times and President twice- having lived in a Democratic ward. His person was immediately placed on freighter carrying used Government Chevrolets bound for Greece.

 Jimmy learned fast and daily accounted for many new customers. He was diplomatic, firm and had a sharp sales pitch. Bob thought he was eminently worthy of Nathan's Coney Island. He was a great find. Again Kay rewarded Nick the Walk with a hug and a kiss.

 The bread they cast upon the waters, came back not as Haralumbus had predicted- soggy, but in the form of money. Business shot up daily. They were selling — wrapping up for home delivery, first forty chickens a day, then forty-five, then fifty-five...75...80…85...90...up, up, up...100, 150, 175, 200. And further and further they skyrocketed...210, 215, 230...250. Each day got better and better. Every week business boomed. The machine strained and groaned, like some animate monster spewing forth hundreds of broiled chicken every day. There were no more slow days. The snack bar where customers waited for a quick lunch became jammed, two or three deep at all hours of the day.

 Money rolled in, oiled by Jimmy's sleek sales talk at the door. They saw that they would be rich and they were pleased. Their fame spread daily far and wide in Athens. Bob and Bill's became the place to go. They had to refuse scores of hungry people because they had so little room. They had turned a 765-1 shot for failure to an odds on favorite to break the bank.

The customers didn't mind the crush and the shoving inside the small store and waited patiently for the chickens to cook, fascinated by the new system.

But it was obvious they would have to expand.

"We can't go on like this, Bill," Bob said, one busy Saturday morning. He was elbow deep in raw chickens, helping Chris. "No kidding, we've got to have more space. This is ridiculous. We clean over 300 chickens a day in this thing." He pointed with disgust to where the sink was buried under a mass of slimy chickens. "I'm telling you it's going to hurt us, these birds need refrigeration and we're losing a lot of good restaurant trade. You can't even get an elbow on that bar."

Sweatingly they ran up to Grapus, exercised their option and rented the stock room behind the wall.

In only ten days, setting a record for swiftness in Greece which amazed Theo, they knocked down the wall, set-up a cleaning kitchen with three sinks and iceboxes, outfitted the back room restaurant with sixteen tables, hooked up a hot water machine for washing glasses, hired two waiters, and assistant for Jimmy and another chicken plucker.

Under Kay's tasteful direction, with the use of dark wood beams and lanterns, the restaurant took on a rustic American look. The overhead soared but was more than compensated for with a splurge of restaurant business.

Bob and Bill had made a complete reversal of the Saying: "When two Greeks meet they open a restaurant."

Chapter Seven

Not long after the opening of the back restaurant, they received unwelcome callers. Bob, Bill and Kay were sitting at a table, counting money and discussing in quiet but elated tones, the brilliance of Bill's idea of coming to Greece. As is the wont of the nouveau riche, they were making plans for the spending of their money—renting mansions, more maids, and the relative worth of butlers. Kay had a French fashion catalogue posed on her lap, and was carefully selecting styles for a completely new fall and winter wardrobe.

Jimmy, dropping his work, joined them, a worried look on his face. He was followed by a black uniformed, thick set police officer and a thin plain clothes man. "Mr. Bill," he said, "we in civilian trouble!" Jimmy's years in the States had not given him a precise or even adequate command of English. Bill wondered what severe trouble they were in.

"These cops want to see the licenses to run."

The three Americans stared dumbly at Jimmy and the two serious law enforcement officers.

"They say they gonna close the store, if you don't got no licenses."

"Do they speak English?" Bill asked.

"Milate Anglika?" Jimmy asked them.

The uniformed policeman's eyebrows rose, his eyes turned back in their sockets and he made a clicking sound with his tongue - no!

"Then milate Ellenika?" the cop asked contemptuously. Don't they speak Greek?

Jimmy looked down and said, "Ohi."

The uniformed man made a long speech, jabbing his finger in the air to emphasize each point. He shouted every word, and when he was finished he glared at Jimmy, challenging him to translate.

Jimmy took a deep breath, "Mr. Bill, they want to see the permission to open and operate, but he said they know that we don't have it, because that if we did have it they would know about it, because it's their job. And, they very mad because we didn't even apply for a license, but even if we did, he says we couldn't get one because no foreigners are allowed to work in Greece, that's the law. There's not even enough work for Greeks in Greece, and he says he doesn't care about foreign aid or stuff like that, you can't stay and they're closing us up and we're getting sued." Jimmy, exhausted, fell into a chair.

Bob asked, "What's getting sued?"

"Fine and jail," Jimmy morosely answered, "They also want your passports."

"Jimmy, certainly these men are not going to close us up," Kay said. "I mean, they don't mean today, do they? We'll get all the papers they want avrio, tomorrow." The plain clothes man evidently understood what Kay said and let out a loud guffaw. Then he turned solemn and shot an order to Jimmy.

"He says you don't understand, you never be able to get the papers. He wants you to go with them."

"Now wait a minute," Kay said indignantly, "just one minute. We didn't do anything wrong. Tell him that we didn't come all the way here to open and close the store for our health." She said something to the policeman in Greek, throwing her head back in defiance when she finished. Her chin jut out determinedly and she demanded of Bill, "Give me Theo's phone number." She marched to the phone. Kay's tenacity had an effect on the policemen and they waited quietly for her to finish her call. With the intuition peculiar to their profession, they sensed she was a formidable opponent. Her voice, clear and precise, came back to them over the noise of the customers and the ring of the cash register. After a few moment, she called, "Jimmy, ask the uniformed one to come to the phone please."

Angrily the policeman left the table for the phone and returned almost immediately, his neck a bright red.

"Me sinhorite, me sinhorite, parakalo," he said respectfully. He grabbed the detective and they hurriedly made for the door.

"What the...what happened..." Bob stammered. He was flabbergasted, the cops did not look the type to abjectly back down.

Jimmy, too was amazed. "Gee, Mrs. Kay," he said in wonder, "What happened...I know about those police... they don' fool aroun'...they mean."

Kay looked very pleased with herself. "I don't know exactly what Theo told him but when I told him what they wanted, his voice got very low and mean and he said not to worry about anything, Yaya would talk to them. Then he put her on the phone." Kay picked up her fashion book and resumed marking her fall selections.

Chapter Eight

By hiring the new help for the restaurant themselves they violated Theo's strict injunction, but they went merrily ahead, selection people for the back. When only the snack bar was functioning, it was comparatively easy to check on and teach the employees the system, but now they were big business. Jimmy was good, they made him manager after only a few weeks. Katina and Chris continued well in their work as Theo had foreseen. The new people were the ones that exemplified the Americans' ability as personnel managers.

Since they needed chicken cleaners desperately, they delegated Jimmy as hiring agent and sent him one morning to the Agora to get someone who might do.

"I know exactly where to go, Mr. Bill and Mr. Bob," he said, tearing from the store in fear that he might be recruited to clean chickens.

"Come back with a guy who won't faint, eh." Bob requested.

"Oriste," Jimmy cried in triumph when he returned with what he had found.

"What's this?" Bob asked.

"This is Spiro," Jimmy said, formally introducing them. "He has no last name, just Spiro."

Their eyes were unable to leave the apparition at Jimmy's side. Spiro was about five feet tall but wore a shirt—a woolen sport shirt—

made for a man much taller. The shoulder seams were at the elbows, and the sleeves, of necessity, were rolled up into thick balls of cloth at his wrist. An open collar revealed a stained yellow union suit buttoned to the neck. The heavy trousers he wore were also too large, the crotch ending at the knees. It was very hot and Spiro should have been extremely uncomfortable with all the wool encasing his body, but he gave no visible hint that the temperature bothered him because his face was completely covered by bangs of hair extending down past his mouth and ending about one inch below his chin. Thick bangs of black, oily hair, trimmed evenly at the back of his neck, covered the rest of his head.

"Should I put him to work?" Jimmy asked enthusiastically.

"Wait a minute, Jim, the interview isn't over." Bill said, parting the front bangs gently and looking into the face hidden underneath. He wondered if, like certain type sheep dogs, Spiro would be blinded by the light. He jumped back immediately, closing the curtain of hair quickly as he did.

"Wanna give him a couple drax for a haircut, Mr. Bill?" Jimmy said, "Don't look good with all that hair, working on food."

"No, no," Bill shouted, "It's OK the way it is. Just keep him out of the public eye as much as possible.

"Check boss," Jimmy said and guided Spiro to the kitchen and mounds of chickens.

After a few days of on-the-job training, Bob and Bill observed that they had an excellent man in Spiro.

"My God," Bob exclaimed, at the end of Spiro's apprenticeship, "I've never seen anything like it. I had a part time kid in for the holidays in the Bronx who could clean chickens like mad, but this Spiro...what production. Do you know he's cleaned 340 chickens so far today and it's only noon."

"He is so quiet too," Bill said, taking a look at the machine and the turning chickens. "Need another spit, Bob, if we're going to handle the two o'clock rush."

Bob shouted, "Spiro, pende," toward the kitchen, calling for a spit of five chickens.

"Spiro, pende," Jimmy repeated.

"Spiro, pende," Katina relayed from the cash register.

A few seconds later the swinging door of the kitchen banged open and out charged Spiro with a full spit of chickens. He looked neither right nor left, but straight ahead, like a charging medieval knight with lance at the ready, he flew down the narrow store to the machine. His hair parted in the breeze, causing gasps from people standing at the bar. Jimmy took the spit and quickly put it on the machine and firmly led Spiro in a fast retreat to the kitchen.

"I know that someday he's going to impale a customer that doesn't give him the right of way down that aisle," Bob said.

"Jimmy tells me he never eats a thing," Bill said, "He serves him three meals a day but he never touches the stuff."

"I know, I've seen him push the dish away," Bob said. "Another thing...I know we don't need a college graduate...but something isn't right. Every day there's a raw chicken miscounted, there's always one less. I know they're not leaving the store, but I'll be damned if I know what..."

Then like a bolt, Bob and Bill had the same thought.

"No," Bill whispered.

"No," Bob gasped.

That same day Jimmy approached Bob and Bill with a pained expression on his face. "Mr. Bill and Mr. Bob, I think we gonna be in civilian trouble," he began.

"What's the matter?" Bob asked.

"It Spiro, I think maybe he working too hard. He don't complain or anything like that, he never say anything, je jus' do his job, but I afraid law gonna hurt us."

"Why, what did we do?"

"It not what we do, but Spiro works from six in the morning to twelve at night, and the law very strict about that."

"Hmmmm." Bill thought, it had never occurred to them that Spiro was working too long hours, he never complained or said a word, but maybe Jimmy was right, maybe it was rather a long day for Spiro. Since they saw him only when he charged out the back with chickens, they never gave him much thought.

"Well, let's see," Bob said. "What does he get a month, Jimmy?"

Jimmy blinked, "1200 drax, Mr. Bob."

"Hmm." Bill murmured, "forty-dollars, that's really not that much for all those hours when you think of it. What do you think, Jimmy, should we give him a raise? Would that square things with the law?"

"It is not the money...it the hours. I think we got to get some help for him."

As they talked, Bill noticed a figure furtively slinking up the aisle to the table where they sat. It was the figure of a man out of a 1937 melodrama about the American depression. It struck Bill as singularly odd that on this steaming August day, with the temperature well over 100 degrees, he should be wearing an old heavy army overcoat and a wide-brimmed Capone-style fedora. For some inexplicable reason, Bill thought of Sacco-Vanzetti.

The overcoat moved closer. It stopped with the man inside it sat the table and waited. Two beady black eyes, so close together as to seem like a double exposure, imploringly asked for attention. There were drops of perspiration on the beak of his sharp, downward-curving nose.

"Jim, get ten drax from Katina and give it to this man," Bill said, "Wrap up half a chicken too."

The man made no move when Jimmy got back with the handout. Instead of taking the fit and leaving he collapsed into a chair, put his head on the table and broke into anguished tears.

"Jim, what's wrong? What does he want?" Bob asked.

Jimmy bent down over the crying huddle and asked in Greek, "Ti thelis? Thelis voithis, yiero? What do you want? Do you need help, old man?

Only sobs of despair came back.

"Here, take this money and the chicken, old man. Here, accept this." Jimmy again offered the dole.

The man's head rose, once again the double exposure, "ohi, ohi...then thelo doro." No, No, I don't want gifts.

"Tote, ti thelis," Jimmy asked again, less patiently. Then, what do you want?

The old man removed his hat, revealing a head covered with eight or ten fine grey hairs. He tearfully exclaimed, "Thelo doulia, doulia, ti thelo." I want work, work is what I want. "Then imme kakomiro." I'm not a beggar.

"What is he...kidding or something?" Bob said softly.

"He wants a job, Mr. Bob," Jimmy said, rushing up front to take care of some tourists who had just entered.

"Parakalo, Kiro," Bill said, "parakalo...etho then eki doulia." Here we have no work, Sir.

Bob was incredulous that the Cyclops would have asked for work. The man, he felt, should have been in some home for the aged, rather than in the streets seeking employment. "Could you just see him carrying a spit of chickens," he said. "He'd collapse, he doesn't weigh 100 pounds under that coat...I mean...this cat made the scene when they still had Ottoman pot in this country."

With Jimmy gone, the man saw he could make no headway with the foreigners, so he got up, took the chicken and ten drachmas and made his way ploddingly out the front door. He first peeked into the kitchen where Spiro labored neck high in chickens. When he reached the machine, he looked at it wistfully, touched it gently and then disappeared into the crowd outside.

For days afterwards, the broken figure that may have once been young and full of spirit, loitered around the store. His eyes begging for help, for honest work. Everyday he stood in the first row of on-lookers, nose pressed to the window, the brim of his hat turned up like a cub reporter's. Occasionally he would sneak past the busy Jimmy and look into the kitchen, and Spiro, and chickens.

One evening, dining at the store, the three Americans learned what determination really was.

Bob, to prepare for the eight o'clock rush, hollered, "Spiro, pende."

"Spiro, pende," repeated Jimmy.

"Spiro, pende," echoed Katina.

All eyes moved to the kitchen door in anticipation of the charge. Regular customers who knew, moved from between the kitchen and the machine, cutting a respectful path.

They waited.

No Spiro.

"Spiro, pende," Bob shouted again.

And Jimmy and Katina, "Spiro, pende."

No Spiro

"Spiro, pende," Bob shouted loudly.

Still no Spiro.

As Jimmy was going to the back to investigate the mystery of Spiro, the kitchen door squeaked slowly open, revealing a wasted frame struggling and staggering under a burden of a full spit of chickens. It was the beggar.

He negotiated the narrow aisle, fell to his knees halfway to his goal, slithered further down, turned and lay flat on his back. He paused for strength and then determinedly, crawling on his back, cradling the spit of precious chickens on his chest, made for the machine. Slowly, excruciatingly, he dug his heels in and inched forward, using his head to steer.

Bob, Bill and Kay watched not believing.

When he reached Jimmy's feet he was near complete collapse and he pointed to the spit with his double exposure eyes, asking help from the astonished Jimmy. Jimmy quickly took the spit and put it on the machine, nodding apologies to the crowd which had gathered inside to watch.

A young woman, stepping closer, helped the beggar up and as he rose, a corner of his long butcher's apron became enmeshed in the rotating gears of the machine. Very slowly, before everyone's eyes, ever so slowly, the gears round the apron tighter and tighter, dragging the hapless beggar first erect, then stiffly into the roaring heat of the oven, Bob, coming out of his trance, jumped to his feet and clocked the power off, saving the old man from a certain, slow-burning and basting death.

Jimmy administered water, a shot of brandy and carried the limp, corkscrewed figure back to the table.

"Jimmy, feed him and get him out of here," Bob said. "He's hurting business."

The crowd of on-lookers continued to stare out of some morbid curiosity, wondering if the old man would die or not. The curb exchange had odds of up to 100-1 that he would pass on in twenty minutes or less.

The old man started crying, mumbling incoherently through his sobs.

"The poor man. What does he want?" Kay asked sympathetically.

"He wont work, Mrs. Kay," Jimmy said, getting ready to throw the man out. "He say he told Spiro to go home, he was the new night man."

Bob moaned, "One of our busiest nights and Spiro went home. Jimmy, do you know where Spiro lives? We'll have to get him, we have to have someone in the back."

"Are you kidding, Mr. Bob? I don't even know Spiro's last name...I don't think he lives in a house."

"Can't this man possibly work in the back?" Kay asked, looking at Bob. "I mean if he wants a job so badly, that he has to hire himself, wouldn't he do?"

"No, Kay. Absolutely not," Bob cried. "You saw for yourself that the fink can't even hold himself up, no less a spit fully of chickens. This is a restaurant. What would you think if you were a customer and saw that in the window? I know what I'd think. I'd think they either starve the help or that the food did."

"Oh Bob, don't be so miserable," Kay pleased. "You can train him. I'm sure he'll do the job all right. You yourself said Spiro would need a day off now and then."

"Kay, you make it awfully hard to be mean," Bob said, breaking into a smile. "OK, Jimmy help the decrepit one up and put him inside. We'll see what we can do with him." They dragged the old man into the kitchen, gave him artificial respiration and then instructed him in his duties for his newly won job.

Is there a humble man? Panyoti, for all the meekness he showed applying for employment, was something less than meek when he finally landed the job. He turned into a severe problem. They had to struggle continuously to keep him out of the front of the store where people could see him and give the place a bad name. With his hound dog look, emaciated body, advanced age, he was not, they felt, a good advertisement for the store.

As he became more familiar with the work, the simpering, cringing man disappeared. He was replaced by a ruthless, determined, penny-pinching house dick. It came out that many years back he had been employed at a well know Athenian Taverna, where his duties consisted of counting the silverware and saltcellars every night at the close of business and ratting on any busboy who might have accidentally dropped and broken a dish or glass. But, Bob and Bill's had no dishes to break, no silverware to count. The glasses broken since opening amounted to three dollars. The salcellars they wanted stolen, they had designed them as souvenirs, especially to be taken. They wanted peace and harmony with the employees. But Panyoti harassed them horribly, he was sure they were deliberately destroying property. He commissioned himself a watchdog committee of one to make sure the help was working at all times. Despite firm protests he took inventory of the plastic throw-away forks and knives at all hours of the day—ten in the morning, during the height of the noon rush and at dinnertime. He accused Spiro of stealing a roll of toilet paper and through some ingenious detective work, confirmed the suspicions about the daily missing raw chicken.

His pursuit of the perpetuator of the heinous crime—the swiping of two kilos of chicken livers—went on relentlessly until he found that Bill had taken them home himself. Except for the raw chicken each day, he never discovered a real theft, but continued his McCarthy-like probes and character assassinations without letup.

Bob and Bill, to amuse themselves, took to playing the game of hiding the merchandise, in which they would secrete, somewhere in the store, a piece of inventory and then sit back and watch the detective work. It was much like hot beans. They even set about laying false clues and misinformation, but only the case of the missing jar of pepper fooled him.

Panyoti hounded Jimmy, the best man, and tormented the waiters. The cashier wasn't safe from his beady eyes and the beer delivery man was constantly shadowed and watched through a peephole he had bored in the kitchen wall.

Bob came close to a nervous breakdown when he saw Panyoti could only clean ten or twelve chickens in an eight-hour day and before he caught control of himself, took to his bed for four days. But as the weeks and months went by, Panyoti became a kind of an institution around the store and they grew to accept him. Besides, neither Bob nor Bill was willing to fire him for fear of Kay.

Chapter Nine

"This is an idyllic life," Bill said softly, reaching out and pulling Kay closer to him in bed. The warmth and glow of the Grecian morning filled him with life. Two glasses of freshly squeezed orange juice rested on a serving table next to the bed. He thought that since it was such an outstanding day, and he felt so well, he could work something out before breakfast.

"Let me alone," Kay mumbled tiredly, turning around and moving further away. She did not see the magnificent rays of sun dancing about the room, she had not noted the serene and happy blue sky with puffs of clouds floating aimlessly in the yonder. All this, Bill mused, this panorama of loveliness, was hers to see if she would but uncover her eyes and gaze out the window. And seeing, he was sure, she would reflect on his presence and the, carried away with the joy of the day, the romance of it all.

"Will you ring for the maid and tell her to keep those kids quiet. Let her throw them some toys," Kay said irritably referring to the shrieks and sounds of punches coming from the children's rooms. "I want to get some sleep. And will you please move over!" She shot an elbow into Bill's ribs, tucked her shorty nightgown down as far as it would go and hunched toward the edge of the bed. Crushed by this rejection, Bill took a little solace by downing his orange juice, and hers too—to get even.

Life had certainly changed for them in Greece, he thought, as he moved to the floor to begin his daily morning exercise of one push up, a deep knee-bend and a cigarette. Whereas at home he had to throw the children toys and books and crayons in the early morning, now they had servants to do all this. He rang for the maid, took four deep breaths at the window and trotted into the bathroom for a warm shower. In the hall he bumped into a woman he had never seen before, and let out a loud shout.

"Why are you hollering?" Kay shouted, tumbling out of bed to see what the commotion was.

"Who is this woman?" he demanded, throwing his bathrobe on.

"Oh, is that all. That's the new maid, Paraskevi."

"Why don't you tell me when you hire a new maid...I got scared out of half my wits." Now it was his turn to be cranky. "What happened to the other maids?"

Ever since Alike the ox was caught red-handed swiping 5,000 drachmas and summarily fired, their maid problem had been acute. They had run through a succession of women but were yet to come up with anything even remotely approaching Voula, whom they thought the ultimate in domestic help. Their problem was the problem of petit bourgeois everywhere how to handle servants. Everything they did was wrong. As Americans they tried democracy, and as Theo prophesized, it failed. "You cannot treat them" had advised, "As your equals or you will be stolen. They will not work for you as their equal. Once you make them feel equal, they resent having to serve you. It is logical—if I am on your social level, why then do you not serve me one half of the time. They become, therefore unhappy and it is only a small matter of time until you are stolen. Remember, equality always...but only between equals."

But as Americans, it was impossible to adopt the aristocratic traditions of Theo, who had a quality of command they could never attain. His mussed and comical appearance did not for one-minute hide his blood. Born into the ruling class in a country which, whatever its politics at a given time, was always honored, Theo was respected by those beneath him far more than any blue blood could hope for in America.

So, Bill, Kay and Bob bungled along, democratically, fraternally, being stolen, getting little work out of their domestics and losing one after another. The contempt in which they were held by the maids was in direct proportion with the manner in which they treated them. It was simple, Bob said, "the better you are the worse they get. Treat 'em rough. We go along buying them fancy uniforms. Looks at Voula, she's only got that old rag and Maro and Theo don't ever talk to her except when it's an order. She's happy...and for crying out loud, Kay, will you stop telling them they're women and have to smell nice. All my after shave is gone." Bob had violently gone on a binge of breaking broom handles from the stand-up brooms Kay had compassionately bought. "From now on," he had said cruelly, "the maids bend over to sweep like in a Greek house."

Kay went along with Bob on the brooms but to take the sting out she divided the work and hired a governess for the children and what she haughtily called an upstairs-downstairs maid.

Assimina, the governess, was a dyspeptic hag of 65, who because she owned only four teeth - all on the upper left hand side of her mouth - demanded the softest cuts of meat and daily feedings of soppy farina. She was four feet one-inch tall and weighed, including her long underwear which she wore winter and summer, 70 lbs. What she lacked in weight she made up in energy and a dirty mouth. She got the children to do anything she wanted, maintained perfect order, through witch-like screaming and curses. The children quickly learned every curse word in the Greek lexicon.

Bill grumbled, felt she was not the best they could find and swore that all she needed was a broom with a handle to take off.

Kay told him that if he wanted Bridgette Bardot, he should go to the movies and, "what do you expect for $17 a month—a Swiss governess? You are just jealous because the kids know more curses than you."

Crisoula, the upstairs-downstairs maid was a drudge. Since they had no washing machine, and the children consumed acres of clothes daily, she was never out of the washroom. She never did get upstairs, Bill commented. She ground and rinsed all day long and wrung the clothes out with masochistic delight. Her hands were like two raw roast beefs. Her day lasted till well past midnight but she always looked fresh and contented - her face was set in a maloccluded

Neanderthalic grin. Her hands did not look contented though, and Kay bought her a pair of rubber gloves, which she couldn't figure out what to use for and they ended up as catchalls for pins and buttons she found in the wash. She too was paid 500 drcs. a month.

With all the house work being done by other hands, Kay once again swore never to return to America. "I'll never...never do housework again," she cried. "We used to think a washing machine was indispensable, but here all we do is plug in the maid and she washes, irons and puts the clothes away too. Try to get one machine to do that in the State."

Nancy told them that Assimina meant silver and Chrisoula gold and Bob like to say they had silver and gold for only thirty-four dollars a month.

"What happened to Gold and Silver," Bill repeated to Kay.

"Assimina left yesterday in a fit of pique because Bob ate the last of the farina, and Chrisoula quit to work for the American consul across the street who promised her she'd do only ironing and get a quart of Jergens lotion every week."

"Damn Americans with their PX privileges."

Paraskevi was still hovering where they had hit and Bill took a good look at her. Her hair was tied in a neat tight bun and she had an insipid grin on her face. Why, Bill asked himself, must they always grin? Her grin showed thirty-three, old and brown, but usable teeth. She wore Assimini's old uniform which was much too small and much of her hairy leg was visible. She was about fifty. It was the feet though, which were the most arresting part of Paraskevi. Through some accident at birth or the continual wearing of shoes too small, or perhaps even through design, the middle and ring toes of each foot overlapped each other. Her toes were crossed. Because of her deformity she wore open crossed-toed sandals and seemed comfortable enough and, they found out later, never tripped or stumbled.

Kay ordered her to get breakfast and squeeze some more juice and she obediently cross-toed downstairs to the kitchen.

Paraskevi was to the house what Panyoti was to the store. She padded around with her grin and thirty-three teeth, bowing and scraping at every order. Bob grew to hate her violently. "I can't stand her, I swear I'll go out of my mind," he complained, joining Kay and Bill in their room one morning at six. He held his hands to his head, squeezing the pain away. "I just can't relate to that woman."

"What up now?" Bill asked.

"You don't have to worry up here, but my room's on the ground floor. I can hear her pitter-patting around all hours of the night. She's an insomniac...last night she washed clothes at three A.M. and she sang Greek mountain music. I have to have my sleep."

"Well, that's OK," Kay said, "she knows the water's only hot in the middle of the night...if you'd quit taking so many hot baths, she'd be able to do the wash during the day. The singing's innocent...she can sing while she works can't she?"

"But in a deep basso?" Bob said and stormed out of the room to one of his nerve-soothing hot baths.

Paraskevi was a problem with her insomnia and her irritatingly obsequious behavior but they were reluctant to get rid of her because she ate very little and had a salubrious effect on the children. She had only to stand in their presence and they would stop whatever mayhem they were up to and stand for long periods, silently staring at her toes.

One morning Bill and Kay awoke to an unthinkable situation. The orange juice and coffee were not on the table next to the bed.

"Paraskevi...Paraskevi," Bill called.

"Save your breath," Bob answered. "She's not here." He entered bearing the morning eye-openers.

"Where's Paraskevi?" Kay asked panicking. The fear of housework drained the blood from her face.

"Friday," Bob said, translating her name into English, "Has joined the ranks of the unemployed. She is no longer part of the Great Society." He seemed very proud of himself.

"Do you mean you mean you fired her?"

"Exactly!"

"Why, what did she do?"

"Look, we've had ample reason to can her long before this but this morning took the cake. First of all I caught her hovering over my bed at four o'clock shining slippers and they're velvet- and then later I found her eating the dog food out of Schwartz's dish. She said she like it...it tastes like hash one of her old bosses used to make."

"No."

"Yes. She was very abnormal."

"No wonder the dog has lost weight, poor thing," Kay said patting Schwartz' wagging head.

"Well," Bill laughed, "we've run through silver and gold and now we're out of Friday." Then he ducked under the covers, hiding from a fuselage of hot coffee.

That afternoon, to relax from the trauma of firing Paraskevi, they went to the beach. Arriving home they noticed an envelope sticking out of the mail slot in the front gate.

Aside from the shrill dunning letters from Sears Roebuck, who had mysteriously discovered their address, and a few 1924 type advertisements written in Greek, they received no mail at all. They sent the children scurrying to the back yard and sat down on the soft grass of the front lawn as Kay tore open the letter.

It was from Nat, the musician she had hired. She read:

"Dear Mrs. Treekerson,

I sincerely hope that this letter reaches you in Greece because I had a lot of trouble getting your address in the first place and because I will be anxiously awaiting your answer in the second place.

It was very difficult learning where you were exactly and after you didn't write to me after you left for five months, I thought maybe you lost my address and that is why you didn't write to me. Is that why? I hope it is why, because I am still "waiting, and prepared to join you there, where ever you are because you made it sound so nice. Now that you are there, is it as nice as you told me it was?

I hope you don't mind that I visited your mother to find out your address. But she wouldn't give it to me, she said how did she know I wasn't a bill collector or something and that not to bother her anymore because she wouldn't pay your lousy husband's debts anyway. She was very mad at me and also at him and perhaps it was because she is an emotional lady but she told me he was a bum, he could never hold a job and he was crazy for dragging you to Greece. I don't believe her even if she is your mother and knows better than me."

Bill thought of his dear mother-in-law even as Kay continued.

"Then I went down the street from your old home to where we played the piano when you hired me. The man that answered, a Mr. Murphy, didn't understand what I wanted because he told me that he didn't want any, and it was a restricted neighborhood and then "he threw me down the stairs. They are concrete stairs. He mentioned upon my leaving that he would fight to the end any type of block busing.

Before all this about the address happened I did many things to prepare for my joining you at the club you were setting up. You told me to get a passport which I did and because I read about you have to get injections I got them. I became very sick, I didn't know that I was allergic to small pox and it cost me 347 dollars for the doctor and the hospital. I don't have blue cross. Then after I got better I bought all the music books you told me to, the ones about Calypso and like Harry Belefonte. They were very expensive but my father who has his own shoe shine route gave me the money, because I was fired from my teaching job, because I had small pox. The principal was afraid of an epidemic with the kids, I guess, like.

Then all my friends gave me a welcome home party after the hospital, because they thought I was going away. It was a very good party, I mean like it really swung. I got many gifts of merchandise and things (one nice trick gave me her body.) I blend with sweet friends. Only one thing marred the party as a whole and that was when one of the best ivory men in the biz, like, in my opinion anyway, ran out of heroin that night and had a fit and the cops came and because someone had some H. on him we were all arrested and I spent two weeks in Lexington, Kentucky in a Federal hospital before they found out I was not a drug addict. But since then I am. Man, there ain't no kick like it, like in my humble opinion. The police also confiscated the going-away gifts.

Now Mrs. Treekerson, I don't want to tell you all my troubles or trouble you but you know like sometimes you got to get things off of your chest. Whee, man am I high today. Now I am not working because of my criminal record and have joined a swinging little organization in the big G. (that's ghetto like in Harlem). We get paid a little of the dust every time we lay down in front of bulldozers or cranes and cement trucks and gear like that. It ain't bad for a fix, you're laying down anyway. Also I pick up a little spare change throwing Molitov cocktails off of buildings down at cops whenever there's like a thing going on.

Recently I broke my hand so that I won't be able to smash you and your stupid husband and if we met again I can't even kick you right because the small pox weakened my legs. But each night I shine and sharpen my Eisenhower switch blade for you. Like hoping you and yours are well.

    I remain, the swinging,

        Nathan X"

When Kay concluded, they looked up and down the street and ran inside with the children and bolted the door.

Chapter Ten

Coincidentally, they moved from the furnished house not long after Nat's latter. It had been a good house, served them well and they were a little nostalgic about leaving but the furniture had arrived from America and stood in two gigantic wooden crates on the front lawn waiting to be placed. Nick the Walk, summoned from his coffeeklatch at a Pireaus caffenio, playing Rommel to the custom's inspector's Montgomery in a nifty game of hide and seek, buried toasters, fans, motors, transformers and other high duty electrical appliances in baby carriages, toy chests, and mattresses and got the furniture out of customs with nominal cost.

Bob delegated himself in charge of all the details of finding the new house and raced about Athens and its environs in a fever of excitement. Bill couldn't figure out why he seemed almost half crazed about getting a new place but willingly and lazily took Bob's hours at the store himself.

A few days into September, Bob bubbled into the store after a week's absence. He was trailed by a short, ugly man dressed in a long, one-button lounge, shark skin, Scotch-plaid suit jacket, blue flannel trousers and very narrow blue patent leather shoes. His face had a mashed up look about it.

"I have found the house of our dreams," Bob declared. He needed a shave and looked as if he had been working very hard house-hunting.

"Where have you been?" Bill demanded. "You have to take a week to find a house...I've been killing myself here. Ask Jimmy, we've been busier than ever. A real nut house." Jimmy, wrapping up an order for four chickens, chuckled at the thought of Mr. Bill killing himself working.

"Aha...but partner, what a house," Bob sighed. "We can't even call it a house...it's a mansion...a villa of villas... a place perfectly suited to our personages." He nudged the short man at his side, "right John."

"Who's that?"

"That is Honest John the real-estate mon."

Bill and Honest John stiffly shook hands.

"I got the house with John's help. He was instrumental." Bob beamed down at Honest John the real estate mon. "One of the cabaret owners recommended him to me. Right John."

"Right," Honest John said sullenly, methodically shining his shoes on the back of his pants legs.

"Just wait til you see this layout," Bob said, "It's the house I've always dreamed of living in. There's a beautiful marble front...all kinds of terra cotta and statuary and flowers...inside too...marble...all over marble. It has a big playroom on the ground floor, the whole size of the house. Perfect for the kids...they can ride their bikes and roller skate down there. It's got the fanciest bar I've ever seen...all marble and Doric columns and a cornice over the place for the booze, like the Parthenon...bas relief and all. It's mad...wait 'til you see it. The landlord's painting it now, I hope Kay won't mind, I picked out the colors. And John here, too. No kidding, it's fabulous."

Bill and Kay saw that Bob had not exaggerated. The house was beautiful. It was a mansion. A long winding walk, tiled in multi-colored Grecian marble led to the front steps. Rows of chrysanthemums, marigolds, dahlias and cockscombs boarded the walk. Neat orange trees stood by, waiting their turn and season.

There were four bath-dressing rooms within, with sunken tubs and gold dolphins for faucets and sleek mermaids for taps. Squirt-up douche bowls, antiseptically clean, stood functionally by the toilets. All the rooms were large and airy and the bedrooms on the second floor all led out through floor-to-ceiling French doors to a wide terrazzo terrace shaded by old and twisted, shiny-leaved olive trees.

The rental price included the services of a gardener who kept it a showplace and planted cucumbers and eggplant in a small patch of the very large back yard.

The playroom with it's Parthenon bar, indirect lighting and sleek blue marble floor was large enough to hold 75 guests.

"From now on, here's where we have our morning coffee served, "Bob exclaimed, running up and down the terrace after Bill and Kay had made their inspection tour. "And we can put the dining room furniture out here too." Excitedly, Bob made plans and arranged and re-arranged furniture in his mind.

For the first time in his life, he felt he belonged. Bob had lived, in New York, in a small dingy bachelor's apartment on East Thirty

Seventh Street. Most of his friends and acquaintances, from whom he hid the fact that every morning while most people were commuting into Manhattan to work, he was sitting on a near-empty Pelham Bay local on his way to the Bronx and his chicken store, thought his pad was the bitter end. The address alone, they screamed, was worth two hundred bucks. Everybody loved the apartment itself and Bob found himself being maneuvered into throwing all night parties three or four times a week. Most of his school cronies—young men on the way up—had myriads of contacts with stewardesses, models, secretaries and pretty copy writers at the advertising agencies, and Bob, who was afraid that if he refused somehow the secret of the chicken store would come out, patiently let them come in their respective waves, bottles under arms, stay till the wee hours of the morning and leave the place a wreck. He had grown to hate the partiers so much, their thin ties, thin suits, squashed down hair, the girls- all beautifully the same, that he was almost happy when one night during a particularly wild party a curvy airline stewardess stopped conversation by saying that he smelled like broiled chicken. After that he had cut down drastically on the use of the hall and carefully aired out his clothing every evening after work on a clothes line in the alley-way outside.

For his own living quarters in their new home, he had chosen a bedroom-den on the lower level. It was lined with knotty olive book shelves and had a functioning fireplace which he ultimately came to keep burning winter and summer. The room had a separate entrance at the side of the house- a thick iron door.

"We can't do with only one maid in a house like this," were the first words out of Kay's mouth, "I'll need help running a place this size."

"That goes without saying," Bill nodded.

"Don't worry, I'm arranging that with Honest John the real estate mon," Bob said, having taken care of all the details.

Except for the colors of the rooms, which Bob and Honest John had selected bright blues and reds and yellows they could not but be satisfied with the villa.

It took a week of solid work, uncrating and de-accessorizing the furniture, placing it and pictures, draping the windows and cleaning up, but at the end they felt permanence all around them. Also helping in setting up the house was a small army of temporary maids that John had thoughtfully hired.

Just as Bob was putting the finishing touches on the terrace, lining up aluminum lawn furniture and tables facing the sun side, Honest John the real-estate mon crept up.

"Mr. Newman, I think it's time to settle up with me for my help," he said dishonestly. A pink gladiola was pinned to his wide jacket lapel.

"Of course, John," Bob said, "We've been so busy, I completely forgot. Look...you've been terrific and I'm grateful, here's 3,000 drachmas." Bob handed him the equivalent of a hundred dollars. Over fair to be sure, but Bob felt that in light of the house he had to be lavish.

Honest John's face turned the color of his gladiola and his mouth puckered up into his nose, "What, are you kidding me...3,000? I got new for you. As a accredited real estate man I get ten percent of the contract...and you signed a three year lease for 7,555 drax a month...here, I got it all wrote down." He shoved a slip of paper into bob's hand. "It all comes to...hmm...we'll eliminate the cabs I paid for and telephone calls...it all comes to 38,000 drachmas or if you want to pay in dollars...1,260. I mean you're not talking to any tin-horn...I been in the States."

"Honest John," Bob said menacingly, getting up from his chaise lounge, "you are not an honest mon." Then he threw him off the terrace.

Chapter Eleven

Over the violent objections of the Grapus brothers, who predicted disaster, and Haralumbus, who condescended to join them in courts, they chose Tikidoras and his fingernail to represent them when the case of Honest John the real estate mon vs. Robert Newman was calendared.

Tikidoras got them to the Athens municipal building on time, paused with them in the hallway outside the courtroom to read a list of the days' cases, ascertained their number - 12 which he considered lucky, and confidently guided them inside.

The courtroom was small, crowded and a dingy, dirty cream color. It smelled like a high school gym after a triple header basketball tournament and victory dance. Two naked 60 watt bulbs hung from a high, ornately plastered ceiling on two black rubber chords and looked like purged phalli. There were no windows in the room and in the resultant dimness, witnesses had difficulty reading the pledge to truth in front of the bench. They squinted, halted and stuttered, trying to make out the unfamiliar words on the dirty finger-stained card which was placed in their hands. Nevertheless, with the proddings of the three judges sitting above the court at a large dark wood bench, the pledge to truth was reluctantly extracted from everyone involved in the cases.

The three judges were sour, drab-looking men, belligerently critical of lawyers. The one centrally seated—the proderos or president—looked like a garbage cleaner after a busy day. In front of him were a pile of papers and a cowbell, rung to call the court to order.

Plaintiffs, defendants, witnesses and lawyers, sat on hard, backless benches lined in four rows facing the judges. Since it was a civil court, only one policeman was in attendance. He was a heavy, mustachioed man with an air of sloppy boredom on his face. His duties consisted of guarding the judges from the assault and battery of losers and protecting the winners and their lawyers from vendetta within the confines of the room.

Bill, Bob and Kay were fairly certain they would be freed of the charges of embezzlement and assault with intent to maim that Honest John had preferred against them.

After all, they argued, Greece was the country which had originally given justice to the world and therefore the tradition must be most strong there. Tikidoras, who had not argued a case for six years—and then only losing ones—was absolutely sure of victory. Haralumbus quietly said they would lose and lose bad. As they took their seats, wedging themselves onto one of the benches, he tried to get Tikidoras to agree to a settlement out of court and said he would act as go between if Tikidoras thought it beneath his dignity. "We should pay that animal," Tikidoras shouted, loudly so that Honest John who was sitting in the next row, could hear, "never...we have an open and shut case. Let me show you." He showed Haralumbus his brief - all the key words, precedents and pertinent lay book quotes were underlined with dents and scratches from his long fingernail.

As they entered, case number eight was just being adjudged. During case number nine, the President was attacked by a disgruntled defendant who forcibly disagreed with the court's decision. The President received a cut nose when the irate loser clanged him with the cow bell. The next case involved a laborer who claimed his employer owed him two days pay (140 drachmas) and was settled out-of-court and in the hall, when the expected fight broke out and the laborer, using a neat half-nelson, dragged his ex-boss out of the jurisdiction of the municipality.

The policeman, for his lack of wits and agility in the performance of his duties was summoned to the bench and slapped three times by the President.

Case number eleven was extremely touching.

The plaintiff, a wholesome girl of seventeen, accused the defendant, a skinny eighteen-year old with thick, olive-oily hair, of destroying her virginity. The girl's outraged mother, a fat, aggressive, bitter widow, had hired a lawyer but insisted on trying most of the case herself. She kept getting up from her seat and punching the principals and lawyers around every time she wanted to make a point or when she thought the case was not being tried right. The President, intimidated somewhat by her righteous indignation, kindly and quietly rang this bell for order when she broke up the proceedings. The mother screamed, cursed, wept softly, pounded her large chest in despair, and with watery eyes pleaded with the judges. She was intent on getting the boy; she wanted to beat him and nothing less would be satisfying. The boy, who was obviously embarrassed by the whole sordid mess, attempted to hide behind his dour, stern-faced mother—also a widow—who was convinced of his innocence. The opposing lawyers played a secondary role.

It was apparent that the sympathies of the court and the spectators were with the girl. It was generally assumed that the boy had done it to her—she was very sexy in a village sort of way.

It was brought out that the boy and the girl had been clandestinely seeing one another for over a year. Both families knew each other for years and were opposed to the union primarily because the girl had no pricka or dowry. The girl would never have dragged her own lover to court had it not been for her mother's discovery that something was amiss. Every month, since her puberty, the mother had analyzed the various evidences to make sure her bodily functions were in keeping with maidenhood. When, suddenly, the mother found they were not, she tortured the girl into admitting that it was the defendant.

The boy was not asked to testify on his own behalf—it would only waste time, the President said—the boy would naturally lie. But the girl was requested kindly to step forward. Her mother and lawyer joined her facing the bench. In a half whisper she read the pledge to the truth. To give her some courage, her mother punched her lightly but firmly in the kidneys every time she faltered.

The President looked her up and down appraisingly and asked in a loud voice if she had, in fact, been violated. Bob, Bill and Kay with their eyes on the girl and their ears cocked towards Haralumbus, followed the case with avid interest.

"You have been seeing this man for one year?" the President asked.

"Yes," came the soft reply.

"Against your mother's wishes," he admonished, wagging his finger. The President was a father himself. "You slept together?"

Softer still, "Yes."

"For how long?"

"Six months." The reply was barely audible. The spectators leaned forward in the benches.

"Six month, six months," shrieked the mother. She lunged at the girl, then, held from striking her by the lawyer she ran to the defendant and hit him in the face.

'The President rang his bell frantically and the policeman slowly separated the mother from the cringing boy.

When order was restored, the President, fingering the papers in front of him, a perplexed look on his face, said, "But the complaint says you lost your maidenhood only one month ago...exactly five weeks. How can this be?" He motioned the two other judges to lean toward him and they held a muted conference. He resumed questioning. "You slept with him for six months?"

Timidly, looking sorrowfully at the mother the girl replied, "Malesta."

"Hmmmm..." said the president, turning to the mother. "You have gravely miscalculated. When was the first secession of blood? She does not look six months with child."

The mother, for the first time, lost her aplomb. She was confused. She knew her daughter could not be six months pregnant, there was proof. Could it be, science had erred?

The President again huddled with the other judges, then he said, "There is only one other explanation. We will need an examination to see if it was bros or piso."

"Front or back," Haralumbus replied. "you know...the Greek way."

The President called the policeman forward and ordered him to accompany the mother and the girl out of the court room, to another part of the building where physical examinations were performed. After a short recess they returned with a doctor. He was sworn in and the judge asked, "You have examined the girl?"

"Malesta."

What do you find? Bros or piso?"

"Both, Kirio proderos."

"Both. Both bros and piso. Back for five months, front for a little over one month."

"Absolutely, you may ask her. They did it piso while they slept together, but one time he slipped. She is pregnant."

With a ring of his bell, the president dismissed the doctor and the opposing lawyers. He called the two mothers to confer with him.

"What are they doing now?" Kay asked.

"They are arranging the pricka, the dowry," Haralumbus said. "Even though she is pregnant, there must be a dowry. The case was open and shut, she's no longer a virgin...they'll be married before the week is over.

He looked philosophical, "The boy tried, he really tried to keep her whole, but you know how those things are. So now he must marry the girl. I think the boy's mother wants a bigger pricka—after all he is marrying a girl without a membrane."

They looked over to the two young lovers, holding hands and cooing on one of the benches as their mothers completed the contract for the pricka.

When it became their turn, Tikidoras, still thinking of the sodomy of the boy and girl, bungled his presentation, was easily euchred into one untenable position after another and they were charged not only the 1,230 dollars Honest John demanded, but all lawyers fees and court costs as well. At the outset Tikidoras alienated the court while delivering his opening address by absent mindedly carving his initials on the judge's bench with his fingernail.

When they told Theo, his cherub face took on a I told you so look and he said, "You don't believe me when I told you—you will be stolen. Now you have painfully learned that this is Greece...you must be careful...or you will be stolen.

Chapter Twelve

From the terrace, Bill observed the children at play below him in the backyard. The five-year old Billy seemed genuinely intent on destroying the cucumbers in their patch near the back fence. With a toy shovel, he was busily severing the low crawling vines, separating the fruit from their placentas and mother earth. Actually, thought Bill, it was time for harvest anyway, the gardener had missed up—the cucumbers were all outsize and blown up with air...perhaps that was why the salads were a trifle bitter lately. He remembered reading somewhere, sometime, that when cucumbers or radishes are left in the ground too long they get bitter and hot. Other than bringing in the crop a little late, Bill had no complain with the gardener. He kept the place looking neat and trim—no mean task with so many children to undo his labors.

Bill sighed contentedly and thought of the small patch of weeds and crabgrass and seedy, rusty evergreens that surrounded the old house on Pine Oak Lane. It was pleasing now to see borders trimmed squarely, trees pruned correctly and various flowers and bushes bloom as God had intended.

He watched his oldest son release the last of the cucumbers and then turned his attention to the other children. Nicholas, four years old, was, as usual, tormenting his younger twin brothers. He gave a shot here, a poke there, probing for weak spots. He was just too fast for the babies...babies...almost three. Bill mused, and we still call them babies. Nick was too quick for them to strike back and get even. He was too agile for the older one too, but had recently been floored by a big roundhouse-right so he left that one alone. He was no fool, not smart, but no fool. The sing of the punch from the older, more lethargic boy was too fresh in his memory for him to want to tease for awhile.

Bill did not like to see the children fight, but he saw no way he could prevent it. And he was secretly pleased that Nicholas, the prettiest and most athletic of the family, got his just lumps. Surprisingly, for four boys, the children didn't fight that much, they usually had too much to do. They were rarely confined inside or in a small area where friction could result. And Bill and Kay had so much more time with them now, the store ran itself well enough not to require a constant presence. Fighting was not the problem as Bill saw it. Bad language was. Cursing! Bill discovered that the children were foul-mouthed and diabolically clever. They knew all the bad words existent in modern Greek and, he would never find out how, they had learned a considerable amount of the more colorful ancient Greek words. They cursed in Homer. A rare thing in ones so young, Bill thought proudly, but nevertheless, not nice.

But they were diabolically clever in the use of forbidden vocabulary; they never let on they were cursing at their father. This was the frustrating part of it. Their fulminations were delivered in soft voices, with sweet smiles, and amiable head tiltings. Their Delphic delivery confused Bill since he didn't understand the language as they did, and hence had nothing to go on.

Since he couldn't pin them down, it was difficult to hit them when they called him shithead in Greek. Innately they seemed to sense which words he knew, or could figure out, and stayed clear of those. Vlakas was one such—Bill found out that it meant stupid and they hadn't been calling him it for awhile. They used it more no Bob now. Zorn, animal, was another. They had stopped describing him as a zorn when they overheard him using it in reference to Alike. It was good to be close to one's children. Bill wanted it and encouraged closeness, but it became sticky when they knew the language better than the father.

It was all the fault of the maids and governesses, pure and simple. There was no doubt of that. Bill sighed again. The kids were good at heart, bastards like all kids, but good basically. It was the damn maids. In the States they would only be influenced by TV, but here it was the maids.

He glanced down to where this week's governess, acnied, homely girl of thirty, who wore blue jeans under a billowy peasant skirt, was sitting in the warm afternoon sun, squeezing blackheads onto a mirror she held in her lap. It was in the cards that she would go...like all the rest. She wasn't even watching the twins, he noticed, as the two little boys started to dismantle a prize rosebush the gardener had borrowed from one of his rich clients. "Crap," Bill said aloud, that rosebush belonged to one of the richest ship owners in Greece. Don't we have any respect. "Renna," he shouted down to the governess, who had just gotten a juice one off her chin, "sas, para kalo, ta laludia...ta pedia." If it pleasest thou, the flowers, the children.

Renna, annoyed at being disturbed during her home facial, looked up at him sourly, her pimples flashing and blinking in the sun, "Malesta Kirio." Then slowly she gathered the children together in a tight little circle to tell them a story. Undoubtedly, thought Bill, a dirty story about rat fink fathers.

Kay joined him on the terrace, looking like fresh peaches and yogurt. "Hi," she said, pecking at his cheek before she sat down.

"Hi babe. You sleep?"

"Just got up now. You ought to nap too."

"I get a headache."

"You sound like Bob. If you try it, You'll get used to it and won't get headaches." Kay took a small bell from a table near her chair and ran for the maid. "You want some coffee?"

"Yeah, but tell her not too sweet. If you don't tell her she really lays on the sugar."

"Dio cafedes, Maria," Kay said to the maid when popped her head out on the terrace. "Chi glico, parakalo."

The maid, a small rat faced, timid girl, nodded and left. She was a left-over from the domestics Honest John had hired, which had included a butler and cook. The butler, with his tux and diffidence made Bob and Bill uncomfortable. Everybody was happy when Bob caught him with the cook on the living room couch without his tux on and fired them both. We don't really need a butler or a cook, "Bob had said to Kay, "we eat out every night...besides they were killing the springs on the couch, I just sat down and one sprung through and ripped my pants."

The left-over maid, for some reason, was terrified of Honest John and even the mention of his name would bring on hysterics.

"Not sweet, remember," Bill shouted after her," or I'll call Honest John."

"You're cruel," Kay said.

"Hon," Bill said seriously, "we've got to get better help." He nodded to the circle in the yard, "All that one down there does is pick her face all day...I don't know...I feel, maybe we're not doing well by the kids. Maybe they're turning out bad."

"They were worse in the States. You don't remember, you were never home during the day. They're fine, don't worry." Kay knew, despite her husband's fears that the children were actually developing more fully in Greece in every way. They ate only fresh vegetables now, as contrasted with frozen and canned in America. When did she ever have time in America to clean fresh spinach or cook vegetables out of their plastic bags? That was the key, she knew - time. Here she had more time to spend with them...and just as important...energy. She wasn't tired all the time, she was more relaxed with them. They had ceased to become a chore, an assembly line to run through quick-cooked TV dinners, television chairs and hasty prayers at bed time.

For the first time in her life, she could honestly say that she enjoyed her children.

Looking beyond her own pleasure in living in Greece, she saw the benefit to the children. They were in a position now to get the language tutors for French and German—-Greek was taking care of itself—that no one in their income bracket in America could afford. And they were taking full advantage of one hundred percent of the culture available in Athens. True, Athens was no New York, but what Athens had to offer culturally was eminently available to them. The distance, in time and money and baby sitters and commutation fares that Kay and Bill were from cultural New York when they lived only thirty-three miles away, was as great as the distance across the sea. The children might call the Parthenon a pile of rocks—-but that would change, and they were aware of its existence—they felt it, hit it, bit it, it was five minutes away by cab or one flight up to the roof by sight. For all their proximity to New York, Kay had never taken the children to a museum—the thought of the crush of people, the disorderly automat lunch and the cost of the baby sitter for the younger children had always deterred her.

When her husband now talked of the children not turning out right, she knew it was his devious way of soliciting a compliment from her...a reaction. He wanted her to articulate what he really felt, that culturally the children were much better off in Greece. The children's formal education in the low-slung modern suburban school back home was now replaced by tutors in French and German plus classes in a rickety Greek school, where the light was poor but the Homer good.

Not to count the intangible benefits accrued from associating with people with different customs, religion and manners...even the maids, in that sense were of value.

"I don't say they're worse than in the States," Bill went on, "or that they're rotten through and through. It's mostly the language they use. I never know whether they're cursing or not."

"Nancy never curses," Kay said.

"Nicholas is the guy...he keeps calling me a pukka... I mean the kid is really some kind of nut. The other day he looks at me so beautiful and innocent...all scrubbed and clean and tells me...Papa isse pukka."

"He calls everybody pukka," Kay said.

"I know...but what is a pukka?" At that moment, Maria the maid came back with the two Turkish coffees. At the work pukka, her rat-face filled with fear. She recoiled, dropped the tray and tore off the terrace, down the stairs and out the front door. They never saw her again.

"We need new maids," Bill repeated, kicking the broken coffee cups aside. "If we could only get something like Voula," he said, wishing on the first star he saw that night. Ah Voula...a goddess among maids, epitomizing the best Greece had to offer. Quiet, never sick, obedient—-he longed for Voula. The expressionless face and the long arms were aesthetic blots that could have been ignored after a while.

Chapter Thirteen

In Hollywood, when the screen heroine has a precious announcement to make to her husband, the whole affair is handled with such realism and taste that it is a wonder pictures are losing money.

Doris Day sits delicately on a floral printed couch wearing a peignoir which blends perfectly into the slip covers. Her legs are gently tucked under her and she expertly holds a pair of knitting needles in her hands. She is working on little things.

Rock Hudson masculinely lies sprawled on his favorite chair, one leg thrown over the arm. He reads the evening paper—sports section. There is soft cradle music on the sound tract

"I saw the doctor today, darling."

"Oh...how is Doc. Morrison?"

"Wonderful," she says and smiles knowingly.

"That reminds me, we've got a bridge date with the Morrisons this week." He ruffles the paper and turns to the funnies.

"Yes, I know. But he told me I should get to bed early from now on and not have too many guests."

"Why?"

"Darling..."

"Darling," he said, glancing at the knitting, then back to the paper, then stupidly to the knitting again.

"Darling, is it true?"

"Darling, is it true."

"Oh, darling." He gets up and softly bends to kiss her, accidentally digging his elbow into her belly. "Oh, darling, I'm sorry...we must be careful now, for him."

"Oh, darling."

Gentle, brotherly kiss, music louder and all sing rock-a-bye-baby.

With Kay and Bill it was never thus.

The two men were enjoying their early morning coffee on the terrace when Kay joined them. She looked like a college sophomore in riding breeches and a pretty green turtle neck sweater. That morning she was scheduled to take the three older children to their riding lesson.

"Guess what?" she said, taking Bill's coffee.

"What?"

"I missed."

"You missed what?"

"Guess what." Bill detected a little bitterness in her voice.

He thought and said, "Can't guess. What did you miss? The maid's been stealing again?"

"We're going to have to get a new passport, stupid."

"You lose yours?"

"Idiot," she said and stormed off. Bob, unaware of marital bliss, looked up through half-closed, sleepy eyes.

185

Later that day she told him, "I was just talking to the attaché's wife and she told me that all the Americans go to the Air Base in Lebanon or Germany to have their babies."

"Yeah, but they're with the government, they can do that. What do you want to go to Lebanon for, you don't know anyone in Lebanon."

"They don't trust the Greek doctors."

"Why?"

"She said they're not too sure about their methods."

"How can there be such a difference in methods. I mean...there aren't too many ways to have a baby."

"I don't know...The Americans here are afraid."

"They're always afraid. Unless they can have their PX and American doctors, they collapse...crap. We've been living off the Greek market for months. I don't see the kids with TB or anything. They're been having babies here a damn sight longer than in the States. Anyway, didn't Theo say he was one of the best doctors you can find?"

"For me it's fine. I just was telling you what the American community here thinks," Kay said.

"So who cares what they think? We'll go to Theo...you'll get the best of care."

Theo was rich. By Greek standards—or any others—he was completely, economically sound. He owned his swank apartment, a car, sent his son to the finest private school in Athens, indulged his wife on clothes and cards and had real gold, in the form of English sovereigns, salted safely away in various safe deposit boxes in Athenian banks. He owned property which was constantly appreciating in value and had a fair interest in a small but busy hotel on the island of Spores. He ate well and plentifully and could easily afford allowing Maro to lose four or five thousand drachmas in one of the all night poker games she was addicted to. His suits, rumpled, unpressed, were nevertheless of the finest English wool fabric and fitted to his large frame by one of Athens most expensive tailors.

IN addition, Theo was by heritage of the elite...the plutocracy in Greece. On both sides. Yaya's forebears in Constantinople had for centuries made money and political deals and wheels working on and between the various Ottoman Sultans and the sharper Athenian merchants. Theo's father had come from an even more impressive and respected line. True Athenians, they were Brahmins for thousand of years. Theo's father claimed descent from Timeon of Athens. Dead for ten years, he had been, in life, a quiet, austere, conservative old gentleman, the type found in any better men's club in a large leather chair, reading the London Times or Wall Street Journal, sipping a brandy and soda. He had never worked a day in his life but had managed, by adroitly buying and selling rich olive groves and grape vines at times when world market conditions were most ripe, to quadruple his considerable inheritance. His greatest stroke, and one he loved to recall, was when he supplied the Government of France with 60,000 barrels of grape mash one year when the crop failed in Burgundy. He had carefully saved clippings from English and

American gourmet journals which raved about the quality and bouquet of the wine—-the best in a decade from France. As a good father he showered education and tutors and trips abroad on Theo and his other son—the ne'er do well who ran away to America.

Theo, in short, had the blood, cultural heritage, inclinations, disposition, aplomb, distinction of any New England Peabody, Lodge or Cabot. Of course, he acted differently—customs differ—but it could be just as well said: Athens, land of the olive and grape juice/Where the Nomarchs speak only to the Theos and the Theos only to Zeus.

Knowing all this of Theo, Kay and Bill were shocked and horrified when they first saw his clinic and found it almost impossible to reconcile it with him.

The clinic was located in a once fashionable but now run down section of Athens. It occupied the upper floor of an old five story apartment house to which the years had been most unkind. The building was too old to have elevators and the only way up or down was a steep, worn, marble staircase. A squeaky wooden banister along the stairs was a distinct help in negotiating the climb unless the clumber bore down with too much weight in which case it would fold back and snap him into space. Bill could not believe that the 80-year old Yaya made the climb a number of times each of her busy days.

The hall and stairs were actually a delight when they compared them with what waited above.

All the rooms of the flat led off a large, high ceilinged, octagonal shaped entrance hall. The hall served as the doctor's waiting and reception room. It was furnished depressingly with two long, black mahogany benches with corkscrew legs and two matching side tables which held two ugly pewter vases containing dusty, fake plastic flowers. The benches looked like pews in a poor Mott Street parish church. And like pews they were exceedingly uncomfortable, the waiting patients sat stiffly upon them like West Point plebes at dinner.

In the direct center of the hall stood a rusted kerosene furnace, for heat in the winter. Its corrugated chimney tube extended straight up about seven feet and then ran horizontally across the room to disappear into a cracked and crooked wall. Wrapped around the chimney was an electrical chord which ended in a naked light bulb.

Theo's office was the first room on the left. It was large, almost as large as the hall. The floor was carpeted in worn brown linoleum which had taken the pattern of the wood parquet floor underneath. Facing the door was Theo's desk, a blond, thick-grained chunk of wood encumbered with telephone, telephone pad, telephone directory, a device which enabled use of the telephone without the handling of the receiver, a checkered cigarette box containing Pez candy, a Bunsen burner, a chromium vaginal dilator and a large set of ivory worry beads.

One wall of the office was lined with tall, glass-doored bookshelves, holding yellowed collector's copies of National Geographic magazine, old editions of Life, a number of finger paintings by his son Antony, strips of canvas which Bill recognized as Antony's de-painting and hundreds of toy soldiers. Hooked on to a knob of one of the glass doors was an oil portrait of a famous Greek-American gynecologist under whom Theo had studied in Italy

Ringing the desk were a few canvas beach chairs, worn and torn and pockmarked with cigarette burns—showing the stress and torque of squirming expectant fathers. The office, like the hall, had not been painted for many years and had turned from cream to beige, then tan and finally brown.

The door furthest down the entrance hall-waiting and receiving room opened to the operating room. It functioned also as labor room and examining room.

The examining - delivery - operating table—ugly and foreboding- was cemented to the floor in the center of the room. Pitted metal stirrups hung from the feet end, dangling on worn leather straps. The table was antiseptically covered with wax paper. There was a small washbasin for scrubbing down, in one corner.

Its dripping cold water tap stuck out of the wall and looked like a hooked nose with a cold.

Theo had made an attempt, years, back, to modernize the delivery room, but the project was given up for one reason or another after only three walls were lined with shiny green formica. The fourth wall was plastered with a dull blue oil cloth. Against this wall sagged a cot with a thin, lumpy mattress. Opposite, leaning forward precariously was a chipped bakelite instrument case with cracked windows held from shattering to the floor by a patchwork of adhesive tape. Inside were three boxes of cotton, an open box of Kotex, another vaginal dilator and a pair of scissors and a large box of cheap, unreliable, Greek prophylactics.

Next to the operating room was the kitchen with a small, old fashioned gas type refrigerator and a two-burner stove for boiling instruments and cooking food for the patients. Yaya, in her position as dietician, supervised the preparation of all the food reluctantly doled out to the patients. She had a staff of one maid and a registered nurse under her.

Around the octagon, to the right of the kitchen, was a dirty bathroom with a continual flush toilet. The overhead water box leaked and the pull-rope dangled down to tickle the back of anyone seated on the bowl.

The remaining rooms were taken up with wards and semi-privates. The wards held five beds each and the semi-privates—much more expensive—three. They were painted a cheerless, dirty, gunmetal grey.

After their first visit and Theo's examination of Kay, Bill cried, "Kay...honey...I can't let you give birth there. I mean let's not be ridiculous. He may be a nice guy...and I love him dearly, but did you ever see a hospital like that? I think maybe the Americans are right...we got to take you somewhere else."

"It is kind of horrible. But he is good...I know that. I've had enough experience with doctors to know. He's gentle. Besides, Yaya's there to take care of me. I'll get better treatment at the clinic than at Flower Fifth."

"Yaya, " Bill shouted, "Yaya...what re you telling me...Yaya. She's 80 years old...she needs a nurse herself."

"She's an excellent midwife. Do you know how many children she's delivered? She told me thousands."

He slapped his head in despair, "Midwife...hon...this is the twentieth century. What do we want with midwives. No, I mean it...I can't allow it. Did you see the bedrooms...and the kitchen? The joint just isn't hygienic."

"Oh, stop being an old worry wart, everything will be fine. Theo's a good doctor. I'm not going to stay there a month you know...it's only for a few days."

In their visits to the clinic, Kay and Bill became aware that it was not wholly used for the delivering of babies—-it functioned also as a safeguard against the population explosion. It seemed odd to them that so many of Theo's patients had miscarriages—he himself volunteered the statistic that fifty percent of them lost their babies. But he guaranteed the nervous Bill, that they had nothing to worry about.

They first became suspicious, when during one of their visits, they noticed a healthy-looking, buxom young woman fidgeting on one of the pews. She went in to be examined and after a few minutes reappeared being dragged by Yaya and the staff nurse Dina to one of the bedrooms. Later, after Kay had been checked by Theo, while chatting with him in his office, they saw the young lady shakily leave.

The anxious look she wore on her face when they first saw her was gone. She had not, obviously, only been examined.

Further evidence consisted of the fact that many of the patients were not married. Theo's clientele included a famous movie star, whom they recognized immediately and any number of young beautiful, chic young girls in their early twenties or late teens. They'd sit patiently on the pews, wait their turns, go in to be examined and were carried out by Yaya and Dina. They never returned for further check-ups or to give birth.

The final proof that Theo was performing more than simple vaginal examinations occurred when he proudly invited them in to witness a gynecological scraping. "You will see a true master's touch," he said, forcing Bill into the room.

On one occasion, Theo seriously told them, "I have many, many patients who wish to become maidens once again. They only go to the best doctors." He showed them with detailed drawings how it was possible to surgically restore a hymen which a bride could palm off as virginity. "You see, with us virginity is very important. Even when an engaged couple sleeps together they guard the lady's innocence." Bill thought of the girl in court. "But sometimes," Theo said, shaking his head, "they slip and fall into error. Then they come to me."

Bill said, "It seems kind of silly, Theo, I mean if they've been so close... and they're getting married anyway...

"Oh, no..." Theo said, rolling his eyes, "not silly...oh, no. We are not like the northern peoples, here the man will not marry if the girl is not a virgin. It is terrible...and a disgrace. I do the operation perfectly. The next time I will let you see."

Theo's frankness with his patients, his jovial spirit and his matter-of-factness, combined to create a remarkable relationship and rapport that Kay said could never be captured in the States. His very appearance in either his white hospital gown or, more often than not, his T-shirt, lent an atmosphere of easiness and informality. He joked with the patients, warned them they were too fat, patted their bellies, got them to laugh and giggle, and somehow convinced the unmarried girls that what had happened was after all part of the game when the blood was Greek and hot.

He was a plump, happy, parish priest to his patients—they worshiped him.

For the first-time mothers, he used a simple, natural bedside manner and put them entirely at rest. There was no white tile and gleaming chrome in the delivery room to panic a woman and with Yaya chatting amiably at the head of the table while he worked efficiently at the bottom, births were effected with the naturalness that was intended.

He explained to Kay what would happen when her time came, "Here, my dear, we do things much more modern than in America," he said pompously. "You will receive no drugs, I do not allow it...it is not good for the child."

Kay paled. "No block?" she squeaked.

The click of the tongue and rolled back eyes, "Ohi."

"No gas?" she tried.

Again the click, "You will not need pain killers, I use a new method. You have nothing to worry for...you are in Theo's hands."

Chapter Fourteen

Due to Kay's condition, Theo felt she should take a vacation. "You must take care of yourself," he prescribed. "And I have a megalio idea. You will join us at our summer house for the next two weeks. Everyone will be there. It is always so beautiful in Mati the first days of October. It is there where you can eat and rest well."

Bill thought of the maids…home whiling the days away washing, ironing, cooking and Kay supervising. Yes, she needed a vacation.

"Of course, you and Bob will come too. It is forbidden that you stay away," Theo said to Bill.

Bill thought of Bob and himself, lounging on the terrace drinking Turkish coffee and orange juice everyday till noon and with the store running itself nicely, smoothly, only visiting once a day to pick up the cash.

"At Mati it is magnificent in the late summer. We wanted you to visit us before but you have been so busy with the store. Now I, as your doctor, order it. We will have a wonderful time. The water is till warm for baths."

"Can I go swimming?" Kay asked. "In America they won't let you go swimming pregnant."

"At Mati you may go swimming," Theo said. "The water there is pure." He beamed with pleasure. He wanted the Americans to enjoy themselves with him.

On their way out to the summer house, Theo explained that the stretch of seacoast on which Mati lay was considered by many to be the finest in the world. The small lazy village itself was a picture postcard, he said. It was just beyond Marathon and as they drove along the highway, he described with vigor and pride, the wonderful run Phidepedes made to inform Athens it was saved from the Persians. The highway took them through gentle rolling country, where grape and olive were the only vegetation. The gnarled and twisted olive trees with their small shiny, silver-green leaves, Theo claimed, were hundreds of years old. They dotted the countryside—living monuments to the tenacity of the Attican farmer who for time immemorial urged and dragged a precarious living out of the dusty, rocky soil.

As they approached the sea, the olive trees gave way to graceful cypress and pine and grass became visible. They left the highway for a short stretch of dirt road, bounced along for a few minutes and stopped in front of a sumptuous concrete and brick mansion.

"Get out, get out...exo," Theo boomed happily. He was as bright as the morning, sunny and clear. It delighted him to play host—to give some part of his ebullient spirit to his guest.

The house was two stores high—Bill estimated quickly fifteen rooms. Completely encircling the upper story was a modern, dark wood terrace. Patches of sun hit the shiny wood through the pines, creating a sparkling, dappled effect.

This, thought Bill, more than made up for the schlock of the clinic. It was more in keeping with aristocracy in Greece. The house was worthy of an Onasis. He was deeply impressed. Bob, who thought their own Villa, the last word in luxury, saw they had still some to go.

"Oh, Theo...this is beautiful," Kay exclaimed, starting up a pebbled walk to the house.

On the left of the mansion stood the servant's quarters—an old, thick, rough cement building of about six rooms. It had small, slits for windows. The red tiles of the roof were cracked and loosened from their cement beds.

The two buildings rested between the dirt road and the sea in a thick grove of pines which shielded the ground from the hot sun.

Theo, grunting, took a suckling pig and a small mild fed lamb out of the trunk of the car while Bill and Bob followed Kay up the path. Aspasia, their new governess, tumbled behind with the children who, upon their release from the car, shot back and forth excitedly. The vacation was timed perfectly with the opening of Greek schools and Kay and Bill felt good about the children stocking up some sun and salt water before they settled down to school.

A little boy, neatly dressed, with a Prince Charles haircut, stood at the front of the house and Nancy and Bill ran for him.

"Stop," Theo's voice boomed. An English-accented voice echoed, "Stop."

"Stop," the English voice shouted again. "Herbert, come inside immediately."

Beel, Katina...ohi...ohi aki," Theo said, joggling up the walk. The still bleeding lamb and pig cradled in his arms were giving him a difficult time. "This is not the house...our's is dipla."

"Herbert, get in here, now!" the English voice continued. It contained a noticeable tremble. "Kirio Klones, I've told you many times, this is private property. Please now." The owner of the voice, a thin long-headed English woman, looked down from the terrace at Theo.

"Amesos, Kiria...it was only a slight mistake," he said apologetically, looking up at her. The blood dripping down from the animals in his arms splattered on his pants and shoes. "These are my nieces from America...they are American."

"I do not care what they are. Now please Kirio or I must call the police again. And will you please move your car."

Theo led them quickly out the walk and to the left, past a ten foot high barbed wire fence which was camouflaged by the pines. They made for the servants quarters. Bill glanced back and saw a uniformed man foundling a truncheon, take up a position at the gate of the mansion. Obviously, he thought, they don't like trespassers.

"I always make the mistake of parking in front of her house," Theo said gravely, shaking his head in lack of understanding of his own actions. "Then birazi...those people are peasants, they don't have any fun."

He walked quickly, rocking back and forth like a pear-shaped pendulum, to the front of the concrete shack where Voula waited with outstretched arms for the pig and the lamb.

Bill looked around and wondered. The house was not really like a house at all. It had no doors between any of the rooms. The bathroom was the only place that offered any privacy—a thick curtain nailed to the door jamb divided it from the rest of the house. The floor was cement, cracked and split and chipped. Toward the left of the entrance way was a combination kitchen and maid's quarters. Cots for the maids were stacked next to one another, facing a concrete sink and a row of three wooden iceboxes. Bill was amused but not surprised with Theo told them that the house had been a German Pillbox and observation post during the war. It was built along with a whole string of concrete bunkers when the Nazis thought the invasion of Europe might hit the soft underbelly rather than Normandy. There was a commanding view, from the rear slits Theo called windows, of the jagged coastline, the sea and the island of Euboea.

The property was Yaya's, and had been the plot next, willed to her by her father. By promising the English Embassy, which wanted a summer spot by the sea for ambassadors and VIPs, that she would tear down the pillbox, build a new summer villa in its place and rent it only to other foreign embassies, she upped the value of the land considerably. After the English had built their mansion, she, of course, reneged on her promise, over their protests, and challenged them to take her to court. She had wisely not signed anything. The embassy, knowing that she would bribe the judges, win the case and issue a statement to a hostile press that the rich English were exploiting the poor Greeks, philosophically noted that it had been jobbed by a Byzantine mentality more astute than anything it could muster and took some satisfaction in the barbed wire fence and a body guard, letting the mansion be used only by minor clerks and attaches.

Under the house, a remnant of its pillbox days, was a deep tunnel. Theo used it now to store a tempting, locally-made retsina and for the curing of meat and figs.

The condition of the pillbox-house was of no importance to any of the vacationing family since all meals were taken outside under the pines near the water and no real Greek, Theo told them, would think of sleeping inside any house during the long summer. "In this we are no different than Onasis when he lives at Glyfada. He too sleeps out in the clean air—and he has a big villa."

They walked through the pillbox to the rear of the property and the beach. The family was gathered there. They were dressed informally, properly for the lazy vacation they enjoyed. Chins and Vinegar-face were sitting on their cots, still in pajamas, Mora, in her specially constructed, oblique, three-piece bathing suit and Nota, in a daring St. Tropez bikini, were ready for an early morning swim. The day was already hot. Yaya, Theo apologized, was taking care of the clinic and hence not free to holiday with them.

An undercurrent of gaiety emanating from the ground, the sea, the people was evident to the three Americans. They couldn't define it but felt the brightness all about them. As they approached, everyone gathered around them and made them feel welcome.

Voula came out of the house with two cotton mattresses which Theo took and threw under a tilting pine tree. "Beel, you and Bob will sleep here. You will have protection from the sun for your nap." He put Kay up in a cot near him and ordered Aspasia to arrange for the children in a walled-off area near the house.

Aspasia was given a cot in the kitchen alongside Vinegar-face's sullen domestic. The maids were allowed each night to drag their cots outside to sleep, but so that the fine line between master and maid was never crossed, were not formally given permission to do so. It was as much of a vacation for the maids as anyone. There was no housecleaning to speak of and their duties consisted primarily of cleaning vegetables for meals and making cots. They swam in the water with everyone else— a boon granted mainly to keep them clean.

That evening everyone tried a hand at turning the pig and the lamb on their spits over a glowing charcoal fire. It was a hypnotizing setting, the flames jumped and hissed like strange orange cobras at the melting fat. Chins strummed at the strings of a bouzoukia—the tinny, eerie notes filled the air with a soft peace. Theo hummed along an old Greek melody with him. The moon was full and the stars were tree-top level. The smell of the cooking meat and the clear breeze coming in off the water combined with the day's swimming to give everyone a hearty appetite.

The maids scampered around setting a long wooden table. It began to groan under salads, cheeses, donut-shaped loaves of fresh, chewy village bread, olives, fried eggplant, garlic sauce, steaming rice and Theo's pill boxed-cooled wine.

Theo, sticking his thumb into the meat, announced it was ready. "Sit...sit...we must eat. Grigora, while it is burning." Chins quickly dropped the bouzoukia and slid onto one of the wooden benches straddling the table. His stomach was up and ready. Nota, sitting down next to him, had, in deference to the outdoors, replaced her powder puff with a swatch of pine needles. She thumped her breast excitedly as Chins tore off a piece of bread for her. Theo sat down and said something to Voula. She efficiently de-spit the meat and carried it to the table where she dropped it on a carving block. With deft hands and fingers, stringy with taut ligaments, she hacked and sawed and passed out big chunks of lambs and pork to the waiting dishes. Wine was poured, bread passed—dinner was served.

The people next door were having their dinner too. Bill saw between mouthfuls that they were sitting on the patio at the back of their house, being attended by a uniformed maid who was expertly serving food and wine. Only the lady who had thrown them off the property and her husband were seated. They had no guests, and he could see there was no conversation. Just a meal like any other, anyplace else. The night, the stars and the sea didn't seem to touch them. After a few minutes they finished and went inside. Bill felt sorry for them. He wondered if perhaps Theo should invite them over, after all if hospitality didn't exist in Greece—where then?

Theo, noticing that he was observing the neighbors, said, "They always go inside when we have a feast, they think we are disgusting." He scooped up some eggplant and loaded it onto his dish. "They are supposed to be ambassadors of good will, but I think they do not like Greeks...they do not wish to mingle with us. It is very strange to me why this is so...oh, not only in their country, but in many others as well. Only in Aust5ralia will they let Greeks migrate...and there merely because they need people. There was a great man in your country who did not see Mediterranean people as dirty...but he died."

He nodded at the mansion, "I am sorry for them, because they do not know what real lamb tastes like. They have no kefi."

Nick wiped his chins and said, "After, when we sing and dance they will call the police and accuse us of being drunk. It's all right for them to drink a bottle of gin at five o'clock and call it cocktails, but they call us drunk because we have wine with our meals."

"Then birazi... the police are our friend and they will join us," Theo said, clapping his hands for Voula to clear the table and bring the fruit.

Later, on a patch of hard-packed dirty near the fire which Voula now kept supplied with sweet-smelling pine logs, Bill and Bob were taught the various Greek dances. They drank and they danced—-sloppily at first, but under the guidance of Nota and Chins whose accompaniment on the bouzoukia was surprisingly competent, they ultimately were able to negotiate the intricate and wild steps of the Greek snake dance. It was like the Jewish Hora, Bob said, calling on his past in the Bronx.

Chins was proud of his accomplishment on the difficult bouzoukia and when they took a breather and Bill complimented him on his playing, said with a pleased look on his face, "You know, we Greeks may not have much to offer anymore...but the little we do possess, we keep a tight hold on. The bouzoukia is a good example...I don't know of many men who don't know how to play it, even a little. I know my son will learn."

Chins' words impressed Bill. He had only thought of him as simply a glutton. He was that, but he was more—he was Greek. He possessed a strong love of country and its traditions and a fierce pride in the gifts to the world that Greece had given. He liked to say, "We gave light to the world...and now...we're in darkness ourselves—but we did give light to the world."

When Bob first heard that he wryly commented, "Sure they're in darkness...they use the crummy bulbs Nick makes."

As the wine glasses were replenished, the party picked up steam. Vinegar-face, usually quiet, amazed everyone with a Kasapiko—the butcher's dance—-and actually smiled in recognition of the applause when he finished. It was a difficult and demanding dance and at the end everyone shout Zorba...Zorba.

Theo, not to be outdone by his father-in-law and later kidded about it, got up suddenly, grabbed the first one walking by, which happened to be Voula, who was bringing out some more wine, forced her to the dance floor and began to perform a wild Chifatelli—belly dance for two. The dance reeked with sex —modern Greece's legacy from the ancient Dionysian Bacchanalia. Theo's belly quivered, rocked and ground erotically as he threw it forward at the stunned Voula. Entranced, he clasped his hands tightly to his mate's, extended one thick leg slightly ahead of him and minced forward on his toes. Nick went berserk on the bouzoukia, hitting the six strings with a full fist. A circle formed around the dancers and everyone picked up the beat and clapped Theo on. Voula, confused and thrilled that she was selected as Theo's belly mate, shuffled back and forth as well as she could on her flat feet. Her arms, self-consciously never left her sides. When they were done, Theo, panting for breath, threw himself into a chair and waved the applause away. He wanted air to breath. Voula reveled in the glory of center stage. An expression, hardly distinguishable in the flickering fire light, came over her face. Her eyes, mirrored a strange glint like the hopping sparks of the fire. For the first time in her life she had kefi—that state in which the Greek soul oozes with love of life and uncontrollably seeks expression, that state which forced Vinegar-face to dance, and roly-poly Theo to exhaust himself. Kefi arrived in Voula like a typhoon, it made her eyes sparkle, her bone marrow expand—it revealed that perhaps there was after all something behind her Orphan Annie face.

Kefi found its way into Bob, Bill and Kay during every moment of their stay at Mati. Each day increased their love of live. Becoming one with the Greeks was a tonic of awareness.

Nothing of Bob's problem remained, he lost all of the inhibitions that plagued him in America. He could face any of the previous circle with a bland confidence not produced by the retsina. Greece had been a frontal lobotomy to him.

They laughed and san and swam. On the clean, pebbly beach they stared in utter disbelief when Voula first appeared in a bathing suit—a misfitting Maro cast-off, canted and ruffled. Her arms, they saw, seemed much longer than when she was dressed. They marveled at her skill in swimming, as with strong overhead strokes she made it to the raft anchored off shore and back more quickly than Bill who had been a star on his college team. Her flat feet, like the cardboard feet on a Mickey Mouse balloon, gave her an unfair advantage, Bill claimed, and "I could only make thins even if I had a good pair of flippers."

Bob and Bill took turns driving into Athens with Theo every other day. They checked on the store and Panyoti, while Theo spied on Yaya and what she was up to at the kliniki. He could never be sure, when he was away, that Yaya, using his facilities, would not go into business for herself. She had slowed down with age, he knew, but lingering in his memory was the incident a few years past, when, while he and Maro were vacationing on Rhodes, Yaya competitively cut his prices for scrapings and deliveries and had built up a tidy side-trade for herself out of Theo's clients.

Every evening after dinner the group gathered slowly around the fire to sing and dance and talk. Every night, Voula hovered at the fringe of the circle, apart from the attending maids, edging closer to the masters. She began to order Aspasia around and shunt her duties on Vinegar-face's maid. The first night's belly dance seemed to give her that right. Bill mentioned to Kay that he couldn't understand what was coming over Voula, he had seen her drinking the better part of a kilo of retsina in the kitchen. The perfect maid, he puritanically felt, should not juice it down on the job.

The last night of their stay, Theo presented Bob and Bill with colorful Evizone costumes, with long whit stockings and slippers and bright red pom-poms. They immediately put them on and led the last wild Snake dance—around and around the fire, through the trees, along the fence and finally into the water.

While they were drying out near the fire, Theo, offering Kay a big glass of wine to combat any chill she might catch, said, "You know, Beel, women when they are with child in Greece become almost sacred." He hugged Kay tightly. He had allowed her to join the dance only because she insisted and threatened that if he didn't she would lose all kefi. "A woman with child can be refused nothing. I know you are wonderful to Katina—you are a real Greek." He laughed. "Even the poorest of poor know this and they treat their wives like a princess during pregnancy. Of course, after they resume beating."

"I've noticed that down at the store," Bill said. "Many times a pregnant woman will stop because of the smell and their husband's always buy them a piece of chicken."

"Aha...veveos...of course. When the woman craves something it must be given. It is "...of course. When the woman craves something it must be given. It is "ya ta guri"...for the good. We must seem very old-fashioned to you. Americans are so young and modern...but it is important that we be thus...we want to be old-fashioned. Even if you see the young women of Athens in short dresses and Paris fashions...they are...inside old-fashioned."

Kay glanced at Nota and Maro. Just that morning she had gotten up enough courage to ask them why they didn't shave the hair under their arms. They were surprised at the question. Nota, who was wearing her bikini, lifted her arm and twirled the long hair underneath fondly. "My father would never allow it," she said, he would get very angry...it would not be natural. Anyway...it excites Nick."

"Some of your old-fashioned ideas are great, Theo," Bill said. "I wish we had the pricka in the Sates."

"The pricka is a very old tradition...and an important one. We don't make as much money as you do in America...there is not that much work. The man has need for his wife's family to contribute something. How could a man who makes 2,000 drachmas a month be able to feed and clothe his family and pay rent? Sixty-six dollars, even here is very little. That is why the pricka has now taken the form of a house or an apartment. At least the young know they will have shelter."

"What about Bob, Theo," Bill joked, "Can we fix him up with a girl with a big pricka?"

"Veveos...yati ohi? Yaya has made many arrangements, she would be happy to work for you."

"Thanks, Bill," Bob said, "But all the same I'll take care of myself. I'm here in Greece to get rid of problems. With all respect to you and Kay...I mean...like...I think marriage is a migraine."

"See what I mean, Theo," Bill said, "The guy won't do anything for business. Well, I still think the pricka's great."

Theo nodded toward Voula, who was listening intently, understanding nothing. "It is great...take Voula...when it becomes her time, I will give her the pricka. I made a promise to her father when he sent her from the village...we will find her a good man...give her some gold...a place to live. She will be happy. She deserves it, she has been good...as you say... the perfect maid."

Theo, so perceptive, so wise, was nevertheless human and fallible—he was incredibly mistaken. For, a year from Mati, he would learn that Voula was not happy, was not the perfect maid and would not accept his pricka. He would learn on his own festive nameday, when Voula was most needed in the hustle and bustle of preparing for fifty guests, that Maro would discover her not preparing the hors d'oeuvres, not cleaning the champagne glasses, not dusting bric-a-brac, not sweeping, not throwing out garbage, not working at all, but sitting on the living room couch with her legs chicly crossed, having her hair coiffured by Maro's own, expensive hair stylist. She would be wedged into a tight, sky blue rayon dress, the hem high above her knees and wearing her first pair of high heels—very high heels.

Maro would stare, shocked, her eyes pressing hard at her glasses, for a long time, not believing, while Voula would direct the hair dresser to place each bristly lock of hair precisely where she wanted it. When speech would finally come to her, Maro would rant and rave and scream for Voula to put on her old housedress, put on her sandals, forget her illusions and return promptly to the kitchen. She would be answered curtly with a cold stare, a smart slap in the face from the new Voula and in complete shock watcher ex-perfect maid over-tip the hair dresser 100 drachmas, and teeter out of the apartment on her high heels—very high heels.

In the recriminations that would follow, Theo would lay the blame on Maro and Maro would weep in absolute lack of comprehension—her breasts heaving up, up, down, down, up, up, down, down. That Voula would leave and leave in such a manner, wreck Theo's nameday and strike Maro was inconceivable until Nick the Chins astutely pinpointed the cause as the belly dance for two and the subsequent applause at Mati. Theo, his aristocratic philosophy shattered, would wear the scar of Voula for years to come...and would always quote the story of Voula as proof that there does not exist, nor will there ever exist, a satisfied maid.

Chapter Fifteen

"Mr. Bill and Mr. Bob, we in civilian trouble." The perennial look of disaster on Jimmy's face was intense as he greeted Bob and Bill when they entered the store one morning.

"Come on, Jimmy," Bob whined. "It's too early in the day for trouble. Save it for later...avrio."

The summer, swimming and Mati were months behind but Bob was still having difficulty getting into any kind of working routine. Never, in the past, had he been able to relax, take a day off from work without losing needed revenue or give up the hard drinking parties at the apartment and he now reacted strongly to his new life in Greece. He dropped into the slow and easy pace like a batch of soft dough into a bread pan. He was not yet a complete sloth, but Bill patted him on the back and teased, "You're getting gmore like me every day. Keep it up and I won't know the difference. I was right, wasn't I ...work isn't everything."

"It's kind of abnormal," Bob said. "I'm not yet used t making a living without killing myself. I don't know...sometimes I get pangs of conscience."

"Everything's abnormal. You consider your life back in the States normal? You were the only person I ever heard of who commuted uptown to work. I wouldn't worry about feeling guilty...it'll pass.

You're not hurting or exploiting anybody. The only problem you should worry about is...how to relax."

"I know...but it's hard. For you it's different, you're always relaxed."

"Yeah, but I got caught - it was a sin. I had to work too hard at relaxing. Do you know how I used to sweat...hiding from the boss...never knowing when he'd show up at the movies. Even not cutting the lawn or missing the God damn PTA was work. Here relaxing is a way of life...there's no crime in it. Work's not everything...think of the lilies of the field. Guys like us can change the world too." Bill paused, his rationalization done. "Anyway, I'm working hard now in school."

Bill, with so much time on his hands, had enrolled, with noble motives, in the Athens University School of Archeology. He hired one of his classmates to tutor him in Greek and old civilizations and plunged into his classes with a vigor that made Kay shake her head in wonder and disbelief. She was curious how long this present craze would last. "Deep," he had said, when he announced that he was going to school, "are the interests of man...hidden in the recesses of the body. I always wanted to know which rocks and bits of jars came from what period and why. I'm not content with the Parthenon - it's too high above ground."

"Well, I wish you luck," Kay had said, "but I think the only thing you have deep in the recess of your body is a sex urge."

He answered, "Archeology is very sexy...you learn all about old time phallic symbols and everything. The ancient fertility rites alone would make most of our political scandals look puny."

Jimmy, distressed that his bosses didn't want to hear about the civilian trouble they were in, raised his voice, "No kidding, Mr. Bob and Mr. Bill...I think we gonna have to shut store tomorrow."

"What do you mean shut the store? It's not a holiday."

"It ain't that, Mr. Bob...it's Spiro and Panyoti. They tole me they marching tomorrow and ain't coming to work."

"Marching?"

"Yeah, we gonna have elections next month and they gotta demonstrate."

"Spiro's going to demonstrate?" Bill asked. "What is he going to demonstrate...hair curlers?"

"Oh, no, Mr. Bill," Jimmy said seriously. "Spiro...he very interested in politics. He tole Panyoti, he used to make a lot of money demonstrating."

The next day the store was closed for demonstrations. Never having witnessed a political demonstration aside from some low-keyed Engels style speeches at Union Square, Bob, Bill and Kay rushed down to the store early. Jimmy had arrived before them. The night before, he had warned, "We gotta be here early to protect the store. You never know about these things...they start off peaceful, but sometimes they get out of hand." He had lugged a few feet of boards from home with him and began to board up the front window. All the shops on the square were similarly boarded...like Times Square on New Year's Eve.

The streets were relatively free of pedestrians but the curbs were lined with grim-looking, black uniformed policemen. There was a cop stationed every ten feet. A long row of paddy wagons and army ambulances ringed the perimeter of Omonia Square. Police officers, gold braid all over their shoulders and caps, holding walky-talkies, busily ran back and forth across the boulevard and Square, stationing police, directing the placement of wooden barricades and trying to clear the area of the few pedestrians that were present. By forcefully striking and kicking the strollers, the police were able to empty the streets in a very short time.

Bill, Bob, Kay and Jimmy watched and waited behind the boarded up window.

They waited for two hours. Nothing happened. There were no speeches, no parades, no candidates, no brochures, no cheering, no heroes. Nothing.

"This is politics?" Bob scoffed. "How do people know who to vote for? Where are the people? Where are the candidates?"

"The people already got their minds made up who to vote for, Mr. Bob," Jimmy volunteered. "This is just a show of power."

"What power?" Bill said. "There's none around except the cops. This is a farce...Jimmy go sneak next door and get some coffee, they're open...I saw the cops going in. We'll have a cup and go home, this is a waste of time."

Just after Jimmy slipped out the door, a policeman carrying an army type radio telephone on his back, ran up to an officer who had more gold braid on his uniform than anyone else. He gave the phone to the chief, who listened for a moment, nodded his head into the phone and then blew a loud blast on a whistle. The police at the curbs adjusted their feet and seemed to brace themselves. Out of hidden pockets they withdrew short, heavy, black billies. From up the boulevard, faint sounds, like those of a shuffling arm, came down. As the sounds of shuffling got louder, the police braced more. And then chants could be distinguished barely at first, then clearer and louder "...Haaaah...Haaaah...HaaaaH...HAAAAH...Kato...Kato...Nato...Nato...Nato..." The last syllable of each word was hit with a roar from thousands of throats. Every moment the sounds of marching and chanting increased in volume.

Then, Bob, Bill and Kay saw the marchers coming down the boulevard. From curb to curb, as far up as they could see, people were massed—marching slowly—chanting..."Kato...Nato...Kato...Nato..." They chanted in iambic pentameter. Two steps in front of the first wave of humanity walked a black robed priest carrying an ikon of the Madonna. He wore a neatly trimmed beard. Following him, arm in arm, were row after row of demonstrators. Giant portraits of candidates for Parliament floated above the crowd. Large cloth banners, blazing with slogans, were held on long poles by flankers along the curbs. "Kato...Nato...Kato...Nato..." The mob chanted over and over and over and over and over again. "Down with Nato, Down with Nato."

"It's the left," Bob exclaimed.

As the first rank passed, the mob took up a new chant, "Kato...Ameri...iki...Kato...Amer...iki...Apano...Rus...sia...Apano...Rus...sia." The whole contingent, six blocks long, took up the new chant, roaring, "Down with America, Up with Russia."

Watching intently, Bill suddenly made out Spiro in the second file. His hair was wildly flying out behind and above him and his face was uncovered—-a terrible revolutionary look was imprinted thereon. He carried a portrait of one of the candidates, a political prisoner who was running in absentia. "Spiro's a communist," Bill shouted.

A group of leaders broke from the crowd and signaled for a new chant. From the midst of the horde cars on long poles went up...CHANT NUMBER 10!

Then the police went into action.

Politely, the police chief approached the first rank...the candidates themselves. Linked arm to arm, they were well dressed, dignified, evil-looking men. The chief asked them for a permit...they had one—it was for a religious demonstration. An argument ensued, first orderly, then disorderly. The people up the street ceased marching and began to tramp march time, roaring slogan after slogan.

The candidates, showing dissatisfaction, pushed on past the chief—the horde began to march again. After all, it was a free country, a democracy.

The chief, in his demonstration of power, ran to the priest who was still holding the portrait of the Madonna and now chanting, "Down with the Turkish infidels," and smashed him in the face. The priest fell to his knees, got up shakily and ran away. With the priest removed, the chief argued that the permit was void and the demonstration had no reason for being. At his signal the policemen lining the curbs squeezed onto the street, pressing into the crowd. Reinforcements from the paddy wagons quickly took their places.

The leftists' spokesman, their main candidate, hurriedly followed the busy chief, demanding the demonstration be permitted to continue. Bob reading his lips, said, "He called the chief a fascist." Angrily the police chief struck the candidate a karate blow to the back of the neck. The mob, enraged, surged forward and the police surged inward, squeezing tighter, flailing with their blackjacks. Blood began to flow. The chanting gave way to one word—-Fascist. The mob broke into unruly pieces, people ran helter-skelter, shouting and screaming Fascist. The police, excellently trained, squeezed and squeezed—every time they moved deeper into the crowd a new rank took up positions at the curb. They squeezed till finally the marchers were stretched into one thin line in the center of the street, on the double white line. The chanting lost its force, it was hollow, like an aria sung by a hoarse tenor with one vocal chord.

At another signal, the police beat the line into submission. It was all over—the demonstration was terminated. In a few minutes the paddy wagons were loaded, ambulances dispatched to hospitals and the remnants of the leftist party, bleeding, beaten, disappeared.

Jimmy staggered back with the coffee. His head was cut and an ugly bruise lumped over his right eye. "Got caught in the demonstration," he gasped.

As soon as the streets were deserted the police resumed their positions. Some were bloody, limping, hurt—all had cruel looks on their faces.

Next in the schedule of political demonstrations, came the right wing party. Numerically superior to the left, they filled the boulevard with a solid wall of people for ten blocks. They chanted and tramped in much the same manner as the left, although Kay noted that they seemed a trifle more dignified. Their slogans were in direct contradiction to the leftists' "Down with Russia...Up with America and South Africa. Down with Red China...Up with Portuguese Angola." The only slogan in harmony with the Communists was—"Down with Turkey." Bill was puzzled at the international aspect of the slogans— he thought with so much needed to be done in Greece itself it would be more realistic if the parties concentrated on domestic affairs. He said nothing, though, not wishing to interfere in the internal political affairs of a nation friendly to the United States.

When the right wing leaders, rich looking, banker types, evil, reached the police chief, they stopped confidently and their leading candidate—a dignified, grey-haired department store owner— presented a paper. The chief studied it and then rejected it out of hand.

Bob, again reading lips, said, "He said the permit is for a picnic gathering, it's no good in Omonia because there's no grass." Amid chants of down with the Communist police, the police moved in. The mob of rightists fought back stubbornly, bravely and dirtily. They swayed against the police, hoping with sheer numbers to crush the black uniforms. The police, weakened already, took more time, were less efficient with them. All of a sudden, as the fight swirled madly in front of the store, Bill cried, "Look, it's Panyoti...he hit the chief with a slogan. He's a fascist." Before the other could recognize their chicken plucker, he had fallen beneath a flood of feet at the store's doorstep. His skinny old arm shot up for a moment and his hand clutched desperately at the smooth glass door, trying to get a finger hold. Then it disappeared—Panyoti was in danger of death by trampling and Bob shouted, "Jimmy, go get him." Jimmy opening the door to rescue Panyoti, was instantly clubbed back inside. His ear was torn.

 The Anachist party, a small but volatile group, followed on the heels of the right wing party. They had no leader, no candidates. All the followers were evil looking, undignified and unkept. They used only one slogan...Down. Since the Anachists didn't recognize the present caretaker Government, or the police as legal entities, they didn't bother showing a permit. Their presence, Bob read, was their permit. The chief blew his whistle and the Anachists were dispatched brutally, unceremoniously and speedily. A few right and left wingers, lying around the sidewalks, trying to stop their bleeding, picked themselves up and helped the police in the destruction of the Anachist party.

The only party which did not present itself in the center of town was the Center Coalition, a moderate group of dignified, evil men which believed in dividing the power of government among themselves and the police quid pro quo. Wisely they confined themselves to ink and brick throwing at the American Embassy and three weeks later won a landslide victory. Bob claimed it was inevitable. "All the other party supporters were in the hospitals and couldn't vote."

Chapter Sixteen

After the elections life resumed its Greek crawl. As Bob said, "How do we follow an act like that?" So they sat back and enjoyed the house and the mild Greek winter. They toyed with the idea of opening another store—Bob and Bill's was doing so well there was a real opportunity to sock it away with two or even more stores—and they agreed they would—avrio.

Bill stayed with his archeological studies, surprising both Kay and himself. He took her on a six-day student dig in Corinth where nothing new was unearthed but Bill did learn that Corinth, judging from the evidence of the amount of brothels which existed there in ancient times, was one of the wildest spots in antiquity. The dig was harder work than he anticipated and afterward he and Kay took a week's rest in a small isolated village near Sparta. Bob was left with the responsibility of the store and the children. For all his dismal view of marriage he enjoyed the children. They worshipped him and his indulgences.

A short time after their return from Sparta, Bill was awakened in the middle of the night from a deep sleep by a blow to his ribs. He turned and moved over. He received another blow, this time to his spine. "What the...?" he mumbled sleepily. "I didn't do anything...I wasn't even near you."

"It's not that," Kay whispered. "I hear noises downstairs."

"I didn't hear anything."

"Of course, you didn't...you were fast asleep. Go look."

"Bob's down there, he can look," Bill complained. "It's only your imagination." If Bob wanted the room with the private entrance, he could certainly protect his part of the house.

"Go see what the noises are," Kay insisted.

Bill got up drowsily, "This is stupid," he grumbled. And then he too heard a noise. It was muffled through the thick concrete floor, but it sounded somewhat like furniture being pushed around. "Come on Schwartz," he said to the sleeping dog, and poked him. The dog slowly got up, stretched, yawned, blinked his eyes stupidly and then sat down wagging his long furry tail. Bill looked at him with contempt. Slob, he thought. This is going to protect me and my family? He pushed the reluctant dog out the bedroom and to the stairs, whispering encouragement, "Come o, boy...come on...good dog."

Bob's room was located at the end of a small hall at the bottom of the stairs. As Bill descended he heard more sounds and soft voices. For a moment he had a vision of Honest John the real estate mon and some hood friends slicing up his partner in vendetta. He hastened down the remaining stairs, gave the dog a big shove and threw the door to Bob's room open.

Instead of Honest John and a group of thugs, the first thing he saw was a tall, long haired, gorgeous young woman bending over attaching a frilly garter to a black mesh stocking. A good deal of her smooth thigh was visible, and as she bent, her breasts, large cones, hung forward, trying to push out of the low neckline of her dress.

Bill's eyes darted from décolletage to thigh in a swift attempt to absorb everything at once.

"Oh, jeez, it's you" Bob grunted. "I got scared out of my skin." He sat rigidly on his bed, surprise on his face. A cigarette was in his hand and he had just been about to light up when the door burst open. "Don't ever do that...heh. You want me to have an attack of trauma or something?" He lit the cigarette, took a deep relieving puff and said, "I'd like you to meet Muni," he waved his hand in the girl's direction. She had secured her stocking and she smiled at Bill and turned to the bureau mirror to comb her gleaming black hair. "She's a show girl," Bob said.

Bill looked at Muni the show girl. She wore a tight black sheath, very low at the neck and held up with two thin spaghetti straps, one of which had slipped down sexily off her shoulder. Her breasts were urged forward and up by a brief French brassiere, forming a cleavage so tight that a sheet of flimsy could easily be held in it securely. Every curve and ridge of her hard body came through the dress in bas-relief- her bikini panties were outlined on her buttocks. As she combed her hair, the buttock muscles, taught and firm, flexed with every stroke. Bill observed that she was an old-fashioned Greek girl—-under her upraised arm was a sheer, gentle pile of black down. Her skin seemed very white, like Pentelic marble, against the black of her dress. Bill licked his dry lips with a tongue that felt like a fish file. "We thought there were robbers," he said in a cracking voice. He felt like an intruder but the hair combing was so interesting that he was loathe to leave. To be sociable he asked Bob for a cigarette.

"Go put your pants on first," Bob laughed.

"What do you think we're running here?"

Only then did Bill notice he had nothing but his shorts on, and reluctantly, because propriety demanded, he left. He kept his eyes on Muni till Bob closed the door behind him. As he was going up the stairs, Bob stuck his head out and whispered to him, "Now, for crying out loud, don't go and tell Kay about this. She might not understand...what with the kids in the house and all. She might not trust me with them...I swear all the time you were gone...everything was fine. I mean it-it was all family—no fooling around. OK?"

"Of course," Bill said. "What do you think I am? We know the kids were fine. Don't worry, my lips are sealed."

The moment he got into bed, Bill squealed everything. "I think it's disgraceful, this kind of behavior...especially what with the kids in the house and all."

But Kay had fallen asleep and didn't hear any of his complaints.

He tossed and turned all night long, and when he finally fell into a restless sleep he had fitful pictures of flexing and combing...flexing and combing...flexing and combing...

The next morning, after Bob had left for his weekly golf date with a Greek Army officer he had become acquainted with, Bill suggested to Kay they discuss Bob's future.

"What's to discuss?" she asked. "He's happy, isn't he? For the first time in his life he has a family...easy living...a soft life. Greece has been a tonic for him."

"I'm not talking about his happiness or his mental health...I'm talking about his future."

"Let's not go interfering in other people's lives. We're all finally free and you want to line up futures. We don't know what the future holds...if we wanted to know, we'd have stayed home. Sometimes you sound just like your mother."

"I don't want to interfere" Bill persisted. "But don't you think it was time Bob thought of settling down? Perhaps even get married?"

"When he wants to get married, he'll get married."

"Yes, I agree...but...well, you were asleep last night and don't know..." Bill told her the story of the night before and Muni the show girl. If he expected a strong reaction from Kay, he was mistaken. She only said, "Bob's a big boy now, Hon. You can't go getting him married off just because he has a date once in awhile."

"That's OK, but you know how these showgirls are...gold diggers. They're just waiting around for a rich American sucker."

"Hmmmm. You may be right there. Perhaps Bob should at least be exposed to the right type of girl. God knows there are thousands in Athens...good family and upbringing. Maybe you ought to talk to Theo."

"Yeah," Bill said. "We can fix him up with a Greek heiress...someone with a big fleet of ships."

Bill felt very proud of his motives and interest in Bob's future and even though he had recurring fantasies at night about bombs, flexing buttocks, black underarm hair and garters, he congratulated himself for being such a good friend.

Theo was very interested when Bill told him he would like to expose Bob to some deserving, nice rich Greek girl.

"I am glad you are turning into Greeks," he said. "I think Bob is wise wanting to marry here. Yaya has a great deal of experience in matters of this nature...she knows of many young people who are available for matrimony and what is important—she will represent your interests well."

"What about Bob, Theo," Bill asked, "will he have any dates with potential finds?"

"Finds...finds" Tin Afto" Do you mean young ladies?"

"Yes, doesn't he get to go out. In America he'd date the girl first...you know...dinner...shows."

"Apogarevete," Theo hissed, rolling his eyes negatively.

"He will have no contact until after many details are discussed. And then only with the family of the betrothed. Here, he may not...what do you say...take the girl around until the pricka is agreed upon and a written contract signed." He nodded gravely at Bill, "You...along with Yaya will represent him. She is in her room; you may see her now if you wish."

Yaya slept in and used as headquarters for her business affairs, any room in the Kliniki which had an empty bed. Busy seasons hit her hard—she either set up a cot in Theo's office, or if, as sometimes happened, the office too was filled with patients, she would be forced to go to a hotel. She hated hotels, impersonal dormitories she called them. And they cut into her pocketbook. On more than one crowded occasion, Theo had caught her craftily doubling up in a bed with an understanding and kind patient.

Bill entered her room and caught her sitting quietly on the edge of one of the old iron hospital beds. It was impossible to tell from her reflective old face what she was thinking—whether of days of riches and glory past, or yet to come.

Within arms reach of the bed, against the wall was a large, old-fashioned, carved wood armoire. It had two curved doors, locked and bolted securely. The armoire was almost as important to Yaya as her life itself, Theo said that if it were taken away she would soon wither and die. It was her Shangri la. It served as her kitchen, bar, file room and office. Locked behind the doors were sweets and bottles of brandy, ouzo and light sweet wine for guests; underwear, assorted shawls in black Spanish lace, a spare set of teeth for good wear, creams, ointments, powders, perfumes, exotic soaps smuggled through customs from the orient. The section not allocated to toiletries and clothing, held records of business transactions, consummated and pending, ledgers, certificates and rolled parchment contracts showing her holdings, earnings and depreciation allowances. There were also Government bonds dating as far back as 1924—unredeemable now, but in the future one could never tell. Deep in the recesses of the closet were fruits, nuts, legs of lamb—in season only—and jewelry which she never wore. The closet had hidden drawers and was laced with secret panels. In one such compartment lay quietly a leather sack holding English gold pounds—the ultimate in monetary stability to her ever since she witnessed the devaluation of the Greek gold drachma in 1902.

The armoire was never opened except by Yaya. Once, ill with high fever, she had chained herself to it in such a manner that if the doors were opened more than three centimeters she would have been yanked from bed and able to call alarm. Whenever she left the room she sealed the doors with chains and strong iron bars. Whenever she changed rooms or went to a hotel, Theo, resigned to the expense, hired two men to move the armoire along with her.

Bill thought Yaya looked depressed, her wrinkled face was fallen. The white hair around her chin mole drooped. She wore the same shade of black as always, but for some reason, most probably a lull in business, it looked blacker.

When he told her what he wanted her ancient eyes took on a new luster, color flashed through her face, her wrinkles slowly smoother and the whiskers stood out arrogantly. In halting Greek, the syntax all discombobulated, he explained that he was in the market for a wife for Bob. As he did, he realized that Bob would never go for the idea, that he was barking up the wrong tree, but the sight of Yaya, fidgeting in her seat with kefi, made him continue. She waited impatiently for him to finish, then cut him off, "To xero...to xero...eho pola koritsia." I understand, I understand, I have many girls.

She excitedly started to jabber away at Bill, not caring that he understood only about ten percent of what she was saying. He politely interrupted her and asked if she could adjust her teeth or insert the good set to help increase his comprehension. She went on and on, telling him how many wonderful matches she had made...that the parties involved were invariably satisfied...that she had a strong interest in genetics and scrupulously tried—by mating dominants with recessives—to weed out bad strains in the race. Never, she lied, had she brought together any pair closer than second cousins. She picked up momentum as she made her sales pitch, rubbing her hands, gesturing, throwing her head back dramatically every time she cracked a joke and rapidly crossing and uncrossing her legs in excitement. She sensed doubt in Bill and worked hard to dispel it. He became so fascinated by her undergarments as she crossed and uncrossed her legs that he lost another five percent of what she was saying. He saw she wore many layers of underwear; there was a black slip, another black slip, another black slip and still another black slip. Under the weight of petticoats, encasing her legs to her knees, hung a blousy pair of black rayon bloomers. They were prevented from rolling up her thigh by an exquisite set of Syrian garters. Bill sat, his eyes bouncing back and forth in their sockets, frantically following the swiftly crossing and uncrossing legs. Things became a whirring blur of black. Tossing silk and rayon, slips and bloomers swished noisily. It was like a wild badminton game played with shiny ravens.

Abruptly she stopped, uncrossed her legs one final time, smoothed her slips, bloomers and dress, placed her hand demurely on her chest, clenched her fist around the keys to the armoire hidden therein and dozed off.

Bill nodded goodbye to her sleeping figure and left. On his way out Theo said, "She always tires herself whenever she discusses something of great interest. No matter, she will be of great aid to you in your quest."

Bill had many clandestine meetings with Yaya in the subsequent few weeks. They'd huddle, head to head, speaking softly, in the room she currently occupied at the clinic. As Bill gained her confidence, she offered him ouzo and sweets—syrupy baklava and powdery koorambientas—which she took from the closet. They became such fast friends that she felt free enough to permit him to stay in the room when she unlocked the doors. She was extremely orderly and organized and because she trusted Bill, she showed him her files—cheeseboxes packed with cards, written on with fine, shaky hand. They contained such diverse information as: sex, age, weight, height, wealth, physical deformities, genetic abnormalities, school transcripts, habits, skin condition and notes about sexual behavior when a) stimulated and b) not stimulated. After drawing the blinds she showed him that the file boxes were cunningly hidden in the closet inside the legs of her spare bloomers. With Bill's approval she set up a tight weekly schedule of meetings with prospectives and their families.

She suggested softly, and Bill agreed, that it would not do to get a very pretty girl because such a case would bring a lower pricka. Her idea was to arrange for a homely thirty year old, possible virgin, healthy and relatively sound of mind. What she called, grinning like the witch offering Snow White the apple—overlooked. The fathers in Greece, she winked, really pay big to marry off an over-looked daughter. Looking Bill straight in the eye, she brazenly told him that her cut would be fifteen percent, payable immediately upon receipt of the pricka. So he wouldn't hurt her feelings, Bill signed a number of papers, none of which he understood, but all of which were properly witnessed and endorsed.

The first interview was held in a luxury apartment in Kolonaki, with a very rich and affluent merchant. In addition to the floors, the walls were paved in marble. Any sound in the flat produced a loud echo. Hence the conversation was muted and subdued. The father tried to act matter-of-factly, but his anxiety crept through to Yaya who leaned over and whispered to Bill that they had a big opportunity to clean up if they played their cards right.

The daughter was presented formally. She seemed rattled, to Bill, unpoised —when she bowed to him. She was in striking contrast to Muni the show girl and he thought a potentially good mate for Bob. Her name was Hondri. She was thirty, extremely dark in a Turkish way, had a well-shaved face except for long sideburns and weighed about 200 pounds. She had obviously been on a diet because her clothes were very loose around her belly and Yaya's card had her down as 230. Her father opened her mouth to show that most of her teeth were in place and those that weren't were pure gold. Bill reveled in her old-fashioned chic—her under-arm hair, which he made out through her nylon blouse, was neatly tucked into the side strap of her brassiere. The fact that the hair was like so many wire springs and kept fighting out of the strap, showed him she had character and tenacity in shoving them there in the first place. Bob, he reasoned, wouldn't mind the hair on her body so much as the back of her head was balding and kind of evened things out a little bit.

"Ti kanete," she giggled at Bill.

"Ti kanete," Bill said, turning quickly to her father.

The pricka was very high and Yaya wanted to close the deal on the spot but Bill asked for a short delay—he thought Bob should at least meet Hondri.

The father sensing hesitance, threw in the use of his own twenty-two year old mistress for one year. He passed her picture around to make the cheese more binding.

Suddenly, Hondri, sitting with her thick legs akimbo on a petite Hepplewhite chair, under the terrific strain and pressure of arranging for a husband, started gurgling and frothing at the mouth. She rigidly fell to the hard marble floor, her feet and hands twitching spasmodically. Her father ran to the kitchen and came back with a long spoon which he crammed down her throat. He apologized for his daughter's indigestion—he had warned that fried foods were hard on the stomach, "but you know how young girls are now-a-days, so modern...they don't listen to their fathers."

Yaya said, "Bravo," then turning to Bill, "He is good at first aid...a worthy father-in-lay."

Bill was very low that night when he told Kay, "I don't know...I don't think Bob'll go for the idea too much."

"Why? Didn't you say the girl today would be perfect?"

"Yes, but it might take her weeks to recover. I'm afraid it's not going to work. I feel like giving up the idea...even if Yaya gets mad. It was stupid to begin with."

Just then he heard delightful squeals and titters from downstairs and clenching his teeth renewed his determination of find a girl more worthy of Bob.

The next few meetings were unrewarding. Yaya stuck with the high pricka girls because of the fifteen percent and they met nothing that Bill thought Bob would even remotely accept.

One was not allowed by her father to talk at all and Bill became suspicious when she tried and he punched her in the mouth.

Another, suffering from acute asthma, was wheeled out and fainted four times while the pricka got higher and higher.

Most of the girls they saw were hairy and dark except the asthmatic whose lucosities were in complete control of her blood and skin pigment.

Finally, Bill timidly suggested to Yaya that they quit for awhile. After all, the effort had not been totally in vain, he argued, as she had lined up the epileptic with another client at a high profit. She was bitter, caused a row and cursed him with five fingers. She claimed the excuse he gave for calling off the hunt and having wasted her time was inadequate. "But, Yaya," he pleaded when she threw him out, "Bob's on vacation in Corfu...he won't be back for two weeks...he ahs to be at least consulted a little...he's American."

Of course Bob took Muni the show girl with him.

Chapter Seventeen

One of the most fascinating times in Greece, Bill, Kay and Bob found, was the period which directly proceeded the Lenten season. Mari-Gras or as it is called in Greece—Apokries. Nowhere is this period more fun and nowhere do the people enter into it with as much of the spirit of Dionysius—with greater gusto and less reservation. Everyone has kefi.

Virtually every night Bob, Bill and Kay went with Theo and the crowd to a new and more exciting taverna. Every night kefi consumed them, they sang, danced, threw dishes on the floor wildly in search of relief and expression. The dishes they broke were of course paid for— even in Greece kefi has a cost and in the forty day Mardi-Gras it was estimated that they broke 914 dollars worth of china.

The best of the tavernas, judged by common consent, were located in the medieval Plaka—and the best of those was the Taverna Of The 16 Brothers.

On the way there, Theo told them about its phenomenal success. The Taverna of The 16 Brothers wasn't always called by that name, he said. It started out by being run by a buxom woman who was tragically left a widow by her husband who was careless enough to allow himself to be run down by a donkey cart in the narrow streets of the Plaka. The widow, an excellent cook, decided, in order to earn a living for herself and her brood of seventeen sons, to open a small taverna in her home right under the Acropolis.

The food was so good and the service so outstanding—there were at first only four tables and seventeen waiters—that the place caught on with Athenian society in a big way. The business grew and grew...and so did the sons. When they came of age, using nefarious legal means, the sons yenced the mother out of her controlling interest in the million dollar operation. Being good and grateful sons, however, they kept her on as head cook for 600 drachmas a month. The sons became equal partners and quit waiting on tables to stand around suspiciously watching one another...lest they be stolen.

When one brother was taken to the hospital for an emergency operation, his last words before losing consciousness were to his wife, instructions on what position she must occupy at the taverna to successfully watch. But, not being used to such a grind, she fell asleep one night after four days of watching 18 hours a day. While she slumbered her husband lost not only his appendix but his one seventeenth interest in the taverna as well.

He was hired back as an ordinary waiter and received a straight salary like his mother. The sign outside was quickly changed to read 16 Brothers instead of 17.

The remaining bosses resumed watching.

Because there were sixteen partners there were sixteen points of view on how the taverna should be decorated. There was a lot of straw and garlic cloves hanging from wooden rafters. Brass pots, plates and guns were on the walls. Murals done in fresco, depicted donkeys, drunks, chesty women and barrels of wine in a state of motion, doing nothing, harmonizing with nothing, were painted on the walls, ceilings and floors.

"This is one of the most novel places we've ever been to, Theo," Kay said as they were being seated.

"It is beautiful...megalio," Bill said, enchanted by the sixteen different motifs.

"The food is also megalio," Theo said, waving his hand in a small circle in the air—an expression that meant extra-megalio.

Sounds of a crowded restaurant filled the air, chatter, tinkling of forks and glasses, orders cried to waiter and busboys. Bill looked around, there were many people, not one table was empty. Theo had arranged with one of the brothers for a choice one for them on the skirt of the dance floor. Behind the small square for dancing were steps and a small platforms for the band. On a balcony above lay giant barrels of wine—the 16 Brothers own special formula and blend. During Apokries, since the prices were three times higher than at any other time of year, the 16 Brothers forced their waiters and busboys to dress in costume. The waiter-brother was dressed like an Emmet Kelly clown. It was easy to distinguish the owners—suspiciously watching at their stations.

Paper hats and noisemakers were served with the sixteen course dinner and as more and more of the heady wine was consumed the din got louder and louder. By the time dinner was finished, Theo and Maro were blowing gustily into their toy horns—Maro's air-filled cheeks challenged her eyes in a bulging contest—and Nick the Chins and Vinegar-face happily pounded the table with small wooden drumsticks. Nota, appropriately given a paper fan, rippled it open and fanned fresh air into her chest. Her sad-eyed mother, Bill thought, looked sadder than ever before, she had absolutely no kefi. It was as if she wanted to be somewhere else.

During dinner soft music was supplied by the same three-fingered pianist that Bill vaguely remembered from another taverna. His duty done, he fumblingly rolled up his sheets of music and gave way to a sixteen piece orchestra clad colorfully in Evizone uniforms with short pleated skirts, gold embroidered, red jackets and tasseled red caps. The band began whipp9ng up a musical frenzy with sparkling Greek tunes.

They played one song after another and the table-pounding and horn-tooting increased. Twice, while a trio of bouzoukias were playing particularly gay tunes, men got up from their chairs, made fro the dance floor and rendered kasapikos. They twisted and turned and clapped their hands—oblivious to their surroundings, unaware of anything but the haunting music. While they danced, dishes were thrown from the tables in appreciation.

The music, the tinny bouzoukias, the hypnotized dancers, who were not performing for applause but for themselves because they had kefi, the shattering dishes and the wine awakened in Bill an almost overpowering kefi and like a Holy Roller hearing the Voice, he got up suddenly, grabbed a scarf from Maro, jumped to the floor and began a snake dance.

Immediately shouts of encouragement went up from the taverna. Dishes flew to the floor, Theo, smiling—proud of the Bill he had created—tossed himself out of his chair, took the end of the scarf and allowed himself to be led in dance by the en-kefied Bill. Other people quickly got up and joined the line. Nick the Chins, Nota, Vinegar-face all joined hands behind Theo. Kay pushed Bob up and nodded to Vinegar-face's wife, who shook her head no and quietly covered her eyes.

The training at Mati served Bill well at the Taverna of the 16 Brothers. He led the Greek snake line—formed hand-to-hand behind him—hopping and skipping in time with the bouzoukias, violins and clarinets. Round and round, waving crazily in between tables the snake line glided- picking up people as it went. It got longer and longer, first thirty, then forty, then fifty people were stretched behind Bill, the snakes head. The line coiled, turned and twisted and the people vertebrae skipped, hopped and whirled up and down the restaurant. The music got louder and louder...faster and faster. As more people joined the line, the band picked up tempo and made it move faster and faster. Bill found himself hissing wildly at the front of the weaving line. The pace got faster...the harsh stringy sounds of the bouzoukias forced...demanded...faster...faster. Faster, cried the bouzoukias...faster...whirling...hopping...jumping...faster...faster...faste r...turning... spinning. The members of the band, hopping down from the stand, joined the line, shrilling out music for the snake.

Bill went wild, he climbed and danced over tables and chairs...up the band stand steps...down the back...around the tables...in and out of the kitchen. The line, like a palsied boa constrictor, trailed insanely behind, humping and jerking.

The few people remaining at the tables hurled dishes, glasses, forks, knives and chairs at the dance floor. An entire table, set with places for six, was dragged close by a host of one of the parties and over turned on the dance floor with a ferocious glee. The man, not sated with the roar of the broken dishes and glasses, began to tear the table to pieces with his bare hands. When he had splintered it as much as he could he then, only then, joined the line of dancers.

The music became deafening, men and women victims of kefi were tearing fixtures and brass plates from the wall and smashing them to the floor in utter abandonment. With a screaming hiss everyone shouted and screamed, "opa...opa...opa."

The dance ended.

Bill fell into this chair. It was minutes before he could speak. "Wine," he gasped and swallowed a glass of refreshing retsina in one gulp. The band struck up some subdued dance music and everyone relaxed. "Theo," Bill said, "that is the greatest dance yet devised by man."

"Aha...but of course it was invented by the gods."

Theo was breathing hard, in short puffs. He wiped the sweat from his face with Maro's scarf. People at surrounding tables looked and pointed Bill out as the American who led the Greek dance. They tapped their hands together at him, nodded and smiled compliments and bravos. For the Greeks to see a foreigner with so much kefi was an exceptional treat.

"You have done well," Theo said, "to be able to lead that dance."

"Yeah...but I'm dead," Bill said.

Then he was resuscitated.

The lights dimmed, a thin blue spot played on the empty dance floor and from the side of the bandstand slipped a tall voluptuous singer. She took a position right in front of Bill. She wore a black, skin-tight satin gown which ripped with every move and gyration.

Chapter Eighteen

It was a hot day in July, the morning gave every indication that heat records would fall later in the day. For that reason, Kay and Bill decided to call on Theo for an early morning coffee and ask him if it were permissible for Kay to motor up to Mount Parnassus and get some relief in the cool air there.

There were not patients on the pews when they arrived and Kay plopped heavily down, exhausted from the five story climb. Yaya padded out with coffee and orange juice. She was barely talking to Bill anymore, ever since he had dropped the notion of fixing Bob up with one of her girls. She took it as a personal affront, feeling that he had jobbed her out of her fair fifteen percent. Her prestige had suffered.

She almost threw the coffee at Bill and then turned sweetly to Kay, "Ti kanis pedi mou? Po...po...po...ti megalo stomaki. Exi pedio...ti oraia pou ine." How are you, my child...what a large stomach...six children...how wonderful.

She looked over her shoulder at Bill and shot him a dirty look.

"Yorgo...ela tho," she shouted into the kitchen. "Katina ine etho." Bill noted that she didn't cry out he was visiting too.

Theo came out of the kitchen and joined them in the hall. His belly stuck way out in front and his hands were filled with hog intestines. "I am making kokoretsi," he beamed. "Only when you have tasted my home made kokoretsi will you know what real food is." He led them back to the kitchen to see what he was doing.

The scene looked like a World War I battlefield after a murderous bayonet attack. Lungs, brains, spleens and guts were lying around in a mass of jelly-like gore on the kitchen table.

In preparing the kokoretsi, Theo had made an earnest effort to keep all the ingredients sorted but the amorphous nature of the innards made it impossible—they sluiced together indiscriminately like wet garbage, on the center of the table.

One glance was enough to make Bill feel faint and he quickly looked to Kay for her reaction. She didn't seem to mind the sight one bit.

"I am glad you are here," Theo said, "you must help me. Katina, stand over there and hold the intestines tight...we have to stuff them carefully." Theo was deadly serious, preparing and eating food came in just second to delivering babies in his hierarchy of values. Taking a sharp bread knife he began chopping and mashing the innards on a big bloody wooden cutting board.

Kay pulled a chair to the side of the table and taking the slimy intestines, held them aloft as if she were holding salt water taffy. Theo started stuffing the loose flapping end with the spongy glob he had created on the cutting board. As he did she gave him more and more play. He stuffed slowly and carefully, making sure there was a proper proportion of livers to spleens in each handful. His eyes followed the work, but his mind was on the finished cooked product.

Bill left the room.

"Katina," Theo was saying when Bill had recovered sufficiently to return, "you will be due any day now, yes?"

"I hope so Theo," she said, glancing down at her distended midsection. "I'm getting a little tired of lugging Oscar around...the heat's killing me."

"When are your months over?" he asked, winding a long string of intestine around his arm to prevent it from slipping to the floor.

"I think they were over yesterday," she said.

Breathlessly she struggled with an unexpected run in one of the stuffed intestines, brains and kidneys started oozing out. Theo quickly went to her aid, throwing a fresh lump of liver into the breech.

"Hmmm...when did you conceive...what day, do you know?"

"Not the exact day...no...but according to my calculations I'm overdue."

Bill began to get woozy again as Yaya started mashing more spleens.

"Hmm...," Theo hummed putting down the kokoretsi, "let us go into the examining room."

"But the kokoretsi..."

"Then birazi...we will get to it later." He took Kay out of the room, leaving Bill with Yaya sadistically mashing and beating the spleens. She glanced at him for inspiration as she mashed.

Bill closed his eyes to remove the picture of what was on the table. It helped slightly for a few moments he kept his eyes shut, trying not to think of anything. When he opened them, he saw Dina putting a pot on to boil. "Oh, no," he thought, "don't tell me they're going to cook the kokoretsi...we're going to get stuck here for lunch...I can't eat kokoretsi...I hate kokoretsi...I saw it made." He shut his eyes again and tried to think nice thoughts. He thought of Muni the show girl. Muni would take his mind off the kokoretsi. Combing and flexing. He saw her upraised arm, the patch of diaphanous hair underneath...her cones. The sudden clanging of the pot cast the image of Muni out of his mind. He opened his eyes once again, a feeling of disgust and despair mingling inside him. Yaya was gone and Dina was just scurrying out with the contents of the pot. He sat alone, staring at eh kokoretsi. He tried to recreate the image of Muni but the slobby mess on the table fought brutally with the lady and she receded into dimness, badly defeated and grossly outmatched.

Just as he was about to leave for home, Theo burst into the room. Dina followed, carrying a bottle of Metaxa brandy and quickly poured a stiff drink and offered it to Bill.

"Beel...Beel, congratulations. You have given birth to another boy," Theo cried. "I am so proud...a boy. It is wonderful."

"What are you talking about, Theo?"

"A boy...a wonderful boy. Kay has been delivered."

Bill was stunned, he started to rise. "But...wh...do...you..."

"A very easy birth, I must say so myself. A wonderful job...as you say. I saw she was ready and...pooph."

Bill continued to stutter, "But...but..."

"Kay is inside with Yaya...go...you may see."

"But Theo, what's going on..." Bill left the kitchen in a saze. How could the baby be born? Babies weren't born that way. They were just making kokoretsi...it was impossible. He entered the delivery room. Kay was still in her dress lying on the table. It was a lie. "What is going on?" he asked her. She looked pale.

"There's the baby," she said weakly.

Yaya was sitting on the cot against the wall holding a bundle. Bill saw it move and turned to Kay. The picture of the room became clearer...Kay was on the table...her dress was on...there was a little baby with Yaya...Kay did look weak...it was no lie...it had happened. He still couldn't believe it...even in Greece things don't happen that way. It had been only a few minutes since Kay and Theo left him in the kitchen. Could it be that in slow-moving Greece the baby was born so quickly?

Kay's color was slowly coming back to her cheeks, but he saw it had been a tremendous effort. "Honey," he said,

"I'm so happy...I'm shocked. Theo said it's a boy. I can't believe it. How do you feel? What can I do? Do you want anything?"

She squeezed his hand and whispered. "I'm so happy for you Theo was wonderful, he's a great doctor. He said I helped." She closed her eyes and a delicate, peaceful look came over her face.

"Hon, take it easy...don't talk. We'll have plenty of time to talk. I love you."

"I love you."

Theo came into the room. "I have called Bob...he is on the phone now. Katina, how do you feel?" He took her wrist and timed her pulse. "Fine, fine. You are fine. You see the method here...ten minutes...ten minutes." He gave Dina an order and flew out of the room, turning to say, "I must finish the kokoretsi, tonight we will have a celebration. We have a boy...a boy." He was extremely excited. Bill had never quite seen him just this way. Exuberant, yes, but never so excited. The fact that he had painlessly delivered a boy...an American boy was thrilling. As Bill went to the phone he heard him in the kitchen shouting happily that he had brought a new American into the world in ten minutes...only ten minutes. "A boy, Dina...did you see his thing...a great big boy."

Bill picked up the phone, "Bob..."

"What happened, I couldn't understand, Theo. Kay have the baby?"

"Yeah, a boy. Can you believe it, ten minutes."

"Congratulations, Dad. I'm going to set Jimmy up; I'll be right over."

In the operating room, Kay was still on the table and Bill asked Yaya about getting her to a room. She told him it would be ready any moment; Dina was making the bed. He saw her fiddling with the baby on the cot and went over to give his new son a look. The baby was as lumpy as a mattress and swollen and red. As Bill smiled down he screamed. Yaya, with half a lemon, squeezed some juice into the baby's eyes.

"Yaha, ti kanite?" Bill demanded. What are you doing? Where's the silver nitrate?"

She ignored him and professionally went about cleaning the baby's eyes. Then she removed the blanket and gave him a good scrubbing with a cloth dipped into a pot of chamomile tea. She bundled him up once again, lifted him with her shriveled, wrinkled hands and took him out of the room, cackling and chuckling in happiness.

That evening Bill and Bob returned to the clinic to visit Kay. Bill had felt a happy glow of pride all day, for the birth of his son and more especially in Theo's parting words that morning when he kicked them out to let Kay get some sleep, "I will tell you Beel," he had said, back at work on the kokoretsi, "I have never seen such a woman as your Katina. She is truly megalio, not like the whining Greek women...She is truly brave."

The waiting room was very crowded and hot. Sweating patients in varying stages of pregnancy sat limply on the pews. One abortion case, a pretty unmarried girl of about 19, sat segregated from the others, staring worriedly at the kerosene heater.

Kay was in a semi-private next to the operating room, as a special concession there were only two beds in the room. Bill opened the door and they tiptoed in. She was not in bed. She was bending over the baby's ugly metal crib dangling her right breast near his mouth, urging him to eat.

"What are you doing?" Bill asked. "You belong in bed. What are you doing," he repeated, watching her bounce the baby softly in the face.

"Shhh. I'm nursing the baby," She said quietly.

"What do you mean...shouldn't you be doing that in bed, holding him in your arms?"

"Of course...I'm only getting him interested. That's all."

"Well you get to bed. I'll bring the baby over. You've had six kids—-when did you ever hear of getting them interested? They're naturally interested."

Kay got into bed with a sigh. She looked amazingly fresh and well. The heat wasn't bothering her now that her burden was laid down.

"Where's Yaya?" Bill demanded. "Aren't you getting any help?"

"They're very busy tonight. Didn't you see the crowd outside?"

"I don't care how busy they are...you're my wife and I want you to have a little help." He rang the bell for Dina.

She promptly came in carrying a baby bottle. "Tin afto?" Bill asked her.

"Ine camomile...ya ta moro."

"Ya ti?"

"Ya ti etsi."

"They give camomile for everything," Kay volunteered. "Before they bathed him in it, sponged me off and later I got a cup to drink. That's all I've had as a matter of fact. I can't wait till the kokoretsi is ready. Did you smell it? Did they start to cook yet?" Hungrily she asked Dina, "Ta fagato ine estimo?"

Bill gave Kay a tender kiss and said, "Kay...look, hon. I don't want to bother you but don't you think things are just a little too loose around here? I mean what with the baby in the same room as the visitors...you eating kokoretsi..."

"My dearest," she said kindly, cutting him off, "we're in Greece, remember. What's wrong with kokoretsi? I have to eat, don't I? As for the baby...there's only us here...we don't have any diseases...I hope. He's better off with me taking care of him, isn't he. Bob, will you tell him this is Greece."

Dina brought the baby over to Kay's waiting arms and hurried back to work. That afternoon, in addition to cleaning the room she had spruced it up with an end table from Theo's office and a vase full of flowers. The two iron beds and the baby's crib were the only other items of furniture.

"You can tuck that thing back in as long as he's going to have the bottle," Bill said and Bob turned his head.

The baby was swollen and had squinty crossed eyes and a furry topped elongated head. He looked like any new born infant, esthetically ugly but ontologically beautiful. Bob went over to take a good look. "He's cute," was all he could get out.

"The swelling goes down after a few days," Kay said, taking the bottle and squirting a few drops onto his arm. "It's cold. It figures...you think they make it warm for the baby at least. Dina reminds me of Paraskevi." He rang again for Dina, pushing down on the servant's buzzer with a clenched fist.

Instead of Dina, Theo's round body popped in. He wore a sterile white medical jacket and a stethoscope hung from his neck. Little medical, metal things were hanging out of his pockets. For the first time he looked as a doctor should.

"Kalispera, kalispera," He cried pleasantly. "How is the father this evening, Beel?" He went over to the bed and rubbed the baby's cheek with his stubby finger. "Aha...Katina...he is beautiful...he is like you."

"Theo," Bill said, "the chamomile tea is cold. Shouldn't the baby have hot tea? And the nipples...I've been wondering...have they been boiled?"

Theo looked puzzled and stared at Bill for a moment. "Nai, nai, the tea should be warm...veveos. You know, Dina and Yaya are very busy tonight, we have much work tovradi." He turned to Kay, "Katina, you may get up...don't be afraid—go into the kitchen and boil you own nipples." He started out of the room "I must go now, I have much work. And the kokoretsi must be prepared too."

"First time I've seen Theo with something more on than a T shirt at the office," Bill said. "He kills me...he waits for the hottest day of the year to get all dressed up. Must have some big shot patients tonight...or maybe the Health Department is making an inspection.

They all knew that a health inspection was virtually impossible unless the Minister of Health, who was indebted to Theo for thrice having scraped his mistress, was removed from office. Since the

Minister of Health in turn had much on the Prime Minister—that was unlikely.

Later, when the baby had been served his tea and fallen asleep, there was a tap on the door and Nick the Chins, carrying a bunch of flowers and a big bottle of retsina walked in. "Ti kanis Katina," he cried. "How are you...you are wonderful?" He gave her cheek a brush with his lips and chin and tiptoed over to the crib. "Ah...oraia...tosso polli araia...how beautiful."

"Honey, get a chair outside," Kay said. "And bring back a vase for the flowers. They're beautiful, Nick...thank you."

As he was returning with a pair of folding garden chairs, Bill bumped into Nick the Walk. He said Jimmy had told him of the birth and he had rushed right over to see Kay and the baby. He too had flowers and a bottle under his arm.

The waiting room had emptied out, the abortion case was gone and the pews free of patents. On one of them was a large dish of steaming kokoretsi. Dina, coming out of the kitchen, picked it up, pushed past Bill and Nick the Walk and went into Kay's room. They followed her in.

Nick the Walk rushed over to Kay, kissed her noisily, a sucking, toothless kiss, patted the baby and sat down with a gummy grin cutting his head in two.

"I'm starved," Kay said, sitting up in bed and preparing her knees for use as a table, "Excuse me while I eat." Dina gave her supper and she dug ferociously into the kokoretsi.

Chins uncorked his bottle of retsina and looked around for glasses to fill. "You," he commended to Nick the Walk, "get some glasses." His stomach started to gyrate as it received messages from his hose and he asked Dina, "Don't we get any kokoretsi?"

"Veveos, Kirio Nicko," Dina said. In a few minutes she was back with a large tray, dishes, forks, bread and a platter of kokoretsi. Chins filled the glasses Nick the Walk brought in and everyone drank. The visit, Bill thought apprehensively, watching Chins and Nick the Walk digging into the kokoretsi and downing the wine, had all the earmarks of a party. The whispering had given way to normal volume Greek talk, which was very close to shouting.

There was another knock on the door and Bob went to open it. "Jimmy," he exclaimed. Jimmy stood in the hall in his uniform, holding a bag of chickens. "What are you doing here?"

"I wanted to wish Mrs. Kay congratulations," Jimmy said. "I brung over a couple chickens. Chicken is very good in the hospital."

"Who's minding the store?" Bob demanded. "Who's cooking?"

"Panyoti. And Spiro stayed to help." Jimmy stuffed the bag of chickens into Bob's arms and went over to peek at the baby. "Oraia, oraia, congratulations Mrs. Kay...congratulations Mr. Bill."

Chins shouted for a glass for Jimmy and another chair.

The door swung open again. Theo and Yaya, the abortion case propped up between them, feet dragging, appeared in the doorway. "Katina," Theo cried happily, "I have brought you a roommate for company." He dragged the unconscious patent to the other bed, laid her down and covered her with a sheet. "Tora, estimo...now I am ready," he said, turning around and holding his hands out in a gesture of offering. "Po...po...po...what a busy night. She was the last. Could you imagine such a hot night and so busy?"

Dina brought in more chairs and glasses and a circle formed around Kay's bed. The baby and the roommate were excluded.

"Maro called," Theo said to Kay, "She and Nota will e over right away...they want to see the baby."

Yaya's lead in lighting up a cigarette was followed by Chins and Nick the Walk and the room started to become stuff. With all the people and the noise, Bill worried for the baby—now there were others coming.

"Jimmy brought chickens, Theo," Kay said cheerfully. "Give Theo a piece of chicken, Jimmy."

"Aha," Theo exclaimed, "I like your Bar-B-Que chicken even better than kokoretsi." He opened the bag Jimmy gave him, tore off a leg and started eating, sighing loudly in contentment with each bite. Nick the Chins took some white meat as a side dish to his kokoretsi. He sent Dina in for more bread.

When Maro and Nota arrived, everyone moved out from the bed, making the circle wider. Nick the Walk ran out to the hall and brought back one of the pews.

Maro had a necklace of garlic around her neck, like the one Theo had worn at the Engenia. She too was warding off any evil spirits which might dare attack the baby. She went over to the crib and made the Greek sign of the Cross with a fresh clove.

Nota charitably offered Kay her powder puff. "It will help you," she said, shaking her head. "Six children... Panyia mou, Holy Mother...I don't know how you do it."

The outside door bell rang and Theo told Dina to answer and tell whomever it was he was not seeing patients for the rest of the evening. Instead of a patient, Dina returned with Tikidoras. He staggered in, breathless from the climb. "Those steps...are...worse than...court," he said, his nose twitching as he passed Maro. He went over to Kay, kissed her and made his way through the crowd to the baby, bent over and tickled him under the chin with his fingernail. "He is beautiful" he said to Bill who had run over to protect the baby's jugular vein. "A real Greek boy."

"That is right," Theo cried. "He is Greek. I forgot...we have many papers to fill out."

The wine quickly ran out and Yaya, furtively glancing over her shoulder, making certain she was not followed, hastened to her armoire for a bottle of ouzo.

The baby slept on through the noise and excited talk and eating and drinking, seemingly oblivious to his welcoming-in party. Then Bill noticed that he wasn't in the crib and a moment of panic seized him. "The baby's gone..." he screamed. "The baby's not in the crib."

"Dina has the baby inside," Kay said. "I told her to take him and give him a little chamomile. Don't panic. Will you relax and have a good time...pass me the kokoretsi."

The party, as all parties tend, started to break up into little groups and cliques and Bill finally was able to elbow his way to the bed and speak to Kay.

"Hon, do you think all this noise and stuff is OK for you? How do you feel? You're supposed to be resting."

"Don't be such a party poop," she said brightly. "Nothing's wrong with me...I fell fine."

He was amazed at the girl's stamina and shrugged his shoulders and went back to the ouzo. After all, he thought, Kay's all right, the baby was all right, he was in another room drinking his chamomile—if Kay felt well enough she certainly could have a few visitors. Anyway, her doctor was present, and he seemed to approve.

Later Vinegar-face and his wife arrived and another pew was brought into the room. More kokoretsi was distributed and Jimmy left for more chickens.

Theo and Chins, turning in a transistor radio started to comp, clomp around in the beginnings of a snake dance. Kefi, like a bright orange cloud of laughing gas began to fill the room. The abortion case woke up, painfully peeked under the sheet to make sure her genitalia was still there and politely asked for some kokoretsi. Yaya, breaking off her serious conversation with Bob about marriage and prickas and beautiful girls, got up and joined Theo and Chins. When she sat down

Bob had an ouzo poured for her. He liked the way she crossed and uncrossed her legs in time to the music and wanted to egg her on.

The air was thick with smoke and the smell of wine blended sickly with that of the garlic, but when Bill suggested opening a window, someone declared that the damp night air would be terribly unhealthy for the new mother.

Through the haze, Bill saw Jimmy had returned with enough provisions to keep the party going indefinitely. Jimmy had also brought Panyoti back with him. "Bob, did you se what Jimmy dragged back with him?"

"I told him to," Bob said calmly. "You don't want that guy taking care of the store, do you?" He turned back to Yaya's underwear.

Things were getting out of hand. Bill was thinking of escape. It was not that the visit was so different in nature to one in an American hospital, or that four hours had passed and no one made any sign to leave—primarily what bothered him was that the snake dance was weaving in and out of the rooms. There was the baby and the other patients to think of, although three from one of the other rooms had joined the party, dancing and singing with everyone else. He felt perhaps they were making a disturbance.

Kay, propped up in bed, still munching kokoretsi, looked a little peaked to him now. The noise and strain of the crowd were taking their toll. They were taking their toll on Bob too—he had gotten so dizzy from watching Yaya's petticoats and the ouzo that he lay down on the abortion case's bed. She was with Kay, chatting about the joys of motherhood.

About mid-night the party reached its climax. The abortion case was flattered into signing by Tikidoras who was suavely ling her up for the future when she healed. Theo and Chins continued to dance and Vinegar-face fed Nota a second time. His wife quietly wept into her handkerchief.

Suddenly, Kay was out of bed—missing. Bill ran outside past the snake line and called, "Kay, Kay...where are you?"

"I'm in the john...can't I go to the john?"

"You've got to take it easy," he said when she got out. "I don't think all this excitement is good at all. I like parties but this is unreasonable."

When they returned to the room, Panyoti was lying in Kay's bed, his eyes peacefully closed, the shirtsleeve on his right arm rolled up. Theo was checking his blood pressure.

"What happened?" Bill asked Bob.

"Nothing. Panyoti saw That Theo had the pressure instrument and wants his pressure taken. Said he hasn't been feeling to well since the elections."

Bill stared as Theo took the pressure. He observed that Theo was evidently not used to taking blood pressure. He was squeezing the air bulb, pumping what seemed too much air into the pressure cuff. Panyoti's arm above where the pressure cuff was wrapped glowed bright red, below the arm was white and limp. Theo kept pumping away and chomping at a new load of kokoretsi, and when he finally went to take the pressure, Panyoti had fainted.

"Get your things...we're going home," Bill ordered.

He made apologies to Theo and Yaya for leaving the party so early and with Bob, carried Kay and the baby down the stairs, called a cab and took them home.

It was a short hospital stay, he thought, on the verge of hysteria, but a good one.

Chapter Nineteen

Once again Bill was on the terrace, reading and reflecting. He liked his reading and reflecting periods, it was tranquil in the shade of the olive trees with the soft, aromatic breeze patting him in the face. He could watch the children below, too. They no longer had a governess—the children had outgrown governesses.

He had done a lot of moving up and down, from terrace to roof and back again, for his reading reflecting periods. During his archeological and philosophical phases he had used the roof—he sought the inspiration of the Parthenon, visible in the distance. He had been willing to suffer the sun and the heat up there for those studies—Plato had brought with him a wonderful tan—but history and Herodotus required shade.

He looked down at the children, playing near the fence. Little Theo was bringing in the harvest this year. Then, after that, Bill knew he'd go to work on the rose bush. Children are so predictable, he thought, from cucumber to roses—always in that order. It didn't bother him anymore, his study of antiquity kept him unruffled and rational at all times. The deeper he got into his studies of the past, and Kay was constantly amazed that he was getting deeper or at least staying with them, the less excited he became over anything new, any seemingly disturbing idea. After all, they had been through it wagon wheel. He was convinced that there was no idea not articulated, explored, detailed or invented by the ancient Greeks. Perhaps not all, he thought, folding a page and closing the book on his lap. The ideas of the two books he had recently read, Look Homeward Angel and You Can't Go Home Again, the conflicting sense of the titles, would have been an intellectual offense to an Aristotle. He, with his precise, brutal, cold logic would reason, 'a thing cannot be and not be at the same time in the same respect' and then walk on to the Lycium. Bill was still not a thinking man, but he admired logic and reason. He liked Wolfe and enjoyed the books, but he resented the choice of titles.

Kay joined him on the terrace, she had been napping.

"Hi, you look deep in thought."

"Hi, yeah...I guess I kind of am."

"What are you thinking about?"

"The kids."

"What about?"

"I don't know. Lot of things. For one they don't speak English."

"They speak Greek very well."

"They should learn English."

"They will. After all, they're doing pretty well in French."

"They're Americans after all."

"Of course, they're Americans."

"You wouldn't know it really, though, the other day I told little Theo and Nicholas we were going to play baseball and they started kicking the soccer ball around."

"They play soccer in the States."

"S' funny, I've been thinking about those two books I read last week."

"What books? Did you finish with Herodotus?"

"No...my contemporary reading...Look Homeward Angel and You Can't go Home Again."

"What are you thinking about them?"

"I don't know. The ideas I guess. Should we look homeward? Can we go home again?"

"Hmmm. Never thought about it much. At all as a matter of fact." She paused and blinked her eyes. "Oh by the way, we got a letter from Bob. He's going to stay another week in Paris and then go to London. It's inside, want me to get it?"

"I'll read it later. Boy, what does he care...I have to kill myself all alone at the store."

Kay smiled.

"Well, what do you think about it now?"

"What?"

"The books...the titles."

"Oh...those. I don't know," she said ringing the bell for the maid. Kay wanted some Turkish coffee. "I think we might give it some thought...avrio."

About the Author

William G Battista

Bill Battista was Bronx born first generation Italian American. His Father was a proud NYC Union Bricklayer. Bill was the first in his family to attend college, earning his BA in English from Fordham University and continuing into the Marine Corps where he became Sergeant. After leaving the Marine Corps in 1955, Bill went to work on Madison Avenue for Family Circle magazine and joined the ranks of the original "Mad Men" earning his way to become top salesman in 1959. In 1960 he moved his wife and family of 3 children to Athens, Greece with the desire to escape the trappings of the very lifestyle that he was selling to his clients. He wrote two books while in Greece, entitled Chicken In Greece, and The KEFI Machine, respectively. In 1967, Greece became turbulent for American expatriates and Bill moved the family to New Jersey and went back to work for Family

Circle. Bill also pursued his love of education by joining the local Board of Education and also starting a one of its kind Alternative High School in Leonia, NJ. He also used his commanding charisma to teach Shakespeare at night to intercity youth. His wife, Kay became National Teacher of the Year in 1972, but unfortunately, they divorced several years after returning to America from Greece. Bill lived an active life until his untimely death of cancer at age 47 in 1980.

Find more about the author at: http://www.chickeningreece.com

Leave a review:

Other books by the Author:

The Kefi Machine

Made in the USA
Lexington, KY
02 June 2017